Thomas Stewart Denison

Exhibition and Parlor Dramas

Thomas Stewart Denison

Exhibition and Parlor Dramas

ISBN/EAN: 9783337335083

Printed in Europe, USA, Canada, Australia, Japan

Cover: Foto ©Andreas Hilbeck / pixelio.de

More available books at **www.hansebooks.com**

DRAMAS,

CONTAINING THE FOLLOWING PLAYS:

ODDS WITH THE ENEMY; INITIATING A GRANGER;
SETH GREENBACK; WANTED, A CORRESPOND-
ENT; A FAMILY STRIKE; THE SPARKLING
CUP; THE ASSESSOR; TWO GHOSTS
IN WHITE; COUNTRY JUSTICE;
BORROWING TROUBLE.

BY

T. S. DENISON.

CHICAGO:
T. S. DENISON.
1879.

Steam Press of
Cushing, Thomas & Co., 170 Clark St.

ODDS WITH THE ENEMY.

CHARACTERS.

———

Mrs. Linton, a widow in good circumstances,
Oscar Linton, her son, - - - -
Alice Linton, her daughter, - - -
Harry List, - - - - -
Lanty Nixon, grocer's clerk, - - -
Squire Simon Carter, a man of wealth,
Nathan Carter, { his nephew, adopted son } of Mrs. Linton,
Betsey Bluff, Mrs. L's servant, - - -
J. McClure Hopkinson, dry goods clerk, -
Tabbs, colored servant of the Lintons, - -
Phœbe Day, Squire's servant, - - -

———

COSTUMES.

———

Any ordinary clothing suited to the station of the wearer. Soldiers in uniform. A soldier's coat will answer if complete uniform cannot be had.

EXPLANATIONS.

———

R, means right for the actor as he faces the audience; L, left; C, center.

Three years intervene between acts III and IV; about one month between IV and V.

ODDS WITH THE ENEMY.

ACT I.

SCENE MRS. LINTON'S *Parlor. Room elegantly furnished, giving evidences of wealth and refinement. Pictures on the walls. Evening.*

Nathan. I can hardly believe it! What presumption in her to treat in this way, one brought up under the same roof, her equal in every respect, and a little better than she is just at present. But her aristocratic notions which she airs so conspicuously, will soon be humbled, or I'm no judge. Well there is no use fretting and fuming, Nathe Carter. Bide your time and it will all come out right. Humph! I can't help laughing at that girl's high-minded notions. Does'ent she know that her prospects are materially changed since her father s death, She forgets that her father was a spendthrift. A large part of the property which she proudly imagines to be hers, will soon be the property of Simon Carter. Then may be his nephew will not be such a bad catch after all. She is not aware of that yet. How could she know it? I forgot that only two persons know all about that trifling circumstance yet.   But she soon will know it, and may be that will cause her to change her opinion on certain subjects. Confound it! I would like to choke that young List when he comes hanging around Alice with his spoony talk. Hist! I hear them coming now. I can't face them after my discomfiture. I'd like to know how, they do get along together. I'll employ a little stratagem to find out. (*Creeps behind lounge,* R.)

Enter HARRY *and* ALICE L.

Alice. Take a seat Harry. Take this arm-chair.
Harry. This will do as well. That is yours.
Alice. You need not refuse it Harry. You must take it. You know you are partial to that chair.
Harry. Yes, I am partial to that chair because it is yours. (*Takes arm-chair* R. *of table,* ALICE L.)
Nathan. (*Aside.*) I wonder if he will like her as well when she does'ent own any fine chairs?

Alice. Harry, none of your nonsense. How careless I am! I have not taken mother the evening paper yet. Excuse me Harry till I take it to her. She will be anxious to hear the news.

Harry. Certainly. (*Exit* ALICE R.) There it is! Always the same. Whenever I hint my love for her, she changes the subject so adroitly I have not courage to renew it. Yet I have the best of reasons for believing that she cares more for me than her careless manner would indicate. But with what charming indifference she meets every reference to the one subject nearest my heart. To be refused by her would be a sort of pleasure, could one but ask again.

Nathan. (*As.de*) Precious little pleasure I found in it.

Harry. Ask again! How bold I am of a sudden, when I have not courage to ask the first time. I dare not contemplate the possibility of a refusal. Perhaps after all she cares nothing for me, as her thoughtless raillery would seem to indicate. Alas! that is what I fear. Would that I could read her thoughts toward me. Humph! may be she does'ent think of me at all. Verily the hardest thing in this world is to read the intent in the word or act.

Enter ALICE R.

Alice. I've kept you waiting longer than I intended, Harry. But then you like that chair and this room so well, that I presume you have not missed me much.

Harry. Indeed I have. You do not know how much I always miss you, Alice, and how lonely I feel when ——

Alice. When you are alone. Ha, ha, what an idea that you should feel lonely when alone.

Harry. Alice, if you would only listen to me ——

Alice. Now Mr. Philosopher, if you intend delivering a lecture, please remember that the occasion is somewhat inappropriate, and the audience not sufficient to develop any latent powers of speech making which you may possess. (*A p ...*) What ails you to night anyhow, Harry? You are not u   'y so particular about the subject of conversation. Harry, yo   . actually cross.

Harry. Sometimes one does not wish t   k on every subject.

Alice. Quite true, Harry. Let's talk abou the war; we must all be interested in that whether we will or not Did you know nearly all the boys in the village have enlisted under Capt. Wilson?

Harry. Yes; and I wish I could go too.

Alice. Oh don't think of it Harry. I can't bear the idea of your going to the war.

Harry. Why?

Alice. Oh there would be no one to bring us the latest news and we should be so lonesome, mother and I. There would be no one to help us while away our leisure hours which grow more tedious every day. I was just wishing before you came that you would drop in and spend the evening.

Harry Here I am and you have your wish.

Alice. You have not been here for a whole week. Is that the way for one old playmate to treat another? Harry, I shall have to ask you to explain.

Harry. You just said you wished to talk about the war.

Alice. Not when you talk of enlisting. It's horrid. What ever made you think of going?

Harry. I have several reasons.

Alice. What are they pray?

Harry. In the first place I think it is my duty to defend my country, and then father does not wish me to see you. For his sake it were better my visits here should cease.

Alice. Harry you are always welcome here; mother likes to see you often. Then you know we have the claims of old acquaintance upon you. (*Knocking*) Who can that be? (*Goes to door* R.) Betsey, come in.

Harry. (*Aside.*) I wonder if old acquaintanceship is my only claim here.

Betsey. Good evening Mr. List.

Harry. Good evening Betsey.

Alice. Take a seat Betsey.

Betsey. No thank you. I shall not intrude.

Harry. No intrusion at all.

Alice. Nonsense Betsey! I should think you would know better than to talk about intrusion, sit down. Harry likes to make himself at home. You know well enough he comes to see the whole household. Is'ent that so Harry?

Harry. Yes.

Tabbs. (*Enters* L. *aside*) Am dat a factotum? All de house holds. Dat cludes me for a fac.

Harry. Sit down Betsey and we will have a social chat. (*All take seats,* BETSEY L.)

Tabbs. (*Aside.*) Spect dat does'ent clude dis individual. (*Aloud.*) Miss Alice.

Alice. Why when did you come in, Tabbs?

Tabbs. Jes about three-quarters of a moment ago to the bes of my reclection. Massa Nixon's waitin at de dooh. (*Betsey jumps up.*)

Alice. Lanty Nixon? Show him in at once. Don't run away Betsey.

Betsey. I shan't run away, but I'd like to know what he wants here this time of night.

Nathan. (*Aside.*) Hang it who else is coming! I'm confoundedly cramped.

Alice. Oh he has come to deliver groceries perhaps.

Betsey. Groceries indeed! He has been here twice already today with groceries.

Nathan. (*Aside.*) Plague take it! He'll stay all night.

LANTY *enters* L. *ushered in by* TABBS.

Lanty. Good evening to you all.

Alice. ⎫
Betsey. ⎬ Good evening, Lanty.
Harry. ⎭

Alice. Take a seat Lanty. We are so 'glad you have come. Is there any news?

Lanty. Yes a telegram—

Tabbs. Miss Alice may I listen to the news?

Alice. Yes, stay and hear it, Tabbs. (*All seated but Tabbs.*)

Lanty. A telegram has just come stating that there has been another great battle and that the union army is routed with fearful slaughter.

Alice. What dreadful news! and yet in our impatience we long to hear of battles and are disappointed if they do not occur almost daily. Who would have thought a few short years ago, that brothers would so soon deluge our country in blood. And then the bitter end, for when that time comes, the victor will only have bruised his weaker brother.

Betsey. Yes, but an erring brother. God's justice is sure and the verdict of Heaven will be on the side of the right and against wrong and slavery.

Harry. Nobly spoken Betsey.—

> "Truth crushed to earth will rise again;
>   The eternal years of God are hers;
> But error wounded writhes in pain,
>   And dies among her worshippers."

Tabbs. Yes, massa Harry; Miss Betsey inlightened onto our minds in a very plain forid way; and poetry am a mighty good thing to pour goose ile onto de troubled waters of true love with. It's mighty nice to talk about de wardick of Heaven too. But I'd jes like to know when dat wardick is to be given in. Sposen de jury cant agree and de court journs over two or three times, what will become of all dese fighten combatifants den? Gineral Jackson! Dey'ell all be done killed off before dey eber hear of de wardick.

Alice. Have faith Tabbs. The Lord will fight the battles of the just.

Harry. Faith has its sphere, but even the Lord can not fight battles without instruments to carry out his purposes. I feel to night that every one who is able to bear arms should take part and that I should be in the field fighting for my country.

Alice. You Harry! Why how you talk! You know we can not spare you, and there are older hands enough. You are but a boy.

Harry. Yes, I am a boy, but even boys can help defend their country.

Tabbs. Massa Harry am right. His kind of faith would remove the mountains of Sodom and cast them into the sea of Saharry.

Beisey. Mountains of Sodom! Sea of Sahara! Tabbs, Sodom was a city of the plain, and Sahara is a great desert.

Tabbs. Sodom a city of de plain! If dat am a case, why did de Scripter ask Jacob to flee into de mountains, if dere were no mountains to flee into? To save argufyin, I'se jes willin to admit dat Saharry am a desert. I meant de sea of Mediterraneum, and for that matter I reckon it's about as easy to throw a mountain into one sea as another.

Lanty. Stick to it Tabbs. You have the best of that argument.

Tabbs. Thankee, Massa Nixon. You don't catch dis individual nappin whar de Scripter am consarned.

Lanty. Tabbs, are you versed in profane history?

Tabbs. Do you spose dis darkey waited on Massa two years for nothing, while he was sittin on de flooh of de legislater? Massa Nixon, I'm proud to say dat my limited knowledge of profane history, am mostly 'quired by observation durin my public career.

Alice. How very wise you must be Tabbs, if you have profited by all the experience of your eventful life, public and private.

Tabbs. Reckon Massa Linton would have been wealthier and wiser if he had listened to the advice of a sartin cullud person.

Alice. What do you mean Tabbs?

Tabbs. Well, if Massa had'ent had no dealins with Simon Carter, it would have been better for him. Jes like dese genrous, whole-souled chaps. Dey's so awful maganimous deirselves, dat dey never think anybody else is mean till it is too late. Mebbe it aint too late yet to give a little advice though.

Alice. Have you anything of importance to disclose, Tabbs, that you are exciting our curiosity to such an extent! Unravel the mystery.

Tabbs. Squire Carter might'ent want dis individual to unravel *his* yarn. But I reckon if Massa Linton had always put away his papers into a safe place, Missa Linton would have had some dockiments dat would help dis ravlin business pretty smart.

Alice. Do you refer to father's private papers which were lost?

Tabbs. Yes Miss Alice. And I also infer to some papers which de late deceased Mr. Linton *did'ent* write.

Harry. Tabbs, drop your big words and tell us plainly what you do mean.

Tabbs. Massa Harry, I'se been droppin big words round like ripe chestnuts arter a frost. Aint dat a fac? To be plain about it, I mean dat Massa Linton never owed Squire Carter in his life, and dat Massa never gave him those big notes.

Lanty. I've guessed as much for some time.

Alice. Tabbs, are you aware of the serious nature of the charges you make against my guardian, Simon Carter?

Tabbs. Did'ent spect to charge any thing. Shant charge a cent, Miss Alice, for dese facs. It am all true though. Did'ent I hear Massa tell Massa Williams, that week before he died, that he did'ent owe nobody nothing ceptin a few little debts.

Alice. Pooh! Tabbs, you must not let an accidental remark lead you to such serious conclusions. Perhaps father did not know at that time the exact condition of those investments he and Mr. Carter made together.

Tabbs. Jes so Miss Alice. In de opinion of dis darkey, no one will ever know de zact condition of dem vestments ceptin Simon Carter, and mebbe his next of kin Nathe.

Lanty. Tabbs, do you know anything to justify your suspicions?

Tabbs. Yes, Massa, I knows *considerable* more than this individual's gwine to tell, until de indigencies of de case requiahs de facs.

Harry. Nonsense, Tabbs. You need not put on such an air of wisdom with your eloquence, nor speak in such a mysterious way. You have nothing but your own suspicions, and those only because you do not like the Carters.

Tabbs. Nothing but spicions eh? I see de maligencies of de case requiahs a plain enclosure of de facs.

Betsey. You mean the exigencies of the case require a disclosure of the facts.   •

Tabbs. I said exidigencies. But we will not argy dat point. Here am de facs. Did'ent I hear Massa Nathe and his Uncle Simon talking busy about Massa Linton's business?

Nathan. (*Aside.*) The black rascal!

Tabbs. An when I see dey was so desput in arnest, I stopped on the stairs to listen, if it was sort of mean, an I heerd two mighty mean men layin plans.

Nathan. (*Aside.*) Your black pate will suffer for this.

Alice. Well go on Tabbs. We are tired waiting.

Tabbs. Massa Nathe says to squire, says he, "You know Uncle them papers are taken care of, now how's we gwine to fix up matters?" An Squire Carter says, "We'll jes put in plenty of claims an try to get a morgidge on de farm for the present. Afterwards we can tighten de screws jes as we please if dat gal don't come to a favorable clusion."

Lanty. The villians!

Harry. Can this be true?

Tabbs. True as preachin.

Betsey. Neither of them is too good for such villiany in my opinion.

Alice. Friends judge not too harshly. I cannot hear my adopted brother and my guardian thus spoken of. Let us drop the subject. Where can Nathan be to night? It is time he was home, if he went to the village.

Harry. Lanty, that reminds me it is time we were at home too.

Alice. No, I did'ent mean that. Don't be in a hurry.

Harry. Really we must go. It is getting late. Good night.
Lanty. Good night. (*Exeunt* L.)
Alice. }
Betsey. } (*Going to door.*) Good night. Call again.
Tabbs. Good night. (*Exit* R.)
Betsey. I must see to the kitchen for the night. (*Exit* R.)
Alice. And I'll go up stairs to mother. (*Exit* R.)
Nathan. Yes, and I'll go too. A precious fool I've been, ly-ing there an hour or so in that dark hole. Aha! They know our plans, do they? All through that black rascal Tabbs. But his influence does'ent amount to a straw. Alice, herself don't believe him. No, she trusts me still. So much the better. Tabbs is easily disposed of, and then we shall see who wins, Harry List or I. (*Exit* R.) *Curtain.*

ACT II.

SCENE, MRS. LINTON's *Parlor. Time next day, after Act I.*
Table C. MRS. LINTON *seated* R. *of table.*

Mrs. L. Oh, this continual trouble! Since my husband's death, there has been nothing but worry over his affairs. Claim follows claim, until I fear nothing will be left. (*Knocking heard.*) Who is that? (*Goes to the door,* L.)

Enter TABBS, *showing in* SIMON CARTER.

Squire. How are you, Mrs. Linton. I hope you are well.
Mrs. L. Good day, Mr. Carter. I'm quite well thank you. Take a seat.
Squire. (*Takes chair,* L.) Fine day for the soldiers to say good bye. There is a terrible bluster down among the cabins on the creek. Women and children are crying. The men are half-crying too. Should'ent think they would care a great deal, as they don't leave much behind.
Mrs. L. They leave their wives and children behind, and nothing should be dearer to men than these. Those who have experienced such partings, best know how bitter they are.
Squire. Very true. It *is* natural to feel such things. We are *all* human when it comes to that.
Tabbs. (*Aside.*) De Squiah am speakin from observation. Dat las remark don't come under de spear of his personal sperience.
Mrs. L. This cruel war will bring sorrow to many hearts that have never known a care. How can men deliberately and intentionally wrong their fellow men? Is there no better way than bloodshed to settle differences of opinion?
Squire. Differences of opinion may be honest, yet irreconcila-ble. So the sword must decide. But I've come down to-day on a little matter of business. I want to see what can be done toward settling up my accounts with your husband's estate. You know

I have made out my claims entirely from my books, including those old notes.

Tabbs. (*Aside.*) Plaguey *old* notes. Made about las week.

Mrs. L. Yes, I know you were preparing a statement, and I'll be obliged to trust to the accuracy of your accounts, since my husband's private papers have so unaccountably disappeared.

Squire. Very mysteriously indeed. Have you no clue to their whereabouts.

Mrs. L. None. I have given up the search as hopeless.

Squire, And I too. I think there is little probability of your ever seeing them again.

Tabbs. (*Aside.*) Dat am mos entirely likely (*Aloud,*) Dey're gone sure.

Mrs. L. Tabbs, you may go.

Squire. Why, are you here Tabbs? Go at once. We have private business that must not be heard by everyone.

Tabbs. (*Aside, going.*) Not de fust business he did'ent want every one to hear. (*Exit* R.)

Squire. Well, as I was saying, I have those matters in good shape at last, and am now ready to settle at once.

Mrs. L. If there is a balance in your favor, I fear that I should not be ready to settle immediately.

Squire. There is quite a balance in my favor.

Mrs. L. Heaven protect us! We shall be homeless yet.

Squire. I am very sorry Madam, to be obliged to break this unpleasant news to you. But I am not able to lose the money, and, though administrator of the estate, I must present my claims with the other creditors.

Mrs. L. You do but your duty in claiming your own. I will pay you every cent, if my child and myself are left penniless.

Squire. It will not be so bad as that.

Mrs. L. What does the estate owe you?

Squire. A small amount comparatively; only some seven thousand dollars.

Mrs. L. A very large amount considering our other debts. Then my husband was deeply involved?

Squire. He was. He lost heavily in oil speculations. The bulk of my claim is for money loaned at that time. Without my help he would probably have been bankrupt then.

Mrs. L. What settlement can we make without sacrificing everything?

Squire. Oh, take your time. Give me a mortgage on the real estate, and pay it off at your leisure.

Mrs. L. Mortgage the homestead! T'is the last resort, but better than to sell it to strangers. I will give you the mortgage, and trust to Providence for the means of paying it off.

Squire. All right. I'll not be hard at all. Now since we have settled up that business satisfactorily, there's another little affair I'd like to mention.

Mrs. L. What is that?

Squire. You know my nephew, Nathan, is very fond of Alice.

Mrs. L. It would be very strange if he were not, for their relations have always been those of brother and sister.

Squire. Pshaw! There is no brotherly love about it. It is all the real thing. Why should'ent he marry the girl? He will some day have all my property, and will be well to do in the world. As for his bringing up, you know what that is. I think they would make a splendid match.

Mrs. L. To be properly mated, young people must love each other, and I doubt if Alice entertains any other feeling for Nathan than that of a sister's love.

Squire. There is great deal of moonshine about the loves of young people. When I wanted to marry Matilda Williams, I just went and asked her father about it, and he said yes. The girl said something about not loving me as well as she should love a husband. I told her love would come in time, and her father said the same. We were married, and we always got along without any trouble. If I do say it myself, I never knew a quieter, more obedient wife.

Mrs. L. I don't doubt her *obedience*, Mr. Carter, not in the least, but I do doubt the propriety of such marriages, especially between very young persons. Alice is too young to think of marrying yet. When she is of proper age, she shall choose for herself. I shall not attempt to dictate to her upon the subject of marriage. A mother's advice is all I have to offer, and if I were offering any-one advice now, it would be for Nathan to give up all hope of ever winning Alice, for I am sure her heart is already another's. I have intimated as much to Nathan several times.

Squire. You mean Harry List, I suppose? And can you consent for one of your family's most bitter enemies, to marry your only child? Do you not fear the old feud will be renewed in all its bitterness? Can a house divided against itself, stand?

Mrs. L. That feud was a senseless, causeless quarrel, which I hope will be forever consigned to oblivion by its youngest representatives.

Squire. Mrs. Linton, I am astonished to hear you speak so. You hope this for the furtherance of a love match between those representatives, eh?

Mrs. L. Mr. Carter, I beg you will not misunderstand me in a way which reflects so decidedly upon my candor, and implies an intrigue upon my part. Of all things, I depise hypocrisy and intrigue. (*Rises indignantly*)

Squire. (*Rises, aside.*) Hang it, I must not be too fast yet. (*Aloud.*) I beg pardon, Mrs. Linton. I did'ent mean to reflect; never thought of such a thing. But you can see that the conseqences of such a union might prove disastrous. Could you not influence Alice to regard Nathan more favorably? Your influence with her is very great.

Mrs. L. I know it is, but I will never use it to compel her to marry a man she does not love.

Squire. That is your decision then?

Mrs. L. It is.

Squire. Very well. I like people to decide such things in a plain outspoken way. No half-way underhand work for me. I can respect such decisions as that. (*Going.*) Good morning, Mrs. Linton.

Mrs L. Good day, Mr. Carter. (*Exit R.*)

Squire (*Passing out* L., *as* MRS. L. *passes out* R.) Deuce take it, may be when she has no roof over her head, Nathe Carter's would be better than none for her and her high-toned daughter. (*Met at door by Nathan, who enters.*)

Nathan. Well Uncle, what success?

Squire. (*Re-entering.*) Curse it, no success at all. That girl don't care a straw for you. But I did succeed too. The mortgage is all right and that will bring both mother and daughter to terms, or my name is'ent Simon Carter.

Nathan. Uncle, it looks pretty hard to defraud helpless women in that way. I would like to have the girl and her property if they could be had honorably, but I almost wish we had never begun to work by unfair means.

Squire. Bah! Don't turn coward and indulge in conscientious scruples now, when it is too late.

Nathan. You may well say *conscientious* scruples, for what we have begun is certainly wrong in the sight of Heaven. It would be base ingratitude in me, to betray those who have ever been my best friends.

Squire. Nonsense, Nathan! It will be all right when the property is yours and the girl your wife; can't she enjoy it, and can't her mother share it too for that matter? "Stratagem is fair in love and in war." It will all be in the family still.

Nathan. I had'ent thought of it in that light before. May be all will be well in the end. I hope it will since we are into the ugly business. But did you know that Tabbs suspects us; knows in fact that those notes are not genuine?

Squire. The devil he does! How did he find that out?

Nathan. Overheard our conversation. He has already told Alice. but she does not believe him.

Squire. He must be disposed of.

Nathan. But how?

Squire. Trust me for that. I'll find some way.

Nathan. Hush, Uncle! We must not remain here talking. We may be overheard again.

Squire. You are right. I must go at once. (*Exeunt* L.)

Curtain.

ACT III.

Scene, Mrs. Linton's *parlor.*   *Time a few days after Act II.*

Mrs. L. Enters R.

Mrs. L. Simon Carter is rude in speech and manner, but I have never doubted his honesty, even though ugly rumors were afloat many years ago concerning him. Can Tabb's story be true? No, I have good reason to believe that my husband's affairs were involved. Tabbs must be mistaken. That mortgage places us in the power of Simon Carter. His language the other day seemed almost like a menace, but we must meet his claim, and that is the only way left us.

Enter Alice R.

Alice. Mother, have you heard the news?
Mrs. L. No, Alice. What is it?
Alice. George Harley ran away from home last night.
Mrs. L. Impossible. It can't be true!
Alice. But it is true, Mother. Susan Harley has just been here and told Betsey all about it Mr. Harley started this morning to the city, to see if he can hear anything of George, and Mrs. Harley has worried herself sick. She is abed now, and Dr. Berry has been called in.
Mrs. L. Oh, the follies of hot-blooded youth! Could that misguided boy but realize the unspeakable anguish which his perversity has caused his parents, he would pause in horror at its consequences. But his ungovernable passions like a fierce simoon, have consumed his better qualities, dried up the springs of filial love, and left his he rt a barren waste, scorched by its own mad passions. Poor boy! Sometime he will repent his folly. Mrs. Harley's grief brings back to me the sad remembrance of our own poor wanderer, laid to rest in a strange land, your own lost brother Oscar.
Alice. Dear mother, do not call him *lost.* I feel that he is yet alive, and will some day return to us despite his foolish vow.
Mrs. L. Banish the thought. The evidence of his death and burial, is too strong to allow us to cherish such delusive hopes.
Alice. Oh, mother, don't speak so. You know that I cherish the hope that he is yet alive, as dearer than all else.

Enter Tabbs L.

Tabbs. (*Aside.*) Ceptin Massa Harry. How dese women folks will be meanin about one thing when dey's talkin about an-

other, and dat other not on de subjec at all. (*Aloud.*) Beg
pardon for interruptin de felicities of dis occasion, but ——

Alice. Tabbs, go away with your nonsense and ludicrous talk.
Will you never learn to stop your highflown gibberish? What
are you here for? Don't you know better than to intrude?
Our conversation is private.

Tabbs. Private! Dat's what de cruitin officer wanted me to
be. Dis chile prefers to be scused from private life jes now.

Alice. Tabbs, leave this room instantly.

Mrs. L. Alice, Tabbs does not deserve rebuke. His genial
good nature has often sent a ray of sunshine through this house,
when all around was gloomy. His unskilled tongue speaks many
a generous thought with a grotesque expression, but an honest
purpose.

Tabbs. Your pardon, Missa, but the gemman, Massa Harry,
is done tired waitin.

Mrs. L. Is Harry at the door? Show him in at once, Tabbs.

Tabbs *retires* L. *re-enters bowing in* Harry List.

Harry. Good morning, Mrs. Linton. Good morning, Alice.

Mrs. L. Good morning, Harry. We are glad to see you.

Alice. Good morning, Harry. I'm so glad that you have come.
I have been wanting ever so much to see you. We have been
making arrangements for a dinner, for Capt. Wilson's Company,
next Thursday, and we shall need you to help get things ready.
Take a seat, Harry, till I tell you all about it. (*All seated,*
Harry L., Mrs. L. C., Alice R.)

Harry. I have another engagement for that day, which will
prevent me from assisting you in the preparations for the dinner.
I suspect Capt. Wilson's Company will dine out that day.

Alice. Pshaw! An engagement which will prevent you from
assisting at the dinner! The Company will dine out! Of course
they will—in the open air. None of your jokes, Harry.

Harry. I'm not joking. I was never more in earnest in my
life.

Alice. What do you mean, Harry?

Harry. I've enlisted.

Mrs. L. ⎱ Enlisted!
Alice. ⎰

Harry. Yes; I have enrolled my name in Capt. Wilson's
Company. To-day I shall don a soldier's coat for better or
worse, that is for three years or during the war.

Alice. Oh Harry how I shall miss you! We never can endure
to lose you, perhaps forever. I shall go mad at the dreadful
thought that you might be killed or crippled for life. Oh the
cruel, cruel exactions of war!

Mrs. L. Be calm my child, Harry is yet safe. We must trust
to God to preserve him. Harry this is sudden. You have never
told us anything about your intending to enlist. Have you your

father's consent? Why have you resolved so suddenly to leave a comfortable home and brave the dangers of the battle field?

Harry. This morning father asked me again to cease my visits here. I refused. He urged that I should not visit where he was not free to go. I told him humbly and with sorrow that his objections were founded upon prejudices which should have been forgotten long ago, and that I respected his wishes but could not admit his right to choose for me. In a violent passion he ordered me to obey him or leave his house and never more call myself his son. It was a hard choice but honor bade me stand by my convictions, and now I wish to say to you something which I had long hoped to say under more auspicious circumstances and with father's approval. Mrs. Linton, I love Alice dearly and I think that she loves me although no vows have ever passed our lips. I ask you to let her be my wife, if I am fortunate enough ever to return from the army alive. I could not join my youthful comrades in the camp until I had unfolded to dear ones at home, my long cherished hope. As for Alice this boy's confession brings no tidings new to her. Her answer I have guessed already. Alice have I guessed right?

Alice. Yes, dear Harry, yes.

Mrs. L. Harry, you are both young. Alice is too young to think of plighting her faith to anyone for years. And then our future is so uncertain. Her father's affairs are yet unsettled, we may have plenty; we may be left in want. The old feud between your kindred and Alice's can you ever forget?

Harry. Mrs. Linton, I have not forgotten that deep seated enmity. I remember it as a thing which should be forever banished out of sight. Its unhallowed dregs are too bitter for oblivion. It is that alas! which brings me here to-day to speak my love. A boy's love it may be, yes a child's love you may call it, for it sprang up and reached maturity amid the happy scenes of our childhood days. But the man's reflective moods can not forget the boy's sweet preference.

Mrs. L. Have you considered the consequences of this estrangement from your father? They may affect your future welfare and they deserve more than a passing thought. Is it wise to bring into such close relations those whom years of enmity may sunder?

Harry. It were better than to blight two lives with grudges in which they had no part.

Mrs. L. True my brave boy, but there is plenty of time. When you return from the battlefield crowned with honors as I know you must, if God spares you, Alice shall decide.

Harry. God bless you Mrs. Linton. If the foeman spares me I shall return to claim Alice as my bride.

Alice. Oh Harry you *will* return safe. It would break my heart to hear that you were killed. Oh the miseries of war! Why did you enlist, Harry?

Harry. No ties are sacred enough to bind the freeman when

his country calls. But time presses. The company starts at three.

Alice. Must you go to-day Harry?

Harry. Yes, and this minute.

Alice. Oh, don't go yet.

Harry. I must. Good bye, Mrs. Linton. (*Shake hands.*)

Mrs. L. Good bye, Harry; brave patriot, that you are. May you have God's blessing; you have mine.

Harry. Good bye, dear Alice. Should I fall, remember I have only done my duty. I will write. For my sake do not despair. (*Kisses her. She clings to him.*) Have courage. Trust in God and your country's cause. Farewell.

Alice. Farewell, dear Harry. God be with you. (*Harry presses her hand in silence. Exit.*) What will become of us? It is dreadful to think that the innocent must shed their blood in the quarrels of wicked men. What grievances have we to fight for? Why don't they send their own sons?

Mrs. L. Every one owes a sacred duty to his country. You should not complain. Our grief is but a mite in the great woe around us. Others are bearing even heavier burdens.

Alice. I know that, but the griefs of others does not lessen mine.

Mrs. L. It does not, but it shou d teach us not to consider our sorrows alone, while those around us are borne down by sorrows as great as ours. Cheer up my child. (*Aside.*) Her grief prefers communion with itself. (*Exit R.*)

Alice. (*Passionately.*) He is gone, gone. Must every one I love be torn from me. First my Brother Oscar when I was but a child, and now dear Harry is hurried off, perhaps to fill a soldier's grave. The very thought is dreadful. (*Weeps.*) Yet why should I cherish my grief, when Harry must bear his in silence among strangers? For his sake I will try to cheer up and hope for the best. Somebody's coming. (NATHAN *appears at door* R.)

Nathan. I wished to speak a few words with you. (*Aside.*) She turns away. She has been weeping. What can be the matter?

Alice. I will listen to you however painful the subject may be to both of us.

Nathan. Dear Alice you remember I desired you to reconsider the question which I asked you the other day. I hope reflection has softened your heart towards one who loves you as his own life. If you wish more time take it. I will wait.

Alice. I have not hardened my heart, towards you Nathan God knows you are dear to me. But I will speak plainly. I love another.

Nathan. Could you not love me? Is there no hope?

Alice. I love you with a sister's holiest love and you cannot know how it pains me to answer you thus, knowing as I do what misery that answer will cost you. Nathan for your own sake and mine, never mention this subject to me again for we never can be aught to each other but brother and sister. (*Exit R.*)

Nathan. I am decided. Fair means will not win. Fate makes

me a villain. (*Exit R.*)

Enter Betsey R. MEETING NATHAN.

Betsey. Mr. Nathan looks decidedly blue to day. I know what's the matter though. He has been declaring his love for Miss Alice again and has got another refusal for his pains. What stupid idiots some men are! They can't take a hint. Some of them will hanker around and ask half a dozen times if a woman refuses them. Others will keep coming and coming but never have courage enough to ask a plain question. I have no patience with either sort and Lanty Nixon is one of the latter. Why don't he speak his mind? Goodness knows he has chances enough! If he does'ent soon make his intentions known I'll just bestow a little attention somewhere else. Lanty is jealous of that crack-brained fop who calls himself J. McClure Hopkinson. Well *he is* too nice for this world. I don't care though. (*Knocking heard.*) Who's there? (*Goes to door L.*) Come in Lanty.

Lanty. Good afternoon Betsey. I have called in to tell Mrs. Linton I left the groceries at the kitchen door.

Betsey. Very well, I will call Mrs. Linton.

Lanty. No, its unnecessary, Miss Bluff. I'll tell you what I brought. (*Approaches closely.*) There was ten pounds ——

Betsey. You need not get so close, Lanty. I'm not hard of hearing.

Lanty. No, but you see I am responsible for these groceries, and I'm going to see that they are all properly inventoried by some one connected with the establishment.

Betsey. What do you mean, Lanty Nixon, by calling this house an establishment.

Lanty. Well, what shall I call it? It seems to me you are getting a little particular about your language. Call it an institution then, or a chebang.

Betsey. Chebang indeed! Lanty Nixon, where do you pick up all your slang?

Lanty. See here Betsey, I'm in a hurry; so if you please we will go on with that inventory. There was ten pounds of coffee, one codfish (not one of the aristocracy either), and fifteen pounds of sugar as sweet as —— (*Kisses her.*)

Betsey. (*Slaps him.*) Lanty, you're a fool.

Lanty. May be I am. Betsey, but I'm sure of one thing.

Betsey. What is that?

Lanty. I know a good article when I've sampled it.

Betsey. Get out, you good for nothing!

Lanty. Betsey, listen a minute. I wish to ask you a question.

Betsey. Oh, do you. (*Aside.*) He is going to pop the question at last. (*Aloud.*) Go on, Lanty, I am ready to listen.

Lanty. Why did you devote yourself to that addle-pated Hopkinson, the other night at Jones's party?

Betsey. Is that any difference to you? Can't I entertain whoever I please without asking you?

Lanty.   I suppose you can, if you choose to slight your friends.

Betsey.   Slight my friends!   Humph!   Must I sit and entertain you all night?   You don't seem to appreciate it any too well.

Lanty.   You know well enough what that Hopkinson is.

Betsey.   What is he?

Lanty.   He is nothing but a sniffling, stuck up counter hopper.

Betsey.   Yes, he is a counter hopper, but he does not handle cheese and codfish, and greasy bacon.   Lanty, it is so nice to go a shopping there, and have him display his goods.   How charmingly he handles the yard stick.

Lanty.   I'd like to break his head with it.

Enter TABBS L.

Tabbs.   Could'ent do it Massa Lanty, for did'ent Miss Alice read in de Filosomy, dat a hollow tube am stronger than a solid one.   Miss Betsey, here am a card from a gemman below.

Betsey. (*Reads.*) "J McClure Hopkinson."   Show him in, Tabbs. (*Arranges furniture, etc*)

Enter TABBS *followed by* J. MC.

J. Mc.   Ah!   Good aftehnoon, Miss Bluff.   How aw you?   I hope you are well.

Betsey.   I am quite well, thank you.   How are you?

J. Mc.   Very well indeed.   Good aftehnoon, Mistah Nixon.

Lanty.   Good day, Mr. Hopkinson.

Betsey.   Take seats, gentlemen.   (J. Mc. *takes a seat.*)

J. Mc.   Ah!   Yes, thank you; hawdly have time though.

(*Seated* J. MC. R. C., BETSEY R., LANTY L. C., TABBS *stands* L.)

Tabbs. (*Aside.*)   Golly, he am a stunner, sure.

J. Mc.   I thought I would call, ah.   I did not know but you might want to walk down to the depot, to see the soldiah boys off this aftehnoon.   As I passed here, I thought I would stop. Perhaps we might go togetheh.

Betsey.   Nothing would please me better than to accompany you.

J. Mc.   Ah indeed!   Thank you, aw you ready?

Betsey.   I shall be ready in a moment.   Excuse me.   (*Exit R.*)

J. Mc.   Certainly; certainly.

Tabbs. (*Aside to Lanty*)   Massa Lanty your cake am dough for this evening anyway.

J. Mc.   Do you think of enlisting Mistah Nixon?

Lanty. (*Fiercely.*)   No I do not.

J. Mc.   Beg pahdon, I diden't know but you would.   Most

young men desiah to rush to arms but for my part I prefer to stay at home.

Tabbs. And rush into arms. Sometimes it am mighty sweet to rush into arms at home. Dis individual is willin to serve his country dat way too.

Lanty. Patriots of that stripe are as plenty as bad excuses and just as useful. A great many stay at home because they are unwilling to defend the country which protects them.

J. Mc. Oh! ah! Did I understand—(*Indignantly, both rise, enter Betsey.*) Ah! are you ready Miss Bluff?

Betsey. I am ready. Good afternoon Mr. Nixon. You will excuse my abrupt departure. It is time to go and I presume you wish to see the boys start too. Mrs. Linton and Alice will entertain you in the meantime. Good afternoon.

Lanty. Good afternoon Miss Bluff. I'm obliged to you for your kindness but I shant need any entertaining this afternoon.

J. Mc. Good aftehnoon Mistah Nixon. (*Exeunt L.*)

Tabbs. If de enemy'd get him dey would put him in de imaginary wid de baboons sure.

Lanty. Confound the impudent puppy. What a fool I've been! Blind as a bat!

Tabbs. Massa Lanty, excuse dis individual in correctin one little mistake of yours.

Lanty. What is that?

Tabbs. Massa Nixon I'se gwine to state plain facs and you must'nt get riled either.

Lanty. Well, go on, hang it.

Tabbs. Stead of Massa Hopkinson's beein a puppy it was massa Nixon. Why? Case Massa Nixon's eyes was'ent opened at fust.

Lanty. Shut up you black rascal. (*Kicks him as he escapes R.*)

Enter MRS. L. *and* ALICE.

Mrs. L. Why Lanty! what are you doing?

Lanty. Nothing; we were only joking.

Tabbs. (*Re-enters.*) What would he do if he was in arnest? I'd jes like to know.

Alice. Tabbs is always joking and your inclination to levity is little less than his. Lanty, we never know when you *are* in earnest.

Lanty. You hit the mark that time Alice. Excessive levity is my failing. But to-day I cast aside that wretched garb of nonsense and am determined on a manly resolution.

Alice. What is that Lanty?

Lanty. I shall enlist to-morrow.

Mrs. L. Why you said this morning you were not going to the army.

Lanty. I have changed my mind.

Alice. How sudden this is! Is everybody going to the war?

What made you change your mind so soon Lanty? If you must go I am glad you are going with Harry. Betsey will be a sympathizing companion in my grief. Why do you look so grave? Any thing wrong between you and Betsey?

Tabbs.   Reckon Miss Betsey's grief wont——

Lanty.   Tabbs I wish you to understand I can manage my affairs without your assistance.

Tabbs.   Yes massa.

Lanty.   I guess there is nothing wrong. I've changed my mind; that's all. I can't go with Harry though for I am not ready to start this afternoon.

Alice.   Why! haven't you heard that our boys have orders to remain until to-morrow?

Lanty.   Good luck! Then I will go with Harry.

Mrs. L.   Where is Betsey? Did she not tell you of the delay?

Lanty.   She knew nothing of it herself.

Alice.   I was hoping Harry would come home this evening but I suppose he could not get leave of absence.

Enter HARRY *followed by* SQUIRE, NATHAN, TABBS L.

Harry.   But he did though.

Alice.   Oh it's Harry (*Rushes into his arms.*)

Squire.   Zounds! what does this mean? (*Alice starts and screams.*) Mrs. Linton do you approve of your daughter's rushing into the arms of a young man in this way? If you do I as her guardian must express my unqualified disapproval of such unwomanly conduct. I came expecting to see that young upstart urging his preposterous claims but I confess I was not prepared for this scene.

Lanty.   (*Aside.*)   A Spy.

Harry.   Squire Carter, do you dare to insinuate that Miss Linton would be guilty of an unwomanly act?

Squire.   Who are you boy who thus presumes to question me in regard to what I shall say to my ward? You bear the uniform of a soldier of your country but you have yet to learn the respect due your superiors. I'm thinking that will be the first lesson you will get.

Harry.   If you choose to use insulting language in the presence of ladies I shall dare to question your right to do so, even at the risk of being considered a fit subject for receiving lessons on politeness.

Tabbs.   (*Aside.*)   Massa Carter needs a few lessons in de a-b-c's of dat branch.

Lanty.   (*Aside.*)   I'd like to be his teacher. (*Aloud.*) Squire Carter, if you came here as a spy why did'ent you listen at the door where you could hear all that was said without the restraint of your presence? That would be more in keeping with your mission.

Nathan.   (*Aside.*)   Can he suspect me?

Squire.   Boy, I know my place and my business. Who presumes to tell me here what I shall or shall not say?

Alice. Mr. Carter I am sorry if I have offended you.

Harry. Mr. Carter your language reflects not only on Mrs. Linton and Alice but on the entire company. For my part I scorn your insinuations as unworthy of——

Mrs. L. Harry, please keep cool.

Squire. As unworthy of a gentleman. I understand. You cooly insult me do you?

Harry. My language is plain; you can interpret for yourself.

Lanty. Mr. Carter you first offered an insult I think, and can not complain if you are paid in your own coin.

Mrs. L. Gentlemen please do not forget where you are. I am surprised at this unseemly wrangle.

Squire. What is unseemly? Mrs. Linton do you call me to account for plain advice because it was too plain? Remember I have the power to exact satisfaction for these injuries. You well know my power over this house and you ought to know that Simon Carter can resent an insult. Mr. List you will find that my influence is not confined to this neighborhood. I have friends in the 13th regiment who will be only too glad to favor me by granting any little requests I may make.

Lanty. Tools for work which you would'ent stoop to do yourself.

Tabbs. (*Aside.*) Plaguey low work Squire Carter would have to *stoop* to, hi, yi.

Squire. And so you feel at liberty, Mr. Nixon, to interfere here with your meddling impertinence. Your impudence is unendurable, though you are excusable for imitating the example of your superiors. But by Heaven, I'll have satisfaction for all this.

Nathan. Confound it Uncle, can't you stop? What's the use of all this row? Has your honor been assailed?

Tabbs. (*Aside.*) Dat would be sailin an illusion.

Squire. I have been insulted; grossly injured.

Alice. Mr. Carter, it was all my fault, please forgive Harry, and I'll bear all the blame.

Harry. I don't think I shall suffer much without forgiveness.

Mrs. L. Remember, Mr. Carter, that youth is rash and apt to be hasty.

Lanty. And that old folks are sometimes more than hasty.

Squire. More than hasty! What do you mean?

Mrs. L. Mr. Carter, do not be unreasonable because the boys may happen to be inconsiderate. Let us drop this subject.

Squire. We will not waste words. I am unreasonable, am I? So be it. I am a match for all of you, when it comes to the test of power.

Tabbs. (*Aside.*) A lucifer match I spect.

Squire. Mrs. Linton, when you find yourself without a roof to shelter you; when you are deserted, friendless, and penniless; perhaps you will remember that the Carters wished to be your friends, and that you spurned their proffered kindness to accept from others, a delusive friendship which could only prove a curse. Adieu. (*Exit L.*)

ARRANGEMENT OF CHARACTERS.
C.
Mrs. L., Alice.

R. Lanty, Tabbs.   Harry, Nathan L.

SLOW CURTAIN.

ACT IV.

Three years have elapsed between Act III and IV. Scene,—Mrs. L. *seated by a table sewing. Room poorly furnished. Evidences of great poverty.*

Knocking. Mrs. L. *opens door L.* Squire Carter *appears.*

Mrs. L. Simon Carter!

Squire. Good morning, Mrs. Linton. I hope you are well.

Mrs. L. You hope I am well! *You* who have blighted forever the hopes of a once happy household. Dare you speak the word hope?

Squire. Mrs. Linton, I have not come here to call up the bitter things of the past. Let us forget the past.

Mrs. L. You taunt me with my wrongs when you speak of the past.

Squire. I am not here to speak of what might have been but of what may yet be.

Mrs. L. What can you have to say to me? Why do you presume to enter this house? Poor as it is it has never been contaminated by the presence of such as Simon Carter.

Squire. Stay Mrs. Linton. We have been enemies but let enmity listen to reason, may you not have judged too severely? Your lot has truly been a hard one, but who is to blame? Your late husband's property passed to his creditors of whom I was the principal one. Your homestead became mine under a mortgage which you gave willingly and of which you admitted the justice. You and your daughter have hardened your hearts against me and my nephew Nathan, him who once was called your son. It is for him I have come to speak. Whatever slights I may have endured are satisfied. Yes I may say forgotten. *He* has always been your friend. He would again be your son and more than a brother to Alice. Will you accept a reconciliation?

Mrs. L. And is this your mission? Our interview is ended.

Squire Then you prefer poverty to comfort?

Mrs. L. Ay, a thousand times better poverty, than one penny of your hated wealth or this degrading alliance. (*Turns away.*)

Squire. (*Aside.*) Unyielding as adamant. We must have the girl though or our title is unsafe and the boys may come home any day. But I've another plan or two. (*Aloud.*) Mrs. Linton. I have been talking to day with Mr. List about this house, you know it is so close to my property that it really detracts from the value of my residence quite materially. I believe *you* thought it an eye-sore when you occupied the Linton Mansion. If we must be enemies, more than a stone's throw should separate us.

Mrs. L. And you wish Mr. List to turn us out of the house and pull it down do you?

Squire. I have only to say the word.

Mrs. L. Then say it. You are strong and I am weak, but in the sense of duty done, and in the approval of a conscience at peace with its possessor, there is a bulwark of safety which your guilty soul has never known Simon Carter.

Squire. I never knew a conscience which could shelter its possessor from wind or rain. You know Mr. List?

Mrs. L. Yes. I *do* know Mr. List as the livelong enemy of our family, yet I believe for all that, he is a man too honorable to stoop to such a crime for crime it would be.

Squire We will see about that. In the meantime consider the proposition I have made. Nathan will talk the matter over with Alice. . Good day, Mrs. Linton. (*Exit L.*)

Mrs. L. Have our persecutions begun anew! Why is Simon Carter so anxious that Nathan should marry Alice? They have our property. What more can they want? I fear they have some other horrible scheme to put into execution.   •

Enter BETSEY R.

Betsey is it not time for Alice to return from school?

Betsey. Yes, and I saw her coming down the road with Nathan Carter.

Alice. (*Entering followed by* NATHAN.) *Never* NEVER will I be your wife and I never want to see your face again.

Nathan. Ah! good morning mother. Good morning, Miss Betsey.

Mrs. L. Nathan Carter, you will please not call me mother. Once I was moved with joy to hear a sweet good morning mother from one who I fondly hoped would fill the place of my own lost son. But the bitter wrongs which we have suffered at the hands of you and yours, forbid that we should ever be aught to each other again but——

Nathan. Enemies. Let me say a word in self-defence.

Mrs. L. Cruel injustice has been done and no defence can change a wrong to right.

Nathan. No, very true. You may have had wrongs and you will admit that we also had rights.

Mrs. L. Strange rights that will turn helpless women from their homes destitute.

Nathan. Strange yet strict justice. Mrs. Linton, have we claimed more than our own? Was not your husband's property justly forfeited to his creditors? Did we not agree for a penny?

Betsey. For the last penny.

Mrs. L. I do not complain of the payment but only of the manner of payment. Why was our homestead ruthlessly sold at such a sacrifice as ruined us? Why were we not given a little time until friends could have aided us?

Nathan. The mortgage was due and you failed to raise the money to release it. Uncle was pressed for means. What else could he do? Who were the friends you speak of? But those things are done and can not be undone. Let us remember only the happy days when I was one of you. Perhaps the future more generous than the past can make some reparation.

Mrs. L. Say no more. I know of what you would speak. You can make no reparation.

Nathan. I can place you in the enjoyment of plenty, if Alice will only be my wife.

Mrs. L. Your wife indeed! Can you ask a woman to become the wife of one who has deprived her of her inheritance, and sent her into the world degraded and neglected? We are poor but we will never redeem our own with the price of honor.

Nathan. Wherein is the dishonor if she weds one who has long loved her ardently and devotedly?

Mrs. L. And whom she despises from the very depths of her heart. Nathan Carter if this is your only mission here you will oblige us by taking your leave at once.

Nathan. (*To Alice.*) Is this your answer then?

Alice. You have heard your answer. If there is one spark of manhood in your perfidious bosom leave this house at once and never desecrate it again with your hateful presence.

Nathan. (*Aside.*) Baffled again, when sure of success. But I'll win yet. (*Aloud to* ALICE.) So you stubbornly persist in your foolish course. Then if want resumes her sway to humble your proud notions of love and honor, you cannot lay the blame upon me. Heaven is my witness that I have tried to help you. Mrs. Linton, Alice secured her situation as teacher in the village school through my influence. That favor has not been appreciated and I can bestow it in more grateful hands. Must you be compelled to listen to reason?

Alice. Your boasted help you gave for a selfish purpose. I despise the motive and the man. When we hear anything reasonable doubtless we will listen to reason.

Nathan. Reasonable or unreasonable you will soon hear from us again. Adieu ladies until we meet again. (*Exit L.*)

Mrs. L. Until we meet again! When will our pursuers rest satisfied with their dark deeds!

Betsey. Their race will be run sometime. " It is a long lane that has no turning." I don't see any turning for us yet, unless it is where it turns to the poor house. But talking will do no good. I must see about the supper. (*Exit* R.)

Mrs. L. Ever ready for the call of duty. Betsey with all her faults is a noble woman. She has been true to us in prosperity and more than a friend in adversity. Her presence is a daily reminder that generosity and fidelity yet linger on earth.

Alice. Mother why does Nathan Carter persist in annoying me with his unmanly attentions? Is the man a lunatic? I hate the very name of Carter.

Mrs. L. My darling child, the Carters have some new purpose to work out. What it may be time alone will tell. Simon Carter was here this afternoon and asked me as he did once years ago, to use my influence with you in favor of Nathan. Like the nephew he made fair promises. When I spurned with indignation his base proposal, he threatened us with further persecutions.

Alice. Simon Carter was here too! Then Nathan did not meet me by chance this afternoon as he falsely pretended.

Mrs. L. No he placed himself in your way and persisted in following you here contrary to your wishes as a part of their plot. I cannot even guess their purpose. Our future is ominous. May Heaven protect us for we know that Simon Carter is a dangerous man when determined upon evil.

Alice. All we can do is to wait and work. Mother, we can not neglect the duties of the present to speculate about the future. Unremitting toil stares us constantly in the face. The labors of to-day are not yet finished and call me to my task. (*Exit* R.)

Mrs. L. Oh this bitter pinching poverty! How I used to wonder that people could ever become so helplessly, hopelessly poor. God knows I realize it now as I never could when I was the petted child of a rich and indulgent father or the idolized wife of a noble generous husband whose means afforded him the opportunity to indulge my slightest wish. Truly our reverses have been swift and remorseless. Only four short years ago we were in a beautiful home surrounded by every comfort and now we drain the very dregs of poverty's bitter cup, friendless and penniless.

Enter BETSEY R.

Betsey. Mrs. Linton, George Harley has just come home from the army, and Capt. Wilson has been up at the Squire's and Pettus Pettifog, the Squire's Lawyer.

Mrs. L. Harry and Lanty will soon be home too, I suppose, as the war is over. Perhaps George brings some news of them.

Betsey. None! Susan says he has never seen either of them, nor heard from them since he left home.

Mrs. L. Alas! Others' sons may return, but mine is gone never to return. Even he whom I hoped to call my son, by his silence is dead to us. Betsey, can we not hope that Lanty may be to us again what he once was? I cannot believe that every one has deserted us.

Betsey. Whatever Lanty may be to us, if he should return, I do not deserve that he should fill the place he once filled. I drove him to enlist by an inconsiderate flirtation, and proudly refused an explanation until he left me, believing I preferred another.

Mrs. L. Is that the only reason of his silence?

Betsey. I know of no other reason.

Mrs. L. Did you say that Capt. Wilson was at Squire Carters? He could tell us something of Harry and Lanty.

Betsey. Yes, if he chose. But in my opinion you would get precious little information out of him. You remember that Squire Carter said his influence might be felt even in the army.

Mrs. L. I remember that.

Betsey. Capt. Wilson is that influence. He is the cat's-paw of Simon Carter. They are up to something now, or that compound of meanness and deceit, Pettus Pettifog, would not be there. Somebody will have to pay for that visit. Susan says, that Jim Black, Squire's hired man, overheard Mr. Pettifog say, "Deuced ugly business if that nigger should turn up." Of course that nigger is Tabbs. I always believed that Tabbs' story about the forgeries of Simon Carter was true. I am more than ever convinced of its truth since the chief witness against Tabbs has said that he believed Tabbs never stole the coat w hich he was accused of taking.

Mrs. L. Tabbs' story may be true. True or false, it matters little to us now. But would Squire Carter dare to banish a citizen on account of a personal grudge?

Betsey. Dare! These are times when men dare do anything without fear of punishment. Squire Carter knew that there would be plenty to back him in that. Think of poor Tabbs ordered by a mob to leave the country after a mock trial, and glad to get away a ive too. All because Squire Carter was airaid he might tell the truth in regard to some things which he preferred to remain secret. Everybody knows Tabbs was not guilty of theft. But what avails innocence against villainy which has the power to carry out its infamous schemes.

Mrs. L. Suppose Tabbs should venture to return, which is not at all probable, I don't see how he could aid us or hurt Simon Carter in the least.

Betsey. I don't see either, but lawyers don't say such things without some reason.

Mrs. L. Did Susan hear anything further from Jim about the conversation?

Betsey. No: only that they were talking about letters, and as he passed the window he saw on the table some papers which they seemed to be talking about. Susan was in such a hurry to get home that she did not wait to tell me the particulars if she knew anything more.

Knocking heard L. *A boy delivers a letter to Betsey, who goes to the door.*

A letter for Miss Alice. *Calls Alice, who enters* R. Alice here is a letter a boy has just brought for you.

Alice. Why who can have written to me: can it be from Harry? *Takes letter.* No, it has no post mark, and the word "present."
Tears it open, reads aloud.

LINTONVILLE, April 20, 1865.

Miss Alice Linton:

For some time past the Directors of this district have considered the advisability of employing some one else to teach our school. We are satisfied that a change is now necessary. Your successor will take charge of the School next Monday. Very truly, yours,

Simon Carter, Clerk of Board.

Alice. The last blow has fallen!
Mrs. L. No, not the last. They will turn us out of the house next.
Alice. We are indeed at their mercy, defenceless women with no protectors. Oh! when will Harry and Lanty return? What can be the cause of their long silence?
Mrs. L. My child, cease your vain regrets. Harry has evidently forgotten us; then why should we remember him? His coming would bring no joy to our hearts.
Alice. She speaks truly. It must be so, but the thought is a death knell to my last vain hope. How could one, the very type of honor, act so basely without even a word of explanation. I can't believe it. I'll *not* believe it. I *will* hope on till he tells me from his own lips, that he wishes to be released.
Mrs. L. Your hope is delusive. We are indeed forsaken by all who could render assistance in an hour of need.
Alice. Not by all. Heaven watches over the distressed, and will some day avenge the wrongs of the innocent.
Betsey. Well, we have our hands and the wide world to make a living in, if that's any consolation. Help will come from some quarter. "The darkest hour is just before the dawning."
Curtain.

ACT V.

One month has elapsed between Acts IV. and V.

SCENE, *Table C. seated* MRS. L. *R.* ALICE *R.* BETSEY *L. Knocking* L. BETSEY *goes to door. Enter* PHŒBE.

Betsey. Come in Phœbe. We are glad to see you.
Phœbe. Good morning Mrs. Linton, good morning Miss Alice.

Mrs L. }
Alice. } Good morning Phœbe. (*Shake hands.*)

Mrs. L. Take a seat, Phœbe. We seldom see you now. Have you too forgotten old friends and the days when you found a place at our hearth?

Phœbe. No, I have not forgotten you Mrs. Linton. The thought of you and your trials has cost me many a sleepless night, many a bitter tear of regret. Mrs. Linton I never shall forget your kindness to me. Oh! that I had been more worthy of it.

Mrs L. Why do you speak of unworthiness, Phœbe? I always found you faithful in all things.

Phœbe. We all have our faults, and I have mine. I have not always been what I seemed to be.

Betsey. You were always my ideal of perfection in your sphere, Phœbe.

Phœbe. Our most cherished idols are often crushed in the dust.

Alice Along with the heart whose inspiration clothed them with life and beauty. But what has been crushing your idols to dust Phœbe?

Phœbe. You could only hate me if I told you.

Enter SQUIRE CARTER L. (*His knocking not noticed.*)

Squire. Only hate you if you told! Girl, have you been blabbing? Have you? If you have you will pay dearly for it. Go home. You know you are not allowed to visit here.

Mrs. L. It is you Simon Carter who are forbidden to come here.

Squire. By whom?

Mrs. L. By the usages of society and the dictates of self-respect which forbid a *gentleman's* entering where he knows his presence is disagreeable. After the wrongs you have inflicted on me how dare you enter my house. Leave it at once. Your presence is as loathsome as the foulest reptile.

Squire. Save yourself the trouble of racking your brains for further hard words. It is not pleasant for me to be obliged to enter your house. I am here only to bring home a disobedient servant.

Betsey. And hear what she would say to us. But we know enough about you already to consign you to a felon's cell.

Squire. Know what! What did you say? Girl have you betrayed me? Have you? Come with me at once. (*Seizes her, she screams for help.*)

Betsey. Coward, do you dare to lay hands on a woman?

Phœbe. Save me, save me. I never will go with him again. He will kill me.

Squire. Come on (*Drags her forward*) your tongue will learn by-and-by to stop its wagging, or I'm mistaken.

Enter J. Mc. L.

J. Mc. Well really ah! Do 'you want any help Mistah Carter? Is she crazy ah?

Squire. Help! Crazy! No you lunatic. I can manage her myself. She has just run away from her work. That's all.

Betsey. Save her, Mr. Hopkinson, from the hands of Squire Carter. She has dared to assert her right to do as she pleases and he threatens revenge.

Mrs. L. Mr. Hopkinson, protect us from Simon Carter, for he fears that we may learn the secrets of his villainy. Phœbe is no longer safe in his hands.

J. Mc. I am astonished ah! Squiah Carter a villian! Squiah this is a free country. May be you had better keep your hands off this young lady.

Squire. Mr. Hopkinson, I'm slandered, basely slandered. I hope you will not interfere since I am merely claiming my just rights.

Betsey. Rights! What right have you to say where any one shall go in this free land? Mr. Hopkinson, please protect us and I will be forever grateful.

J. Mc. Well it is really a pleasure to hear you say so. I will serve you most willingly. I beg pardon Miss Bluff, but I believe the last time we met you preferred to have some one else as a protector.

Betsey. (*Aside.*) Because he would act the dunce. (*Aloud.*) I was just joking then and did not mean to slight you Mr. Hopkinson. You know we shall always be good friends.

J. Mc. Only *friends!* Is that all? I would rather we were enemies than such friends.

Squire. Deuce take your palaver. Phœbe, come with me. (*Advances towards her.*)

J. Mc. I really can't allow you to take this young lady with my consent.

Squire. I shant ask your consent, nor anybody else's. (*Advances.*)

J. Mc. Look here Squiah. It is exceedingly unpleasant for me to be obliged to hurt your feelings ah, but I shall have to do so unless you modify your demands a little. The fact is you don't take this girl until she is willing to go.

Squire. Mr. Hopkinson, it seems to me you are unreasonable. But we have always been on good terms and I don't wish to quarrel with a friend about a trifle. I will just wait here until the girl is ready to go.

Mrs. L. Mr. Carter, Phœbe shall remain here till she has finished her visit and wishes to go. You can remain too, of course, if you insist on it. But I hope you will excuse Alice and myself from entertaining you. Phœbe, come to the kitchen and we will have a chat. (*Exeunt* Mrs. L. Alice *and* Phœbe R.)

Squire. (*Aside.*) Well I suppose I'll have to go without her.

I'll keep a close watch on this house though. (*Exit L.*)

J. Mc. Squiah Carter seems determined to have his own way in this village, to run things in fact.

Betsey. Yes and he is not very particular about the means he employs to run them either. He has succeeded in getting possession of all Mrs. Linton's property, and now he dares to come here to this poor place to exercise his authority.

J. Mc. This is a poor place. Miss Bluff, I should think you would get tired of staying here. There can't be much inducement for remaining ah.

Betsey. No not much. (*Aside.*) And very little for leaving.

J. Mc. Miss Bluff, you aw sacrificing yourself by toiling here this way. You aw actually *giving* Mrs. Linton your services, pon my veracity you aw.

Betsey. Mr Hopkinson I am not sacrificing myself by serving those who befriended *me* when *I* needed assistance. I am not *giving* Mrs. Linton my services. I *owe* it all to her.

J. Mc. Ah! Debt of gratitude. But really Miss Bluff, would you not like ah to take charge of a house of your own?

Betsey. No I believe not. I think it would be trouble enough to *help* take charge of one.

J. Mc. Oh! I meant to *help.* Of course you could not do it all. Miss Bluff, will you be my bwide. I offeh you my hand and heart. I admiah you so much.

Betsey Admire me do you! Just as you do a new necktie or the latest style of coat, I suppose. When I marry a man I want one who *loves* me.

J. Mc. Really Miss Bluff I *love* you. You know I meant that at first. Will that be sufficient?

Betsey. Mr. Hopkinson, I don't love you. I cannot even *admire* you. I can respect you and that is all.

J. Mc. Is that all? Well that is not as bad as it might be. Could'ent we get along with respect? Some married folks do not have even *that.*

Betsey. Mr. Hopkinson I don't think I shall ever marry. My mind is made up. Such a union as you speak of would lead to a life of misery.

J. Mc. Could'ent you change your mind Miss Bluff?

Betsey. Not without some reasons, and I don't see any reasons just now.

J. Mc. If your mind is made up I shant insist. Well I suppose a girl is not to blame if she dont like a fellah. (*Aside.*) Pon honoh I believe some other fellah is to blame. (*Aloud.*) Miss Bluff I presume you aw very busy to day, so I will bid you good aftehnoon.

Betsey. Good day Mr. Hopkinson. (*Exit* J. Mc. L.) Plague take the dunce; he might have guessed how matters stood. May be I am a bigger dunce than he is after all. I sent Lanty Nixon away in fun and he left in earnest. Now Hopkinson is gone. I guess I'm too particular, "wit, money, and manners," dont often go together. What's the odds now! It's decided anyway.

Enter MRS. L., PHŒBE, ALICE, R.

Mrs. L. For " better or worse"?

Betsey. No.

Mrs. L. Are you acting wisely, Betsey? Offers do not come every day.

Betsey. Wisely or unwisely, I'd rather die an old maid than be tied to that booby for life.

Alice. You may change your mind in a few more years. Phœbe, I think I have guessed the cause of your despondency. Are you thinking of " What might have been"?

Phœbe. I am thinking of what might have been if I had not fallen, miserably fallen.

Mrs. L. Phœbe, you surprise me. What is the matter? What have you done?

Phœbe. I have wronged you so deeply that no repentance can atone for the crime. Your suspicions in regard to your property are correct. The Carters' claims were based on forgery and falsehood. Mr. Linton never owed them a dollar. You have been basely defrauded and I have been the means of enabling them to execute their criminal purposes.

Mrs. L. Oh Phœbe! have you done this? And we have known you so long and trusted you. It is terrible. What have you done to aid them?

Phœbe. I have been their accomplice. I took the missing papers, and Simon Carter forced them from me by threats of imprisonment. I deserve reproach. I deserve to suffer for my unpardonable guilt. Oh that I could atone for my crime by some act of reparation in your behalf! I would walk through fire to serve you. I'll be a slave no longer, and when the proper time comes, you may trust in me. Then Simon Carter will find to his sorrow that a despised servant can wield a power which he dreams not of.

Mrs. L. Deluded girl, you are mad! What can you do to prevent Simon Carter's unholy works? It is too late now.

Phœbe. Too late! Alas I fear it is. (*Musingly.*) Why have I not tried to do something sooner? Miserable coward that I am! It is not too late to die in the attempt. They are both away to day and now is an opportunity which may not come soon again. I'll try it.

Mrs. L. What do you mean Phœbe? (*Exit* PHŒBE *hastily* L.)

Alice. I believe the girl is crazy.

Mrs. L. It is the lunacy of despair. Her story is too probable to admit of any doubt. And what a tale of villainy it is. *For gery* and *falsehood*! What I took for a lack of mercy in selling our property, proves to be a lack of honesty. And the man whom Mr. Linton trusted so implicitly is capable of robbing his benefactor's wife and child! Horrible thought! I was warned in time but would not heed the warning. Now it is forever too late!

Betsey. I always despised the whole set anyway, for I believed they were not trustworthy. Now) (*Knocking which is unnoticed, Enter* SIMON CARTER *unnoticed.*) the evidence is complete and Simon Carter is a consummate villain.

Squire. Villain eh? Who dares say villain? Have a care how you blacken my character. I thought you knew me Mrs. Linton?

Mrs. L. I thought so too Simon Carter, but I find I was mistaken, for each day adds something to my knowledge of you nd your lawless transactions.

Squire. There is one thing you have not learned yet, and that is the extent of my power. Tempt me no further.

Mrs. L. (*With scorn.*) *Tempt* you no further indeed! As if you had not already yielded yourself fully to the wiles of the tempter. You have accomplished your fiendish work of robbery and cruel persecution. You have done your work only too well. Years ago people called you a villain. My husband and I disbelieved them because we thought you a persecuted man. You took advantage of his generosity to cheat him shamefully. Not content with your ill-gotten booty, you set yourself to rob his helpless family. You who was legally their protector. To accomplish your dark deeds you alienated our friends and strove to blacken our fair name. You stole the patrimony which you were sworn to protect. Ay *stole* it! Well might you blush with shame if your hardened cheek were not stranger to a blush.

Squire. Mrs. Linton, you have said some hard things. You may yet repent these hasty words. You may be called upon to prove your assertions.

Mrs. L. Repent my words! Never! No words can portray the depths of your infamy! Dare you ask for proofs? They shall be produced. Simon Carter, I know at last from an eyewitness, the secret of your cunning plot. Where are my husband's lost papers which you so hypocritically pretended to be searching for? Who has seen them since you forced them from the trembling hands of a timid servant whom you threatened to imprison if she did not give them up? Dare you answer that?

Squire. Mrs Linton this is all very fine but it is mere assertion. I suppose that trembling servant is Phœbe Day, who has been filling your ears with slander when she should have been at home at work. I see through it all. It's conspiracy. That's easily settled.

Mrs. L. Base wretch begone! You have succeeded in your unhallowed schemes but you can not subdue a will determined to oppose you to the last. You may *crush*, but you can not *conquer*. There is a limit to all oppression and to all forbearance.

Squire. Who will believe a tattling servant and such as you?

Mrs. L. Oh bitter lot! Wronged, persecuted, and insulted because of my wrongs! Has it indeed come to this? No lower depth can be reached. Traitor I defy you. Begone! Wreak vengance if you choose. You can no longer wound.

Squire. I shall not leave until you allow Phœbe to go with me. But there is no hurry. If she stays, I stay.

Mrs. L. Until Phœbe goes! She has already gone.

Betsey. She has learned her lesson of cringing obedience well. I'd just like to see the man who could rule *me* that way.

Squire. Mrs. Linton, where is that girl? I believe you are plotting mischief and have her concealed somewhere.

Alice. We have told you she went some time ago. Is not that sufficient?

Mrs. L. I know nothing more than you do of her wherabouts and as for plotting mischief, what alas! can we do or plot now?

Enter PHŒBE, *L Excitedly.*

Squire. Can I believe my eyes? *Will* you come here again? What are you up to? Phœbe, you must go with me at once and no words about it. (*Advances to seize her.*)

Enter NATHAN *hastily*, L.

Nathan. Flee from this house, uncle. The soldiers are home and Harry and Lanty are on the way here now. Tabbs is with them and has told them all. Flee at once for you are not safe here.

Squire. Humph! Is that all.

Mrs. L. At last thank God.

Alice. Where are they?

Betsey. When did they come?

Nathan. Uncle be quick. They are almost here.

Squire. Silence coward! You are unworthy the name of Carter.

Nathan. Well I can't be responsible for your safety.

Squire. Pooh! They dare not lay hands on me. I have the law on my side and they have not a line to prove Tabbs' story. Let them come.

Enter HARRY, LANTY, TABBS, L.

Harry. Very likely you will *let* them come. Alice!

Alice. Harry! (*They embrace and kiss.*)

Tabbs. We's jes in force a comin like de bugs on de cowcumber wines.

Mrs. L. God bless you Harry, back again safe and Tabbs faithful old servant. (*Shake hands.*)

Betsey. (*Rushes into* LANTY's *arms.*) Why Lanty! The same old Lanty Nixon.

Lanty. Yes the same Lanty and not very old yet, and I infer from your demonstrations that you are still Betsey Bluff.

Betsey. Yes.

Enter L. OSCAR LINTON, *introduced by* HARRY.

Harry. Mrs. Linton, Colonel Oscar Linton.

Mrs. L. Oscar Linton! Oh God! my long lost son. (*Rushes into his arms.*)

Oscar. Yes a prodigal son who fled from the best of mothers. May Heaven forgive him. Alice, the little pet of my boyhood. (*They embrace.*)

Alice. Oscar! Dear brother Oscar! I always thought you would return to us.

Tabbs. Wish dis individual could jump into somebody's arms for two or three moments. But den de filosomer says man often hugs a collusion. Golly I kind o'think all huggin am a collusion anyway.

Oscar. And Betsey Bluff too, whom I have often led through the deep snow drifts, on our way to school. (*Shake hands.*)

Nathan. Brother Oscar, will you not recognize me?

Oscar. Do not call me brother. You never were my brother and now I loathe your proffered friendship.

Squire. Loathe us then, son of a haughty race. We can endure your scorn. Nathan let us go. Girl, (*Turning to* Phœbe.) will you go?

Phœbe. Never!

Oscar. What! Phœbe our old servant! (*Shake hands.*)

Phœbe. Yes, master Oscar, I am Phœbe. Heaven be praised that you are spared to come back again to shield the helpless.

Squire. Be careful what you say girl. You have learned your place, I think. (*Exeunt* Squire *and* Nathan L.)

Mrs. L. My darling boy, this is a joy unspeakable. But why have you never written in all these years? Seven long years have passed since the report of your death. Why have you been silent when a word would have changed a mother's grief into joy.

Oscar. I have not been silent. I suppose you heard of the fatal accident in the mine, when my comrade Jerry White was killed and several others fatally injured. But I wrote the particulars to prevent anxiety at home, for I knew you would hear of the accident through Jerry's friends. How they ever got me among the killed is more than I can tell, unless it was because I left immediately after for other diggings. I could not bear to stay where poor Jerry met his sad fate.

Mrs. L. Your letter never came. Why did you not write again?

Oscar. I received no answer and my proud spirit construed silence as an intentional slight. I left for California at bitter enmity with my father because I imagined he cared more for Nathan than for me. We quarrelled and I vowed I would never return until the family needed my services. It was a rash and wicked vow which has resulted in nothing but sorrow to the dear ones at home. I say dear ones, for I loved you all at heart and have repented a thousand times of my folly.

Alice. Tell us how you happen to come back with Harry and Lanty, in an officer's uniform.

Oscar. That is soon told. When the war broke out I enlisted as second lieutenant, and have been promoted step by step to a colonelcy. I learn̩d by accident a few months since that there was a Capt. List in a regiment encamped near us.

Alice. A Capt. List! But I asked about Harry.

Lanty. Well, Capt. Harry List then.

Alice. What! You a Captain, Harry?

Tabbs. Dat am a fac. Dis war am a gwine to hatch out a a drefful sight of capens and ginerals. Dis individual will be a gineral too if he was'ent in de wah. He'll not be Tabbs anymore. Jest call him if you please Adjutant Sutler.

Lanty. I thought you were only assistant barber where we found you, Tabbs.

Tabbs. See heah massa Nixon, when a gemman has done got up in the world I think it is mighty small business to cast up to him the misfortunate occurrences of his poorer days.

Mrs. L. Tabbs, you have not got up very high in the world when you return to us. We have reached the bottom of the scale.

Tabbs. Massa Oscar will make that scale tilt pretty lively tother way some of these days, I tell you.

Harry. Things have changed since we left, and we never heard of your distress. Why did'nt you write to us? We could have helped you.

Alice. I concluded you would write to us when you wished to hear from us.

Harry. I did write repeatedly. And you never got my letters?

Alice. None after you left for the seat of war.

Harry. I wrote several. Receiving no reply I feared that my letters were lost in the mails, and wrote at different times until I was forced to conclude that for some reason you wished to consider our engagement broken.

Alice. How strange, that all our letters were lost.

Oscar. That may not be very strange after all. Who was your first Capt., Harry?

Harry. Capt. Wilson.

Oscar. And Capt. Wilson was the instrument of Simon Carter's machinations. Probably the Capt. could give you some information concerning those letters.

Harry. I see it all now. Squire Carter's remark about his influence, the day I enlisted, is clear as daylight now.

Oscar. A remark dropped by a brother officer of mine, who was acquainted with the Capt. leads me at once to conclude that your letters never left his tent when delivered there. The Capt. is said to have quit the service under suspicious circumstances to avoid a court-martial, owing to various irregular ties.

Harry. How stupid I was not to think of that at the time. Well I shant hunt up Capt. Wilson for information just yet, especially since I have more important enquiries to make. Mrs. Linton I have come back from the army safe, as you predicted I should. May I not ask now for the fulfilment of that promise which you made three years ago, that Alice should be mine?

Mrs. L. Yes, if Alice has not changed her mind.

Harry. I think I know what her answer is. Am I right Alice?

Alice. Yes dear Harry. Through all these years I have loved and hoped on in silence.

Oscar. In silence through the criminal knavery of designing men, who deserve to suffer severely for their crimes, so long unpunished.

Mrs. L. By the mercy of Heaven the worst part of their black plot has miscarried, and with loved ones around me again I feel that half the sting of poverty is removed. To see you all once more, strong and happy, is something I never dared to hope.

Harry. Lanty it strikes me you are rather still to night. Are you thinking about your next turn at picket duty, or about your rations of hard tack and bacon?

Tabbs. Hard tack! Dat am de reason of massa Lanty's solemn aspec, dat hard attack he had de day fore he enlisted. Dat enemy am still in de field. (*Looks at Betsy.*)

Betsey. Tabbs I see you still talk in riddles as you used to do. But tell me all about your military career Mr. Nixon. I should like to hear it. I know you would always acquit yourself like a soldier. I'd be ashamed of you if you had not.

Lanty. Would you indeed? I am happy to hear that you think I would not do anything unworthy of a soldier.

Tabbs. (*Aside.*) Massa Lanty am about to fight his battles over again if de enemy don't surrender.

Mrs. L. Lanty, I knew you would be a true soldier, for you were always a gentleman.

Betsey. And the gentleman is the true soldier.

Lanty. (*Aside*) Now or never. (*Aloud.*) Miss Bluff, I think it is about time this thing was understood.

Betsey. That what thing was understood, Mr. Nixon?

Lanty. Betsey, you know what I mean. I want—Miss Bluff it is about time—ahem, ahem, I think—

Betsey. Well go on. How do I know what you think.

Lanty. It is about time for you to choose between me and that Hopkinson.

Betsey. You haven't asked me to choose yet.

Lanty. Betsey, I've loved you for years. Will you be content to settle down with me for life? Don't say no.

Betsey. I'm not going to say no; you could have had an answer long ago if you had only had the courage to ask for it.

Tabbs. Three cheers for Massa Lanty. He has met de enemy and in de langwige of de philosomer, de victory am his. Massa Nixon don t you feel *con*siderable better than when we met Massa Hopkinson goin down de lane as we came up?

Lanty. No more of your nonsense Tabbs.

Harry. Allow me to congratulate you, Lanty, on your success and you Betsey on your choice. The events of the last few minutes would have driven away many a fit of your blues while in camp, Lanty.

Lanty. I doubt that Harry. It seems to me your blues were about as indigo-tinted as mine. Suppose I had asked before I went to the war.

Tabbs. Reckon you'd mos likely never gone at all.

Lanty. That is possible too Tabbs. Suppose I had known my fate, it would only have made the going harder, and then I might have had to endure the painful reflection that Betsey was false, if any letters had been missing.

Betsey. And I that you were false rather than bashful. Of the two evils I prefer the latter, especially as Mr. Hopkinson did not go to the war.

Lanty. See here Betsey we shall have a quarrel at once, if you allude to that donkey again.

Tabbs. Mustn't quarrel yet. Plenty of time for discussin family pivileges and judificatin differences of opinion after de honeymoon am set. When a family settles down to business such things have a reglar place in de orders ob de day as massa used to say about de proceedins of de legislater.

Alice. That is often true Tabbs, though I hope the disposition will be wanting in this instance.

Phœbe. "A word to the wise is sufficient," Betsey.

Betsey. Very true Phœbe, but *you* must not be so despondent amid this general rejoicing.

Tabbs. Speck de cause am Miss Phœbe's soger has'nt come back from the wah yet.

Phœbe. No Tabbs. I am expecting no soldier. I have greater reason than that for despondency.

Alice. Why Phœbe! You have not told us yet all you knew about Squire Carter's defrauding us.

Phœbe. Will you protect me from the Carters if I tell?

Oscar.
Harry. That we will. Speak on.
Lanty.

Phœbe. You all remember that Mr. Linton's private papers mysteriously disappeared after his death.

Oscar. Yes, I remember that you spoke of them, Harry.

Phœbe. I can tell you where those papers are.

Mrs. L. Indeed! Can you? Too true, alas!

Oscar. Where are the papers, Phœbe? Tell us all the particulars. Were they stolen?

Phœbe. In the changes which took place soon after Mr. Linton's death, his desk and papers were removed upstairs, while some work was going on below. I took all the papers and books from the desk to clean it. Looking over the different packages as I took them out I noticed one marked "valuable"—"notes, contracts, &c." I foolishly feared that particular bunch might be mislaid and placed it by itself upstairs on a shelf among some old books. Those books were carried off by Tabbs and thrown carelessly in the garret. When I looked for the papers, I was frightened to find they had disappeared. I could not find them in the garret so I kept the mater to myself instead of telling you as I should have done. When I learned the value of the missing papers at the time you were searching for them, an evil thought came into my head to keep them if I ever found them. Some time after I found them but told no one, for I had an idea I could make money out of them.

Mrs. L. And you sold them to Squire Carter. If you wanted money, why did you not come to me? I would gladly have given you money.

Phœbe. Judge not too harshly. I was not so wicked as I had planned. Nathan Carter had noticed that I was frequently hunting for something, and the Lord only knows what put it into his head to ask me if I did not know something about the missing papers. My guilt betrayed me and I confessed all. Nathan said the papers belonged to his uncle Simon as administrator of the estate. He urged me to give him the papers for his uncle, but I refused, for I never thought of giving them to any one who might use them to injure your interests in anyway. He said no more about them then and left me.

Mrs. L. Why did you not bring them at once to me if you mistrusted the Carters?

Phœbe. You were away from home that day. Besides I was ashamed to c nfess my crime and the Carters gave me little time to reflect, for that afternoon Squire Carter came over in hot haste and demanded the papers as his. He threatened imprisonment and prosecution if I refused. I was so frightened that I gave them to him on condition he would not tell any one what I had done.

Betsey. Precious little danger of his telling anybody.

Phœbe. Afterwards he compelled me by threats to go and work for him because he feared your influence. Since then he has kept me like a slave, constantly in fear of his threats.

Oscar. Where are the papers now, Phœbe?

SQUIRE CARTER *rushes in followed by* NATHAN, L.

Squire. I forbid her to speak. (*Steps forward threateningly.*)

Oscar. (*Steps forward.*) Go on Phœbe, you are in no danger.

Phœbe. Simon Carter I am your slave no longer. I will no longer remain silent when silence would cover up crime. Here are the papers. (*Hands them to Oscar.*) They prove Squire Carter's black and infamous crimes. Take them, and may Heaven forgive me for my part in the dark business.

Mrs. L. Heaven can forgive all in this act of repentance, and so may we.

Oscar. The more because it makes reparation. Well do I know that hand! My father's private papers and a memorandum of his accounts with Simon Carter. Phœbe, how did you regain possession of them?

Squire. Those documents are stolen from my private records. They are mine, and I will have them. (*Steps forward threateningly.*)

Oscar. Stand back. A civil tongue is a knave's best friend.

Harry. You have to deal with *men* now, instead of women.

Phœbe. Squire Carter keeps a strong iron box in his library. That box is always carefully locked, and I've thought for a long time that them papers were in it. One day he accidentally left the key to the box on the table. I took an impression of it and had another key made. I couldn't stand the pangs of my conscience at the misery I had caused a bit longer. When he was away to-day I opened the box and found the papers. Oh! I'm so glad, Mrs. Linton, that you can forgive even me.

Squire. A cursed pretty blunder I've made. That is a barefaced theft. I'll have those papers. Oscar Linton, you are an accessory to this theft; you will have to answer to that charge.

Oscar. So she is a thief, and I am no better. And who has made himself the chief culprit by reaping all the benefits of her crime? Answer that. You are not yet done with this, Simon Carter. You shall suffer the heaviest penalties of the law.

Nathan. Give back the property, uncle. We are foiled. Those fatal papers are our ruin.

Squire. Never! Never! They have the law, but I have the money. We'll see who wins. Besides, I can't dispose of the property better than in defending it. Try the law. Ha! ha! (*Going.*)

Harry. Pah! *You* talk of appealing to law, when you've violated the most sacred principles of law. Wretch! (*Exit* SQUIRE *L.*)

Oscar. His bluster is only the bravado of a bad man in a bad cause.

Alice. Can we recover our property?

Oscar. Our case is clear. No court will refuse us justice.

Nathan. Yes, your case is clear. My uncle Simon has committed a great crime. But what is his sin compared with mine? I have turned against those who loved me dearly. I have betrayed a loving mother and an affectionate sister. With the basest ingratitude I have brought to want those who took me a poor ragged outcast, and made of the wretched orphan a respetable and intelligent member of society. I have proved a viper in the bosom which cherished me. But as God is my judge, my crime began because of my love for her whom I hoped to make my honored bride. I loved her passionately, and hoped to make atonement by restoring all in common ownership. I failed miserably, and have wrecked my own brilliant hopes of the future, and blasted the happiness of others. Life has nothing more for me but to drag out a despised existence. May God forgive me. I dare not ask forgiveness of those I have so cruelly wronged. (*Exit L.*)

Alice. Poor Nathan! He has suffered enough already. I can forgive him.

Mrs. L. Misguided, wretched boy. He is to be pitied.

Tabbs. (*Aside.*) Wonder if anybody will forgive dis chile for bein run away?

Mrs. L. What bliss in this joyous reunion after the long dark past.

Oscar. Mother, I have been a wayward son. I have deserted a happy home. I have brought sorrow to a kind mother and a loving sister. Can you forgive me?

Mrs. L. Dear boy, we have forgiven you a thousand times; and now all is forgotten and again forgiven.

Oscar. Mother, sister, loved ones all, my heart swells with joy when it feels itself once more entwined by the blessed ties of home.

Alice. May we ever hold those ties sacred!

Harry. Comrades of the camp and field, we have survived the hardships of the march, and the dangers of the battle-field. But when we think of our stirring experiences and hair-breadth escapes, may we ever remember that, with silent heroism, faithful ones at home bravely battled for the right while the Odds were with the Enemy.

ARRANGEMENT OF CHARACTERS.

C.

Mrs. L.   Oscar.

Harry. Alice.   Betsey. Lanty.

R. Phœbe.   Tabbs. L.

SLOW CURTAIN.

INITIATING A GRANGER.

CHARACTERS.

"Doc" Sawyer,
"Artist Jack,"
"Pony" Simpson,
"Nestor" Briggs,

"Tip Wiggs,"
Imes Green, } New boys to be
Mike Mullett, } initiated.
"Dig" Wright,

Prof. Rattan, Dr. Needem, Billy Whistler, and two or three others who may enter as "members."

OFFICERS.

Most Wonderful Cabbage-Head, "Doc" Sawyer; regalia, a huge cornstalk wand, and a collar of cabbage leaves.

Knight of the Rake, "Artist Jack;" regalia, a hand rake.

Most Rustic Scribe. "Pony" Simpson; regalia, a paper cap encircled by a hay band; a huge turnip or beet on his table for a paper weight.

COSTUMES.

The Most Rustic Scribe should present a seedy appearance. Imes Green should represent a "Country Greenhorn." "Tip" personates the fast young man. Any ordinary clothing will answer for the other characters.

STAGE EXPLANATIONS.

R means right for the actor as he faces the audience; L left; C center.

INITIATING A GRANGER.

SCENE, *a student's room in an agricultural college. Bookshelves in the corner*, R, *containing a number of volumes. A "Grange" has been organized by the students, and two "freshmen" are to be initiated. Room exhibits various regalia and furniture for the "Grange." A stand or desk for presiding officer occupies C in rear. On this stand or desk, at either side, is a vase or goblet containing a large carrot, beet or other vegetable. At R is a table for M. R. S. On table is a large turnip flattened for a paper holder. On the wall L C is the motto, "Wild oats are a sure crop." R C is the motto, "The early worm catches the corn." Above these mottoes may be hung neat festoons of wheat, oats, hay, etc., or turnip tops, a pumpkin vine, etc. A washtub full of water, and an office stool in corner R. K. O. R. has a chair by the door L. When the "Grange" is called to order, the members take seats L and R.*

Tip. (*Looking around.*) This must be decidely agricultural. It looks like a granger's den, I think, though I never was in the country but two or three times in my life. Blow me if I could tell young turnips from cabbage plants now. But then the governor is going to move into the country and I must have a little preliminary knowledge so I can help with the garden and the lawn. How would I look in the garden with a spade, the ace of spades for instance? Ha! ha! That is one implement of husbandry we know how to use. We are not attending an agricultural school to no profit. (*Knocking heard; goes to door L.*)

Enter DIG WRIGHT.

Why how are you, Dig. I am ever so glad to see you. You seldom leave your door at night. Conterminate your Latin! Why don't you let it go for once. Sit down. (*Offers him chair.*)

Dig. I have no time to tarry. I must finish my essay.

Tip. On the mythology of the Hindoos compared with the Niebelungen Lied. Let the Hindoos go to grass.

Dig. Can't afford to do that for Prof. (*Pronounced "Proff."*), might send me after them.

Tip. George Wright, you have well earned the title Dig. You are a regular dig. There is no let up with you even when you know Prof. is away for a day or two. You learned that on the farm I suppose.

Dig. I believe I did Tip, and it's not a bad habit in my opinion.

Tip. No; you are right, I wish I could work like you, but I can't. It isn't in me. Sit down. (*Offers chair.*)

Dig. Haven't time.

Tip. Of course you will come around to see the initiation. We are going to induct Mike Mullett and Imes Green into the solemn mysteries of our order. There will be fun, lots of it.

Dig. Especially if one of the faculty drops in.

Tip. Oh! the Prof. who runs this dormitory will not be back till to-morrow, and who cares for the monitor. We'll look out for him. We've fooled him often enough, and we can do it again. Imes is well worthy his patronymic. He's so green he never suspects anything. He never heard of *hazing* and thinks our lodge is all O. K.

Dig. Tip, I'm in a hurry and want to borrow your "Synonyms."

Tip. All right, here it is. (*Reaches a book from shelf and hands it to Dig.*) Drop in for a few minutes at half-past eight.

Dig. I shan't come. Tip, you are a jolly fellow but you are too fast. I don't propose to lecture you, but I wish you would not take part in these silly proceedings or allow them in your room.

Tip. "A little nonsense now and then,
Is relished by the best of men."

Dig. Nonsense may do. But this is worse than nonsense. It is wrong. When we engage in such folly we waste our own time and encourage others to waste theirs by our example. Besides, it is not right to ridicule in this way men who are honest in their opinions, even if they are apparently objects of ridicule.

Tip. Now Dig, don't come it too strong in the high moral line all at once, just because some of us wish a little fun. We can't work always.

Dig. I am not coming it strong all at once. We have been carry-ing things a little too far for a good while and I've made up my mind that I'll have no more of it.

Tip. By *we* I suppose you mean *me* chiefly.

Dig. No; I don't mean you alone. I mean the boys of the North Domitory of whom I am one. That motto (*Points to " Wild oats are a sure crop."*) is a fling at morality.

Tip. That's true, isn't it? How can truth be a fling at morality?

Dig. Aye; wild oats are a sure crop but what is the harvest; and what is the market?

Tip. Oh well! it isn't harvest time yet. We shall have a high old time to night. It will all come out right some time.

Dig. Sooner than you expect may be. (*Exit L.*)

Tip. He is a queer chap. You might as well try to turn a trade wind as him. (*Knocking L.* TIP *opens door.*)

Enter ARTIST JACK *and* BILLY WHISTLER.

   Good evening, gentlemen.

Jack. }
Billy. } Good evening Tip. How are you?

Tip. I'm first rate. Take seats. How do you like our decorations? Very appropriate are they not?

Jack. Very. Especially that one. (*Points to "Wild oats are a sure crop."*)

    Enter DOC SAWYER, PONY SIMPSON, NESTOR BRIGGS,
                 and others.

Doc. We didn't wait to knock.

Tip. All right! My latch string's always out.

Pony. (*Looking around.*) Boys, I think these tasty decorations and regalia do credit to our committee.

Jack. Just what I was saying.

Billy. Green and Mullett will think they are at a country fair.

Tip. And *wish* they were there before it's all over.

Nestor. Tip, what on earth is that tub for? Are you going to throw a tub to the granger whale?

Tip. That's it exactly! Nothing like foresight in the agricultural pursuits. That's one of *my* ideas. We have the whale, of course we must save the blubber. That originated in my brain.

Jack. The blubber?

Tip. Ha! ha! You're getting witty, but just wait awhile to see my idea applied.

Pony. The Latin Tutor would like to know that Tip has an idea for once.

Tip. I fancy this one would relax his classic features.

Billy. Boys it's time to come to order isn't it? The candidates are tired waiting may be.

Nestor. Guess Mullett is suspicious. You'll never get him into anything worth doing, Tip.

Tip. We'll see.

Doc. (*M. W. C.*) Let's begin at once boys. (*Ascends stand.*)

M. W. C. (*Raps on desk with his gavel, a potato on a stick.*) Order! (*In a solemn tone.*) Huckleberry Grange will come to order. The officers will take their accustomed places and proceed in the discharge of their duties. Sir Knight, make proclamation.

K. O. R. (*Advances, speaks in a pompous tone.*) Hear, ye tillers of the soil, ye horny-handed sons of toil, ye sturdy-muscled, double-fisted, brawny-minded delvers after truth and low prices, behold the hour is at hand when Huckleberry Grange should open. (*Opens door L and shows in* MIKE MULLETT *and* IMES GREEN.)

M. W. C. (*In a solemn tone.*) I now declare Huckleberry Grange formally opened in regular session. I shall on this occasion dispense with the momentous incipient observations which under our Constitution the Most Wonderful Cabbage-Head has the prerogative to dissemiate. (*In an oratorical style.*) Let me only say that we should all be prodigal in felicitating ourselves that we live in this hyperbolical nineteenth century; located as it were right between jeopardy and the millenium; a century which has reverberated, and will continue to reverberate if you let her alone, with an accruing concatenation of inferential extrications. I may say without tergiversation that heterogeneosity is bound hand and foot to the expatiatory car of incontrovertibility while the triumphant charioteer urges on his' prancing oxen toward the inexorable goal of indivisibility, and an excrutiating public shout till the welkin jingles "Universal suffrage, cheap calico and hot flapjacks for all." I challenge the factory Lord to controvert what I have said. I defy the Middleman or any other man to invalidate my process of ratiocination. They can't do it. Let them try it and let them beware when the people, I say the people [*A voice: We heard it.*]— when the people rise in their majesty to sit down on their pocket books. Still notwithstanding, I say, nevertheless—

Nestor. I thought you were going to adjourn your remarks.

M. W. C. (*Severely.*) Order! We fervently hope that no Brother will interrupt the solemnities of this occasion and cast a blot over the proceedings.

Tip. (*Rising.*) Most Wonderful Cabbage-Head, it's more than a blot. It's a blight, a wilting blight. We should all be duly impressed with the serious importance of the imposing and expressive ceremonies about to take place this "initiation night." It is my sincere hope that we may do no discredit to our Brotherhood which is doing so much to give dignity and importance to rural toil. All honor to the noble institution of which we are proud to consider ourselves members. May she continue to teach farming as long as the scythe is the emblem of Father Time's presence. May she soon elevate the task of tickling the sides of mother earth, till she grins, into a refined and delicate art. In the halcyon days to come the manipulation of the hoe will indicate a taste as refined and artistic as that which guides the brush of the painter or the chisel of the engraver. It is coming to that. I know it. I see with the eye of a prophet. [*A voice: And hear with the ear of the animal the prophet rode.*]

M. W. C. (*Severely.*) Order! order! The Most Rustic Scribe will now read the minutes of the previous meeting.

Tip. Most Wonderful Cabbage-Head, I move that we dispense with the reading of the minutes.

Nestor. I second that motion.

M. W. C. Are there any remarks?

Several. Question!

M. W. C. All in favor will say *aye.* (*Chorus of ayes.*) Those opposed say *no.* (*One or two noes.*) The ayes have it and the reading of the minutes will be dispensed with. The next thing in order is "Words of wisdom from those who ought to know." The Most Rustic Scribe will call the roll and the members will respond with a sentiment. Of course our *candidates* will be excused from this part of the programme.

M. R. S. (*Reads.*) Tip Wiggs!

Tip. (*Rises.*) Our parental ancestors studied agricultural farming by a life-time of laborious experiments in their shirt sleeves. (*Laughter.*) *They* were in their shirt sleeves, not the experiments. We study the science of the soil in fifty easy lessons and are not much the worse for the wear. Who says this isn't an age of progress? Our forefathers and foremothers never feasted their eyes on a scene like this. (*Applause.*)

M. R. S. Knight of the Rake!

K. O. R. Learn wisdom from the Possum. A little pretense goes a long way.

M. R. S. Nestor Briggs!

Nestor. "Late to work and early to quit
Is the motto of him who lives by his wit;
Spice hard work with a little rest
Is the motto of him whose work is best;
To work not at all is just as well
Is the easy creed of the pert young swell;
Early to work and never get through
Is the miser's maxim. Which is true?

[*A voice: Now we should have the Granger's motto.*]

M. R. S. Billy Whistler!

Billy. (*Rises.*) I'll give the Granger's motto.
Philandengookenoben nixandabit;
Pater habet. Mullein sauce. (*Laughter.*)

Tip. A Latin verse for dignified sentiment!

Billy. Latin! That's a Greek *strophe.*

Nestor. A *trophy* I should think, such as Samson slew the Philistines with.

Billy. Ha! ha! Pretty good Nestor, but your logic's lame. My verse isn't the ordinary *jaw.* It's only the *jaw breaker.* So look out for *your* verses. (*Laughter.*)

M. W. C. (*Severely.*) Order! Order at once! The candidates for honors will now retire under charge of the Knight of the Rake, as is the custom until certain preliminary rites necessary to their initiation have been performed. (*Exeunt L,* MIKE MULLETT *and* IMES GREEN *escorted by K. O. R. As soon as they have passed out the others bring forward the stool which is placed in the C and covered with a cloth for a throne. The tub of water is placed in front of the stool and covered with strong boards for a footstool. Over the boards are placed carpet.*)

M. W. C. The Knight of the Rake whose title indicates the duties of his office, and signifies "We will gather them in," will now proceed to inform the candidate for the first honor, namely, Good-Fellow-at-Large, that the society awaits him. (*K. O. R. goes to door L and speaks to those outside.*)

Enter K. O. R. escorting MIKE MULLETT, *ceremoniously.*

Mike. Boys, I've been to college before and know something about what is expected of a freshman. I'm in for fun of course, but don't make it too strong.

M. W. C. I am astonished to my full capacity to think that the gentleman candidate would insinuate that there is any *fun* about the *imposition* of this solemn rite, so imposing in its nature. (*Solemnly.*) We will now take the first step in this significant ceremony and drain the memorial cup of good-fellowship with the Granger's favorite beverage, cider. * (*Pours from a pitcher in goblets and hands around, to candidate last.*) The candidate will now remove his right boot.

Mike. What for?

M. W. C. At once if you please. (MIKE *sits down and removes boot.*) The object of this simple ceremony is to remind the candidate of the uncertainty of human affairs. Many a spreading thistle fringes the path of life, and when we least expect it we may put a foot in it. The candidate will now mount the throne, which ceremony indicates that the rural toiler is indeed a monarch. (*Aside.*) Of all some other man has surveyed. (*Steps upon the tub and assists the candidate to mount the stool.*) With one more simple rite we can salute you as Brother and Good-Fellow at Large.

Mike. I wouldn't care if I was at large now.

M. W. C. The candidate will please preserve a dignified silence as becometh his position. I now veil thine eyes, oh waiting one, (*Bandages his eyes.*) to illustrate the solemn fact that the farmer must plow and sow, and reap and mow, and buy his yankee-notions by faith, that he must occasionally trust to the uncertainties of the syren middleman. I now ring in thine ears the tocsin of alarm to remind thee that the canker-worm may gnaw and the grasshopper pipe his festive lay and it behooves the Granger to be ever vigilant. (*Rings bell. While he is ringing the boys remove the boards and substitute others sawed nearly through.*) I now present thee the parting pledge and pronounce thee a Good-Fellow-at-Large. (*Gives him a cup of soap suds. The "Candidate" tastes and jumps up with an exclamation. Breaks into the tub of water and makes a great splashing. All laugh.*)

Mike. (*Springing from tub and tearing bandage from his eyes.*) Thunder and blue blazes! What was that I drank? (*Coughs and sputters.*) That confounded tub had water in it, eh. How, the Dickens did I break through? What was in that cider?

Tip. That's decidedly good to call soapsuds cider. (*Laughs uproariously.*)

Mike. Soapsuds by jingo! (*Spits.*)

DR. NEEDEM *rushes in wildly L.*

Dr. That's right boys! Give him soapsuds! A sure antidote. Make him swallow another glassful while I get an emetic ready. (*Tears open his pill bags and begins to prepare medicines. Sees tub.*) Had him in the bath! Couldn't have done better if working under orders. Keep him in. Keep his feet hot before the poison gets the mastery.

---

* Cold coffee or tea will serve for the "cider."

How much did he swallow ? (*The boys, who have stared in amazement,* " *see the joke*" *here and begin to carry out the* DOCTOR'S *orders by putting the* "*patient*" *in the* "*bath*" *again.* MIKE *resists energetically.*)

Dr. (*Earnestly.*) Stick to him boys. Merciful Heavens he resists! He is delirious! What if I should lose my first patient ! Lord knows I have waited long enough for some fellow to swallow poison or break his leg or do something of the kind! (*The boys struggle to get* MIKE *into the tub.*) Keep him in a minute longer. Give him more soap and water. (DR. *seizes the glass of soapy water and attempts to pour it down* MIKE'S *throat.* MIKE *throws up his hand and spills the water in* DR.'s *face.*) My Lord! gentlemen. He's mad ! raving. He'll be before his judge in less than ten minutes unless we do something.

Mike. I hope He'll be a more merciful judge than this crowd is.

Dr. Hold him gentlemen. He raves. I'll try the stomach pump. (*Bustles around and produces pump.* †)

Tip. All right doctor ! Be quick. (*Dr. approaches with pump.* MIKE *flings off those who hold him, and rushes at the* DR.)

Mike. (*With fury.*) See here old fellow, this thing has gone about far enough. You bring that nasty old pump near me and I'll knock your ugly apothecaries' mug off your shoulders.

Dr. Seize him somebody. He will escape in his delirium.

Mike. I'd like to see the one that would seize me now. Fun is fun and I can enjoy a joke as well as anybody. But this is what I call a dry joke.

Tip. Not for the want of water then.

Dr. (*Stares; he plunges his hand into the water.*) Good Heavens ! You have had him in a *cold* bath ! He'll die sure.

Mike. I've had enough of *initiation* anyway, but I guess it'll not kill me.

Dr. (*As the truth dawns on him.*) Initiation ! (*Looks around.*) What mean these mystic symbols ? Do I dream or is this a horrible nightmare ? Isn't this No. 42 South Dormitory? I've been victimized.

Tip. No; this is 27 North Dormitory.

Dr. (*With feeling.*) Oh I'm undone ! I'm a ruined man ! I'm eternally disgraced ! Where is the South Dormitory ? Oh my patient ! He is dead before this. I know he is. Where is he ? Do tell me.

Nestor. How in thunder can we tell *where* he is if he's *dead.* (DR. *seizes his pill bags and rushes out, leaving his stomach pump on the table.*)

Tip. (*Picks up the pump.*) Just the thing; may be the next candidate will need this. I call this enjoying an initiation.

Mike. Mighty fine fun ! My pants are entirely ruined.

M. R. S. What's a pair of pants ?

M. W. C. Nothing! Let's go on with the ceremony. The Knight of the Rake will escort the other candidate into the room. (*The boys carry the tub back to R and arrange the room.*)

---

† If a stomach pump can not be obtained, a syringe will answer the purpose, or an instrument may be improvised from some old tubing, etc., which will look sufficiently like a pump.

Enter IMES GREEN *L, escorted by K. O. R.*

M. W. C. The candidate will advance to the front. (IMES *shuffles up to the stand awkwardly with K. O. R. at his side.*) Oh candidate, (*Solemnly.*) you are about to become a member of the Verdant Circle of the Anti-Climax Society. Have you duly considered the momentous importance of the step you are about to take? The answer is: (*Speaks fast.*) " I have cogitated it with multifarious cogitations of a concentric hebdomadal conscience.

Imes. (*Blunders.*) I have agitated it with—with—multiplied aggravations of a chronic conscience. I can't say that.

M. W. C. You mean it, I see, and that will do equally well.

Tip. (*Beckons to M. W. C.*) Shall I apply the test?

M. W. C. It seems unnecessary in this case, but then it will certainly do no harm. Will the society have the test?

Several. Let's have it.

Tip. (*Advances with stomach pump. Speaks in a mysterious manner.*) Worthy brother, in thy response hast thou told the whole truth, all the truth, and nothing but the truth? Far be it from me to doubt, but our Brotherhood has a test which never fails to penetrate the depths of a man's consciousness. It will lay bare that which is hidden in the twinkling of an eye. It will reveal the most profound secret, even to what a person had for dinner.

Imes. Mercy on me! I told the truth. What is that thing anyway?

Tip. It's a cardiac, gastronomic, extenso-flexor. It never fails. Was there any mental reservation?

Imes. Any what?

Tip. Ah! I see there was. This will tell. All that is necessary is to place this tube to the mouth and work this handle and the most stubborn are moved, as if by an earthquake, whether they will or not. (*Makes feint of applying the pump.*)

Imes. Don't! (*Drops on his knees.*) Don't for Heaven's sake! · I told the truth. I told all I know. I'll swear to it if you want me to, but don't try that awful thing. Let me swear. (*All try to restrain laughter.*)

M. W. C. (*Sternly.*) No profanity here if you please young man. Rise and we will proceed with the ceremony. (*The boys now place the tub of water on a chair or box of sufficient height that* IMES *may stoop over it without bending too low.*) Worthy Brother, we now complete this ceremony by observing the symbolic custom of "bobbing for the apple." Our mother Eve was very fond of this emblem of wisdom and implanted a like desire in many of her posterity. This simple ceremony commemorates that famous historical event and also typifies the fact so important to the Granger, that apples are often hard to get but that patience and a constant eye to the end in view will do wonders. As Eve did not obtain the apple until some one showed her how, so we deem it proper that the novice should see before he is asked to believe. Will the Knight of the Rake perform this touching ceremony, as only his artistic skill knows how?

(*K. O. R. produces two apples, one of which has a short wooden peg driven into it. The one containing the peg he places in the water.*

He places a strong wooden stick across the top of the tub at the side farthest from him, and placing his hands some distance apart on the stick proceeds to " bob" for the apple, or try to take it from the water with his teeth. After several feints he succeeds in seizing the peg between his teeth and lifts the apple triumphantly. While he is engaged in this PROF. RATTAN *slips in L unobserved, and squats behind a large arm chair.*)

M. W. C. (*Places the other apple in the water and turns to the candidate.*) Worthy Brother, you will now complete your initiation by performing this simple though significant rite. (*While he is speaking* TIP *slyly removes the stick and replaces it with one sawed nearly in two.* IMES *places his hands on the stick and stoops to seize the apple. The stick breaks and he plunges headlong into the water with a great splash. Jumps up, coughs, and blows through his nostrils.*)

Imes. Gewhillikers! how did I slip? (*All roar with laughter.*) By George, that's a deep tub.

Tip. What made you dive for the apple? Ha! ha! (*All laugh uproariously.*)

Prof. Rattan. (*Jumps up; speaks in severe tone.*) What do you mean, gentlemen, by making night hideous in this way?

Pony. Good Lord! It's Prof. Rattan. (*Dives out of the door L. Others attempt to follow but are headed off by* PROF.)

Prof. What are you doing, I say? I demand an explanation.

Tip. Well, Professor, we were just having a little fun when that accident happened.

Prof. An accident, indeed! Aha! I am here by accident too. I'll finish your *initiation. I will.* There is one ceremony to be performed yet and that is the laying on of the *rattan.* I'll teach you how to play tricks. (*Rushes at the boys; all escape L but* TIP. PROF. *seizes him and plies the rattan amidst cries of "Don't! ooh! stop that! etc."*)

QUICK CURTAIN.

SETH GREENBACK.

CHARACTERS.

SETH GREENBACK,	LARK,
DR. ESTY,	GRUBBER,
FRANK,	MRS. GEEENBACK,
PAT MULDAWN,	MILLIE WINFIELD,
SLIGH,	MOLLIE.

COSTUMES.

Any clothing suited to the social standing of the wearer.

STAGE DIRECTIONS.

R means right as the actor faces the audience; L, left; C, centre.

SETH GREENBACK.

ACT I.

SCENE, *Seth Greenback's sitting room. Furniture mostly old fashioned and incongruous, furnishing evidences of decided peculiarities in the owner. Table in C, sofa L, chairs R and L ; heavy pictures on the walls, one, the portrait of a beautiful boy, over table C, is draped lightly in mourning. General effect is sombre, but conveys the impression of wealth and intelligence.*

Pat. (*Pacing floor.*) Howly saints! was iver a man wrought as I'm wrought? Faith an' not a bit longer will I sarve ould Greenback, or my name is not Pat Muldawn.

Millie. (*Entering R.*) What's the matter now, Pat? You are getting into a pet nearly every day with Mr. Greenback lately.

Pat. An' it's your precious self that's a pet, Millie, shwate rosebud.

Millie. Pat, you're silly; I'm nobody's pet.

Pat. Faith an' ye desarve to be, an' I'll pet ye meself if nobody else will.

Millie. Balderdash! Pat, you have too much blarney. I reckon I'll get along as I have been doin'.

Pat. As ye have been doin'! An' how's that? Haven't ye been rulin' th's house almost intirely. Not but what ye should, for ould Greenback is a mean ould tyrant. But how ye manage him is more than I can tell. I niver was anybody's pet, exceptin' one man, an' that was ve y unfortunate.

Millie. Ha! Ha! He was unfortunate in selectin' his favorites, I s'pose?

Pat. Shure it was meself that was unfortunate in the selection. For he kept borryin' me hard earnin's that I saved, and niver a blissed cint of me wages did he pay me at all.

Millie. Why, Pat, how could you loan him your hard earnin's if he never paid you any money?

Pat. Faith, an' I lint him cash in hand that he should have paid me, but never did. He gave me some quare little slips of paper he called due bills.

Millie. And they are still *due* bills.

Pat. Ay, and we'l named, for I'm thinkin' they will never be *paid* bills, for the poor gintleman died and bequeathed all his liabilities to an ungrateful father, an' by me sowl the ould gintleman intirely refused the legacy.

Millie. So for want of anything better you concluded to try Mr. Greenback's.

Pat. Y s, out of necessity. Now if there is any vartue in larnin' temperate ways, and practicin' self denial, you see I'm makin' a vartue of necessity.

Millie. Mr. Greenback must be mighty virtuous if he can make virtues out of the necessities of other folks.

Pat. Ay, the ould skinflint. He's a paragon of vir'ue. He's above timptation. You might as well try to get a war-whoop out of a tobaccy sign by callin' him bad names, as to try to tempt the ould miser from his beaten paths.

Millie. I wish his appetite would tempt him to get us somethin' fit to eat, I'm nearly starved.

Pat. True, Millie, an' ye be. Ye're gettin' thin and maigre like. (*Pinches her cheek and attempts to kiss her.*)

Enter MRS. G. R.

Millie (*Slaps his ears.*) Keep your distance, you blockhead! (*Turns away angrily.*)

Mrs. G. Dear me! Pat, such conduct is very improper. I can't allow it.

Pat. (*To* MRS. G.) Troth an' I think so too, to be nappin' a fellow's noggin in that style. (*To* MILLIE.) Me distance you want me to kape, is it? Faith, an' I think I'll kape it a trifle further away from ye. (*Rubs his face.*)

Mrs. G. Pat, you should be in the field at this time of day. This is the very rush of the harvest. (MILLIE *busies herself arranging books on table.*)

Pat. Is it indade, mam? (*Aside.*) It was always me bad luck to be unlucky.

Mrs. G. Pat, you prefer talking to the girls rather than pitching hay. Doubtless it's pleasanter, but it don't suit folks who have to hire help to have them employed in that way.

Pat. Indade, mam! (*Aside.*) Begorrah, I can't snatch a minute wi h the girrels but some spalpeen's yelpin', Pat! work!

Mrs. G. Pat, you had better go before Mr. Greenback comes in. He won't like it to see you here.

Pat. I'm off at onct, mam. (*Exit* MRS. G. L.)

Millie. (*Angrily.*) Pat, don't you dare touch me again, you great, impudent booby. What will Mrs. Greenback think? If you do that again I'll break your Irish pate. (*Slaps him again.*)

Pat. (*Comically.*) May I look at ye iver again?

Millie. Sass-box!

Pat. (*Rubs his face*) Millie, just keep your pet names and your carisses for some one else, won't ye? I never could stand such things onyhow. They turn me head entirely. (*Aside.*) An' that last turned me body too. (*Aloud.*) Kape all your purty sayin's for master Frank. Poor boy, he needs a dale of sympathy.

Millie. (*Seating herself R of table.*) Pat, you're a dunce. Frank does not need pretty sayin's as much as he needs kind treatment and good friends.

Pat. (*Stands behind chair L of table, puts one foot on chair round and leans right elbow on chair back, head resting on hand in an easy attitude.*) Now ye've hit it to a *t*. But he'll have one good friend as long as Pat Muldawn's got a shilling, and I'm thinkin' he'll have an ther while yerself is to the fore.

Millie. (*Slightly confused.*) Yes, Pat, we must stand by him, for he has no other friends in the world except Mrs. Greenback, and she is afear'd to speak a word in his favor.

Pat. It's a ragin' shame the way that ould tyrant does bate him.

Millie. (*Starting violently.*) Oh, Pat, has he whipped Frank again? (*Walks the floor in great agitation*)

Pat. He *began* it, but he never finished the dirty job, for I heerd the racket and was in the barn immagitly, and I'm thinkin' me remarks on that occasion were more convincin' than illegant.

Millie. I hope you didn't insult him, Pat He's awful squeamish about such things, and it would only be worse for Frank.

Pat. Niver an insult did I give him. Says I——but I'll not repeat all I said. Says I, "Mr. Greenback, just drop that ould horsewhip, or I'll be afther breakin' ivery bone in your body."

Millie. The old fiend!

Pat. An' says he, "Pat, you're in a passion." Says I, "Shure an' I am. It makes me very blood boil with shame to see you strike that poor crayture who would now be nearly a grown man if ye hadn't starved his poor life out of him." He turned dreadful rid in the face, and I seed I'd raised a breeze an' must stop the rumpus s me way. Says I, "An' it's all about an ould shovel handle not worth a dime. Mr. Greenback, you know I'm perfectly willin' to make a new handle durin' me leisure, and not charge ye a cint." An' says he, "All right, Pat; but be careful you don't say something sometime that you will always regret." As he went out I wondered whether he iver regretted anything he iver did, or iver did anything a dacint man wouldn't regrit.

Millie. (*Indignantly*) The disgrace! To think of his strikin' poor Frank like a slave. But he da'sn't strike him when I'm around. I'd like to see him strike me onct, if he dares.

Pat. Shure and what would he think if he should be after strikin' you?

Millie. Think! I wouldn't give him time to think.

Pat. He'd be after thinkin' he'd mowed into a hornet's nest.

Millie. Well, if I seen such meanness goin' on I could be as spiteful as a hornet without half tryin'. (*In her excitement knocks a small vase from the table and breaks it.*)

Pat. Faith an' I believe it.

Millie. Shut up, you monkey! I mustn't let the old man see this. (*Picks up pieces of vase.*) Frank is too good. He actually likes Mr. Greenback; says he was good to him, and furnished him a home when he had none. A precious home, to be a galley slave for a mean pittance of clothing and coarse food. I'd as lief go to the poor house for my part. And Frank thinks that old Greenback is generous. You know he gave Frank an old gold wa ch. Heaven only knows what made him do such a recklessly extravagant thing. I s'pose he couldn't get rid of the watch any other way. But he must have been beside himself when he gave it away.

Pat. He wasn't beside himself. He was beside the boy. I seed him when he gave it. He handed it to Frank, and says he, "Frank, here's a watch you may have. I had a boy once. He would have been about your age now, if Providence had not taken him from me." An' would you belave it, Millie, he actually shid tears, an' Frank cried like a five year old spalpeen; an' says he, "Oh, Mr. Greenback, you've been very good to me, and I've been awkward, and careless, and ungrateful." An' Mr. Greenback says, says he, "Niver mind, Frank, I haven t done much for y u." An' he left the room so kind o' sudden I couldn't help feelin' sorry for him, for it was one of his awful blue days, when he looks so worn an' sad lookin'. Thin I thought of the day he rapped me over the head for breakin' a wheelborry, and called me a green Irishman. An' I restrained me tears, and rekivered me manhood immagitly. (*Straightens up and tries to look dignified*)

Millie. So you call that manly to hide your tears when your sympathies were excited. Pah! such manhood, Patrick! Smiles may be counterfeit, but tears mean something.

Pat. Shure an' it's meself can testify to that, for didn't me tears have a dale of meanin' when ye pulled my hair and pounded me noggin, because I said you were the purtiest girrel in the county, an' that your rosy lips were spilin' for a kiss, which I was ready to administer. I'm a man of me worred, an' I'm willin' yet to do that same. (*Seats himself, and leans across the table toward* MILLIE.)

Millie. When you get an opportunity, ha! ha! (*Rising, begins to dust and arrange the room*)

Enter FRANK R.

Frank. Have you curried the horses yet, Pat? You know Mr. Greenback is in a hurry to start to town, and we must get to work at the hay. There's not a minute to lose.

Pat Shure M ster Frank, an' ye's in a great hurry. The hay will not be dry for an hour. Take it aisy a bit.

Frank. Take time by the forelock, Pat.

Pat. Be jabers, an' if ye take him by the forelock too early in the mornin' ye must howld him all day. Frank, ye are larnin' the ways of Mr. Greenback very fast. Faith an' ye are as anxious about the hay as the ould miser himself. What interest have ye in the hay? It doesn't pay us to fret about the farmin'. The master will attend to that.

Millie. He will let nothing suffer for want of fussin' over.

Frank. It pays to do right, Pat. Mr. Greenback depends on us to lead in the field. If we don't get out the teams in time, will the other men follow?

Pat. Shure an' are we the main depindence? If I'm the boss in the master's absence, I'll get the worth of the money out of them lazy spalpeens. (*Rises—sticks his thumbs in arm-holes of his vest, and straightens up with an air of importance.*) Faith an' the idlin' rascals wouldn't airn their salt if it wasn't for a drivin' boy like meself to lead them.

Frank. You must have been born to lead, Patrick.

Pat. An' ye be flatterin' now. May I inquire the grounds of your opinion?

Frank. Because it is hard to get you to follow.

Enter GREENBACK *L. All start in surprise.*

G. I think he'll *follow* me. It's confounded queer that servants can't get to work without being watched. I sent you after Pat an hour ago, Frank. What have you been doing? Spending your time here gossiping; keeping Millie from the work she should have finished long ago. I've a notion to shake you. (*Pat behind him shaking his fists at him.*)

Millie. (*Aside.*) The old crocodile!

G. A half dozen men around, and not one on hand when you want him. Here I've had to hitch up myself, when I'm in a desperate hurry. And you lazy louts are gossiping with the girls.

Frank. Mr. Greenback, I couldn't find Pat. I went to the barn to call him, but—

G. No excuse for idleness. Oh! you will all be the death of me yet! (*Fidgets nervously.*)

Pat. (*Aside.*) Amin to that remark.

G. (*Furiously.*) Why do you stand here gaping like a lot of idiots. Get to work at once every one of you. (*Exeunt* PAT *and* FRANK *L,* MILLIE *runs out R. In her hurry drops a piece of the vase.*)

G. (*Calling L.*) Pat! Pat! (*Enter* PAT.) Put the ponies in the stable. I'm not going to-day. It's too late, curse it!

Pat. Shure an' if ye plaze it's only a trifle beyant nine.

G. I said it was too late. Did you hear? Put the ponies in the stable, and get to the hayfield at once.

Pat. Vis, sur, immagitly. (*Aside.*) If not sooner. (*Going L. Aside.*) Begorrah, an' the ould man has one of his tantrums to-day. (*Exit L.*)

G. (*Walking the floor in agitation. Sees piece of vase and picks it up.*) What's this? (*Musingly.*) The work of a careless servant. So much money thrown away! Mrs. Greenback will have such things. Talks of art and its refining influences. Well, I thought so once too, but I should like to see the art that can refine this household. My life is like that vase, once fair, now in ruins. Why didn't I go? I can't stay here. Oh, what can quiet the scorpion-like stings of remorse! They gnaw my very heart strings, and turn my home into a hell, in which I am the presiding demon. The delirious starts of a morbid conscience prey with keener tooth because no penitence comes to soothe the hideous wound. No, there is no repentence for the miser. Miser!

did I say? How that odious word once made my ears tingle with
shame, when first I heard it flung at me in bitter taunt. Oh, God, how
I've changed! I'm no longer the same man. 'Tis well I bear a new
name, the badge of my dishonor, which, partly blazoning my character,
better hides my former self. My eye no longer sees the mocking leer, nor
hears my ear the scornful gibe. My every faculty, like my soul, slum-
bers to all but baser, grosser objects Men despise, and righteously
too, the hated miser. But the r contempt is only a tithe of that which
I would heap mountains high upon my own debased self. But why
despise the creature of our own making? Deliberately I so'd myself
for gold. I signed and sealed the contract, and daily pay to Mammon
his hateful interest, cent per cent. Worse shame, I sought to exalt
and enrich my own flesh and blood at the expense of a father's dishonor. An incensed deity rebuked my idolatry, and took from me my
precious child, but left me the curse. That will never depart. I am
doomed and damned forever.

Enter R MRS. GREENBACK.

Mrs. G. Seth, I thought you had gone to the city this morning.
What has caused this sudden change of mind? I saw the ponies at
the door a moment ago.

G. Ask me no questions. Have you nothing better to do than waste
your time and mine with idle questions?

Mrs. G. Seth, your despondent moods have grown more frequent
lately. You must not give way to them. They bode no good to your
peace of mind.

G. (*Savagely.*) Peace of mind! Dare you speak again of peace
of mind? True, I have no peace, but my mind will hold its sway
while life remains I have been a fool, but I never will be a madman,
even to please you.

Mrs. G. To please me! Seth, how *can* you speak so? Is it possible that you think your own wife can find pleasure in your distress.
Your troubles are my troubles; your grief is my grief; your joy my
joy. Would that your love were mine as mine is yours. It would
make a better man of you.

G. Mary, cease your wretched prating about love. Once we loved
with as strong and holy affection as human beings can know. But that
is past. Stony indifference has taken its place. We are not the same;
(*With feeling.*) God knows we are not. Our love lies sleeping in
the silent tomb, and it were hollow mockery to fan those cold ashes,
hoping to start the sacred fl me.

Mrs. G. Seth, I own your words are sadly true when you speak of
icy indifference. Whatever else may fail let us still cling to truth and
candor. Do you doubt me now, when I solemnly assure you that my
love has sprung into new life, and that I still love you devotedly?

G. Doubt your word? No. But I do doubt the existence of the
feeling that you speak of. You deceive yourself. Remember that we
agreed together years ago that our early love was dead. Was not that
a fair understanding? And do you now censure me for accepting your
own statements? No, we are like two neighboring mountain peaks,

linked together yet distinct and silent, nothing to each other but near neighbors.

Mrs. G. Seth, you deceive yourself; 'tis not I. Since the sad time of which you speak, my love has been born again and strengthened by sorrow. It is stronger, deeper, and holier to-day than was the plighted faith of the young girl at the altar years ago. (*Beseechingly puts her hand on his shoulder.*) Seth, do you still doubt? Can you yet return my love?

G. Never! Can a stone feel grateful because it is set in a corner? Mary, you have wasted your love on a wretch who cannot return it, or a half-man whose better nature has perished, and whose baser parts run riot in the ruins. Your revelation only adds tenfold to my misery, because I deserve no love, and despise to owe anybody.

Mrs. G. Cease your avaricious ways, and be a man again, is all I ask.

G. All you ask! Woman, are you mad? What greater request could you ask of me?

Mrs. G. At least make restitution to those you have wronged. Have your brother Will and his family no claims upon you? Must he be forever wronged?

G. Wronged! And who brought his wrongs upon him? Can he not blame his own shameless dissipation and wickedness?

Mrs. G. But he is a man now, and we have reason to believe a better man. Seth, to repair the wrong you have done him will make a better man of you. Justice demands it.

G. A better man of me! I *am* a bad man. But it is hard to be taunted about one's crimes by those who have counseled their perpetration. Woman, (*Pointing at her.*) my life has rested under one long, baleful curse, and you have not laid a finger to the lightening of that curse. I do not complain, but I speak plain truth. Did you not advise me to retain Will's money, and to stand silent when his enemies drove him to the wall?

Mrs. G. I did. I am willing to bear my full burden of shame. But can we not yet atone for our crime, partly, at least? I have a thousand times regretted our wicked course and its shameful consequences.

G. Wife, it is too late. The deed is done. You wished station in society, I desired wealth and influence for the sake of my darling boy. Where is your station, and where is my influence? Ha! ha! we have a name, 'tis true. I bear the name that was always on my tongue, and among strangers we carry the synonym of our ruling passion. Is it better than the one we dishonored in our native land?

Mrs. G. (*Pleadingly.*) Oh, Seth, it is not too late. It is never too late to repent of sin, and turn to righteousness. Don't continue to harden your heart. Remember our lost Frank. We saved for him. He is taken from us. Let us devote our wealth to the good of others. Can it be that you still await his return? (*Turns toward wall pointing to the picture of the young boy.*) Vain hope! Sad hope!

G. I do not expect the grave to give up its ill-gotten gains. He is gone forever.

Mrs. G. Then why not do justice? His angel cheeks (*Still pointing to the picture.*) would blush with crimson dye could he know what has been done in his name, and what has not been undone. Has the remembrance of him no power yet to bless?

G. None! The worship of Mammon has fretted his sweet image into a mocking phantom, to taunt me in my dreams. The gold hoarded for him has cursed me, though we meant it to bless him. But it shall curse no other soul. No one shall have a penny of it till I die. They call me Old Greenback, a skinflint and a miser, and I shall remain so. You speak of repentance. You will be the better for it, and I will be the worse by contrast. I am past repentance, or the power to feel any of the finer emotions of the human soul.

Mrs. G. If not for Will's sake, think of his wife and child, and when you think of his child remember your own Frank.

G. I have ever remembered him with gall in my heart. His fate was crueler than death. He received no mercy, and I will show none.

Mrs. G. Hard and unmerciful. (*Turns away toward R.*)

G. 'Tis useless to plead.

Mrs. G. (*Aside.*) A madman in truth. Lost to every sense of honor. (*Exit R.*)

G. Mary's conscience, after a long sleep, is aroused at last. (*Paces floor.*) She will no longer allow me a moment's peace until I make full restitution. No longer will we be in sympathy, and the last link which binds me to the past and to my fellows, is severed. Her words are the voice of truth. I know I should be a better man Reason remains to me in full vigor, but AVARICE, the master, nods imperiously to her helpless slave, and moral faculties are sunk in helpless imbecility. Why was our family doomed? A fond father and mother would turn in their graves if they knew the fate of their promising sons (*Enter PAT unobserved, L.*), one a miser, a by-word and a reproach among his fellow-men; the other a prodigal, a reveler, a gambler, a criminal. A criminal! dreadful thought! but what am I, too, but a criminal? Perhaps it was right to withhold his patrimony when he knew not how to save it. At least it was prudent. But what was it to retain it when he plead for his rights? *Crime;* a foul wrong against which a youthful brother and his starving wife and babe have plead in vain. Oh, God of justice, let me be a man again! I swear to Thee (*Drops on his knees.*)—No, I'll not swear. I dare not. In the years long gone, before my manhood ceased to struggle with my baser self, I have resolved again and again, and broken all my resolutions. I'll not swear. (*Rises.*) It would only sink me deeper in the ominous shades which are surely closing over me. It is useless to struggle; all is lost, lost! (*Exit R.*)

Pat. Shure an' here's a pretty rivalation. The ould chap's been chatin' his kinfolk, bad luck to him. He says he won't swear. I'm thinkin' swearin' would be a refreshin' vartue after such thricks as his. (*Enter MILLIE R.*) After all he seemed awful sorry like.

Millie. Pat, what are you talking to yourself about?

Pat. The vartues of the master.

Millie. I did not know he had any to discuss.

Pat. Shure, Millie, an' there's a good streak in his character after all. You know he gets the dumps, and feels sorry like, an' he can be ginerous, too, when he tries.

Millie. Yes, if it's generous to give choice wines to strangers, and feed the family on crusts and old bones.

Pat. Divil take me if I don't think the master's a dissected puzzle, anyway. He got put together wrong. (FRANK *calls* PAT *L.*) I'm comin', sir, directly in haste, as soon as I get a jug of water for the boys. (*Exit* PAT *L* MILLIE *R.*)

CURTAIN.

━━━━◆━◆━━━━

ACT II.

SCENE, *same as Act I.* FRANK *assisting* MILLIE *to arrange the furniture.* MILLIE *dusting the room.*

Millie. Frank, you are down in the mouth about something. What's the matter?

Frank. I've been thinking.

Millie. What are you thinking about, Frank?

Frank. About you, Millie.

Millie. (*Starts slightly, and turns to hide her blushes.*) About me. That's odd.

Frank. I was thinking what a good friend you have been to me, and wondering why you should befriend such an unpromising specimen as myself.

Millie. I've learned one thing, and that is, that it aint always promisin' people that *does* most.

Frank. And you think that mebbe I'll do something because I don't promise. Well, I'm sure I don't know what I can ever do. Somehow I've been awful unlucky. When them fellows stole me away from home they did the business for me. I haint got on the track just right yet.

Millie. And you never will while you stay here. Why don't you run away. It's a shame for you to work so hard for nothing. Pat and me get our pay, but you get nothin', only ill usage. I wouldn't stand it.

Frank. If it hadn't been for you and Pat I believe I'd died long ago. But I'll never run away. Please don't mention that again. I won't sneak off like a thief or a coward. Mr. Greenback took me in when I was a little thing, not able to earn much, and I'm going to repay him.

Millie. You've already repaid him a hundred fold.

Frank. This is my home, the only place in the world where anybody cares anything for me, and I'm going to stay here. Mrs.

Greenback is kinder now than she used to be. Mr. Greenback wants to be kind too if he could.

Millie. But he's so mean he can't.

Frank. Don't say that, Millie. You don't know how he feels. Sometimes he looks so careworn and wishful, like he'd lost something, and acts so queer that you'd nearly cry to see him. I pity him, for I know something awful's happened him sometime. He shows it.

Millie. That's when his tenants don't pay the rent.

Frank. No, it ain't that, neither. It's some grief. He talks to himself, and goes on awfully. That is, he used to more than now, when I came here, ten years ago. I believe Mr. Greenback wants to be good, and knows that he ought.

Millie. Of course he knows it. He's no fool. Ten years! What a long time. I've been here six, but if it wasn't that Greenback is good pay, I wouldn't stay another day.

Enter PAT R.

Pat. Faith, an' I'm thinkin' ye has a different raison intirely.

Millie. What's that?

Pat. Shure an' Master Frank is here, to say nothin' of the other attractions. (*Aside.*) Be jabers, an' I'm here meself.

Millie. Other attractions! Fiddlesticks. Yourself, I s'pose!

Pat. Meself! Howly prophets! I've been called by a good many names in my time, some of them illegant and some of them not, but I niver was called by such a convanient title as fiddlesticks. Faith, an' its appropriate too, for I'll not die with all my music in me. (*Whistles "Pat Malloy."*)

Millie. Pat, you're a fool.

Pat. Begorrah, an' I have it now. Ye called me fiddlesticks, not because of my music, though that is very shwate and inticin', but because I'm always getting into scrapes.

Frank. Hist! You'll get into another soon. Mr. Greenback is coming.

Millie. Goodness sake! (*Runs out R,* PAT *and* FRANK *following.*)

Enter GREENBACK L, carrying a quilt which he throws on sofa, L.

G (*Calls savagely.*) Pat! Frank! come back! (*They turn toward him.*) What are you doing here you lazy louts? Can't I go away from home for an hour without coming back and finding you loafing around the house? Be off at once, both of you. (*They start R.*) Hold on, Pat. Bring in a basket of early harvests which I brought from the orchard. They're at the gate. They are beauties. No finer fruit in this country than my orchard produces. Hurry up, Pat.

Pat. All right, sir. (*Exit L.*)

Enter MRS. G. R.

Mrs. G. Where have you been, Seth?

G. Down at Burns's. Crops are looking splendid. The wheat shocks are thicker than I ever saw them before, I think. If the rain don't spoil them.

Mrs. G. Never mind the rain. We shall have plenty anyway.

G. There's a great risk in farming. There's either too much rain or none.

Mrs. G. Even Providence can't please a grumbler.

G. I'm not grumbling, Mrs. G., I'm thankful.

Mrs. G. If the potatoes hadn't failed.

G. I came through the big orchard coming back. The trees are bending with apples. I brought up a basketful. The first ripe brought a dollar a bushel. The market is glutted now, and I'm afraid we'll have to use them ourselves. It's a pity though. They are too nice to use at home. Here's Pat now. (*Enter* PAT *L, with basket of golden apples.*) Beauties aren't they, Mary? (*Places basket on chair L of table.*)

Mrs. G. Very fine, Seth! Can't we have some for dinner?

G. I suppose so. One apiece will be sufficient, will it not? They are large you see.

Mrs. G. They are not the choicest. (*Holds one up.*) You sold the best. Besides we want some for pies.

G. *Pies!* PIES! Pies are expensive; besides they are not wholesome. Doctors will all tell you that.

Pat. (*Aside.*) Doctors be hanged for such haythenish advice.

Mrs. G. Seth Greenback, what's the use of starving your family when bushels of fruit are rotting under the trees, and you can't sell it. I won't be scrimped to death any longer.

G. I think prices will rise.

Pat. (*Aside.*) Such financeerin' strikes me dumb with admiration.

Mrs. G. I'm going to live if prices do rise.

G. Well, you may use *these* anyway. Pat, I grow the best apples in the country. These have a splendid flavor. Try them.

Pat. Thank ye, an' I will. (*Takes an apple from the basket. Is about to bite it.*)

G. Wait a minute, Pat. Too much raw fruit is not safe at this season. You know they have the cholera in the city. Let's divide. (*Takes the apple from Pat, cuts off a small slice and hands it to Pat on the knife.*) What a flavor they have!

Pat. Don't you think, sir, I'd better only smell the knife? I'm afeerd of the cholera.

Mrs. G. Pat, you deserve another slice for that. (*Laughs.*)

G. Pat, you are too much of a wag ever to succeed in this world.

Pat. Faith, then I'm thinkin' I'll take the praste's advice and keep a close eye to the nixt, where I'll take a fresh start, may be in better company. (*Takes the apple.*)

G. Pat, an empty stomach makes a clear head.

Pat. (*Aside.*) An' a fat pocket-book makes a lean sowl. (GREENBACK *cuts a small slice for* MRS. G., *one for himself, and places the remainder of the apple in the basket. Attention of* MRS. G. *is attracted to the quilt.*)

Mrs. G. I declare if Millie hasn't brought a quilt in here and left it. I never knew her to be so careless before. (*Picks up quilt.*) No, that is not ours. How could it have come here?

G. I got it at Burns's.

Mrs. G. The one the Sewing Society gave them last winter (*Holding it up.*) Did you dare to take that?

G. There was nothing else to take.

Mrs. G. Then I'd do without the rent forever before I'd take away the bed of a poor invalid woman.

Pat. (*Aside.*) Be jabers, he only took the kiver.

G. I'll teach him to go off and work for Jones when he owes me.

Mrs. G. Have you no conscience?

G. If you please, Mrs. Greenback, we will say nothing about conscience.

Pat. Faith, Missus an' I can explain that, beggin' your pardon. Your husband's conscience is ashlape, an' he wanted a quilt to tuck it up in.

G. Get out, you Irish vagabond, or I'll crack your rattle head for you. (*Rushes at* PAT, *who exits R.*) Mary, (*Imperiously.*) take out these apples and that quilt.

Mrs. G. (*Takes up quilt and basket. Aside.*) What shall I do? I dare not return it. (*Exit R.*)

Knocking heard L. MR. G. *goes to door. Enter* GRUBBER, ESTY, *and* SLIGH.

Grubber. Good morning, Mr. Greenback.

G. Good morning, Mr Grubber. I'm glad to see you. Walk in.

Grubber. (*Introduces* ESTY *and* SLIGH.) Dr. Esty, Mr. Greenback. Mr. Sligh, Mr. Greenback.

G. (*Shakes hands with them.*) Very glad to see you, gentlemen. Take seats. (*Places seats.* ESTY *and* SLIGH *seated L C.* GREENBACK *and* GRUBBER *R C.*)

Grubber. These gentlemen are out from town takin' a little rest. They're stoppin' at our house. They thought your grounds looked so snug that they would like to come up and see them. I 'low they don't see no nicer in these parts.

Esty. Very fine location, indeed.

Sligh. And improved with great taste.

G. (*Pleased.*) We don't make pretensions to taste, but we have taken some pains to fix up a little. (*During this scene* SLIGH *watches* GREENBACK *closely, while taking his part in the conversation.*)   •

Grubber. Did it all himself too. Beatinest man in the world for plannin'. Greenback, you ought to spend a little *money* on these grounds. Why don't you bring water from that big spring over on the hillside, and make a fountain and a duck pond, and have some swans and notions like them 'ere city chaps does. I reckon they'd fix it up mighty slick.

G. That would cost too much. Can't afford such things when times are so dreadful close.

Esty. (*Rises to look at pictures. Gazes at picture of the boy. Is observed doing so by* SLIGH. *Aside.*) I think he's in advance of the times in closeness.

Sligh. And then it would look artificial after all. Nothing like rural simplicity, you know, as the poets say.

Grubber. Waal, I reckon you can find enough rural simplicity in this country outside the yard.

G. Quite true, Grubber. Excuse me, gentlemen, a moment. (*Goes to door R. Calls* MILLIE.) I'll have you try a little wine, gentlemen. I think you will pronounce it good for home-made. (MILLIE *appears at the door R.*) Millie, tell Frank to bring some wine and fruit at once.

Millie. Yes, sir.

G. Gentlemen, we have a splendid view of the river in the distance from the piazza. Have a look at it?

Esty. Certainly! (*Exeunt* ESTY *and* GRUBBER *L, following* GREEN-BACK. SLIGH *remains.*)

Sligh. I'm interested in something else more than in the river just now. By George, it must be him. (*Gazing at picture of boy.*) That's the boy sure as guns! (*Looks around the room.*) He has money yet too. May be this discovery will pan out something for somebody. I'll draw the old chap out a little. He's sharp to change his name and put on the air of an eccentric old fish. (*Re-enter* GREEN-BACK, ESTY *and* GRUBBER.)

Esty. Why didn't you go out and look at the view? It's splendid.

Sligh. I saw it as we came in.

Esty. (*To* GREENBACK.) As you remarked, you make your own wine, Mr. Greenback. A good idea. You know then what it's made of; I suppose it's cheaper too?

G. Yes, much cheaper. I can't afford imported wine often.

Sligh. Where did you learn the art of wine making, Mr. Greenback, if I may be so inquisitive?

G. I picked it up myself.

Grubber. As he does everything else.

Esty. (*Aside.*) That doesn't belong to him by right.

Grubber. I'll tell you what, Greenback is a genius.

Sligh. Beg pardon! I thought you might have learned the business somewhere in the wine regions. Judging from appearances, though, I suppose you've always lived here. (*Eyes him for answer.*)

G. No; (*Hesitating.*) I came out here from the East.

Sligh. From Pennsylvany, I should say.

G. No, not exactly.

Esty. You can tell from Mr. Greenback's speech that he is not from Pennsylvania. It sounds very much like our dialect where I was brought up, down in York State.

G. (*Nervously.*) In what respect?

Grubber. There's right smart difference in people's lingo, but dang me if I could ever tell purcisely where a man came from by his gab.

Esty. I can generally guess pretty closely. (GREENBACK *looks uneasy.*) I should say that you came from Rockrib county, New York, Mr. Greenback.

G. (*Uneasily.*) In fact I did come from that region.

Sligh. (*Aside.*) The very same, I'd bet my head. Wonder if Esty suspects him. (*Enter* FRANK *R, bearing a tray containing a pitcher of water, a bottle of wine, and a plate of apples. Sets the tray on the table. Enter* PAT *R.*)

Pat. Mr. Greenback, shall we saw up the balance of the wood now, or go down and repair the fince forninst Jones's pasture?

G. Repair the fence first, Patrick. (FRANK, *in wiping the dust from the bottle, knocks off a goblet, which is broken.*) What are you doing, you awkward numskull? I'll teach you to break things that way. (*Flies at* FRANK *in a passion, and siezes him by the collar. Is about to strike him.*) You'll ruin me yet with your awkwardness.

Pat. (*Steps forward indignantly. Draws back to strike* GREEN-BACK. *All jump up excitedly.* GRUBBER *seizes* PAT.) Hands off, Mr. Greenback, or I'll break your ould pate. Shure an' I've seen that boy abused too long 'alridy. I've parsevered in kapin silence, but be jabers parsavarance has caised to be a vartue. This is more than human flesh and bones can stand.

Esty. (*Aside.*) He's a brute out and out.

G. Pat, do you dare to insult me here?

Pat. Ay, if you dare touch that boy.

Grubber. Gentlemen, don't get excited. Greenback, let the boy go; it was an accident.

Esty. He feels badly enough about it, too. He's a good, faithful boy, or I'm badly mistaken.

Pat. Faith, an' we were both kind o' hasty like. I'll make the price of that all right out of my nixt month's wages.

G. I guess I'm able to lose a tumbler. Get to work at once, both of you, without another word.

Pat. (*Going with* FRANK.) Yis, sur. (*Aside.*) If there was no company prisint, he'd be able to take a dime for it. (*Exeunt R.*)

G. Take seats, gentlemen. Don't let this little affair mar your pleasure. (*Opens bottle and pours out wine.* Passes a goblet to* SLIGH *and one to* GRUBBER.)

Esty. (*Aside.*) I'd as soon drink poison as touch it.

G. (*To* ESTY, *who is still standing.*) Have a seat, Mr. Esty, and try some of this old grape juice.

Sligh. It's capital, Esty.

Grubber. Cleans out the cobwebs first rate. (*Smacks his lips loudly.*)

G. Come, man.

Esty. (*Aside.*) Hang the fellow. I suppose I'll have to drink for manners' sake. (*Coldly.*) I'll try it. (*Seats himself L, and takes a few sips.*)

G. Try these apples, they are finely flavored. (*To* ESTY.)

Esty. No, thank you; I think we must be going. Jack, what do you say?

---

* Cold tea will serve for "drinks." The players should always drink where the sentiment requires it.

Sligh. I say it's deuced unmannerly to snatch a fellow away in this style, when there's good cheer.

Grubber. What on arth's the use of this hurry? We don't visit here every day.

Esty. (*Aside.*) Thank the Lord for that.

Sligh. Well, if we must, we must; that's all. (*All rise.*)

G. (*Passing apples.*) Put one in your pocket to try on the way. (SLIGH *and* GRUBBER *take an apple apiece.*)

Esty. No, thank you. (*Moves to door* L, *followed by others*.) I do but one thing at a time, so I cannot eat and drive at the same time. Good day, Mr. Greenback.

G. Good day, Mr. Esty. (*Shake hands.*) Good day, Mr. Sligh. Sorry to have you rush off so, gentlemen.

Grubber. Well, as fur me, I s'pose you'll see me agin purty soon. I reckon I'll be in these parts a right smart while.

Sligh. And so'll the rest of us too, if I'm not mistaken. (*Aside.*) I guess we'll like the air here. (*Exeunt L.*)

G. I'm glad they're gone. It's queer that Esty should mention York State. He may know too much, and that Sligh knows a good deal more than he tells, I'll bet. (*Paces the floor in thought.*) Can it be possible that some one from down East has discovered my secret and put these men on my track? Impossible! No one from that part ever settled here, and that's why I chose this locality. Pshaw! my fears are groundless. A dozen years are a cycle in this fast age. And then I've changed greatly. Ugh! (*Shudders*) No need to remind myself of that. (*Steps to a mirror* R, *and surveys himself; strokes his bushy whiskers.*) Tut! tut! Seth Greenback, nobody would ever take you for the handsome George Walford of twenty years ago. In truth I'm another man. Twenty years did I say? Aha! Seth Greenback, you're twenty to-day; for just twen'y years ago to-night George Walford clasped his young brother's hand in a hurrie! farewell. He swore to aid and defend that imprudent brother, fleeing from the stern demands of offended justice. The oath passed into the black nothingness of the night, and with it the fair name of George Walford. In a few short months Seth Greenback robbed the one whom he swore to protect. Even poor Will would not know me now. I wonder where he is? In a drunkard's grave long before this, I suppose. Poor fellow! The papers said he left for California, with his boy, after his wife's death. Well, no matter. It's all over now. (*Exit L.*)

Enter FRANK *R.*

Frank. (*Picking up fragments of broken goblet.*) What humiliation! I wouldn't minded a whipping, for I suppose I deserved it for my awkwardness. But I won't stand this degradation before strangers any more. Mr. Greenback thinks it's smart, but I think it's mean. I'll tell him so, too, the very next time he does it. He was good to me when I was an outcast, but I've stuck to him long enough. I've paid him well for that. I'll do right by him still, if he'll let me, but I wont be knocked around any longer.

Enter MILLIE *R.*

Millie. (*Wiping her eyes; has been weeping.*) It's too bad, Frank. Oh! I could tear him to pieces. (*Covers her face with her hands.*)

Frank. Don't mind it, Millie.

Millie. You've never had nothin' but knocks.

Frank. Yes, I have. Father and mother loved me. I don't remember anything about them only that father called me his darling, and said he loved me better than anything else in this world. Then the men stole me away and took me from him forever.

Millie. Your father and mother must 'a been good people.

Frank. (*Picking up plate of fruit and tray.*) They were, indeed. Oh! what *would* they do when I was gone?

Millie. I wish you could live with them again, Frank.

Frank. They're dead long ago, I know, Millie; I can't bear to talk about it. (*Picks up bottle. Starts toward R.*)

Millie. Let me take the plate, Frank. You can't carry all them things.

Frank. Yes, I can. This is my work, you know.

Millie. I don't care a snap whose work it is. I'm going to carry that plate. (*Takes plate of apples. Exeunt R.*)

ACT III.

SCENE, *room in a hotel, plainly furnished ; cheap chromos on the walls, a few chairs and spittoons, two or three small tables with dingy covers and call bells. Seated around a table C,* SLIGH (*rear of table*), ESTY *R, and* LARK *L.*

Sligh. Lark, I tell you what, we've found the queerest old coon up here that ever you saw. You know that old brick house where there's such a large orchard?

Lark. On the right hand, about two miles out?

Sligh. Yes. Doctor and I were up there the other day. Old Grubber took us up and introduced us.

Lark. Is he as queer a case as Grubber?

Sligh. Ten times queerer, but not half as much of a gentleman. But I guess he's been a gentleman once.

Esty. It's a long time ago, I think.

Sligh. You're too crusty about trifles, Esty.

Esty. Do you call that a trifle, to act as he did the other day towards that poor boy?

Sligh. Ha! ha! Lark, deuced if Doctor didn't get into high dudgeon because Old Greenback—that's the old codger's name, by the way—was about to cuff the ears of a gawky butter-weed who broke a goblet as he was bringing in the wine. Blood and pistols! if that wan't a pretty little bit of sentiment on the Doctor's part.

Lark. Yes; almost as sentimental as your oaths. *Blood* and *pistols!* Did you get that at an old ladies' tea party? Have you abandoned the use of all those words that polite printers spell mostly with dashes?

Sligh. Not entirely, but I must defer a little to the Doctor's notions of propriety. He's got very sentimental of late.

Esty. If you call that sentiment, then I *am* sentimental. I tell you the fellow's a brute to act so. If he hadn't been in his own house I'd knocked him down, I believe.

Sligh. Let's look at both sides of that question. Esty, were you doing exactly the polite thing when you refused his hospitality so rudely, after his kindness to us?

Esty. Hospitality be hanged! I can't be polite to a man I don't respect, and I don't want his hospitality.

Sligh. Guests of our stripe oughtn't to be too particular.

Esty. (*Angrily.*) Guests of our stripe! Jack, I know I'm not fit for the society of decent people, but you are the last one to taunt me with my crimes.

Sligh. I don't say it to taunt *you*, Esty. I take my share; but you may have forgotten that two men once left their native village rather unceremoniously, because they happened to put another man's name to a brief piece of writing.

Esty. (*Bitterly.*) Well, and if they did, who suggested the miserable work, and who would have taken the lion's share if the scheme had succeeded?

Sligh. (*Angrily.*) You needn't have followed my suggestions if you didn't choose. You were of age.

Esty. In years, but not in the ways of wicked men.

Lark. Here boys, this has gone far enough. Let's have something to take. (*Rings bell.*) There's no use calling up bygones. Why don't you talk business, Jack?

Sligh. Hush! We're not far from other ears.

Enter MOLLIE *R.*

Mollie. An' what will yez have?

Lark. Cigars and brandy.

Mollie. Yis, sur. (*Exit R.*)

Sligh. Lark, don't talk so deuced loud. Remember **we're in a** hotel.

Lark. Third rate tavern, I'd call it.

Enter MOLLIE *R, bearing tray and glasses, etc.*

Sligh. Mollie, (MOLLIE *going R.*) close the door. There's a draught here.

Mollie. On the brandy bottle did you mane, sur?

Sligh. No; (*Laughing.*) from the doors

Mollie. Arrah thin, an' I'll close them both. (*Closes both. Going R. Aside.*) The bye's are up to somethin'. (*Exit R.*)

(*They pour out a glass of brandy each, which they gulp down excepting ESTY, who merely tastes his, unnoticed by the others.*)

Lark. That goes right to the spot. Now for business at once, before we're interrupted. Jack, state your case.

Sligh. Briefly it is this, that we crack Old Greenback's crib, and see what's to be had.

Lark. Is it worth the trouble?

Sligh. Splendid opening. No trouble to get into that old house, and they say he always has lots of money around him, to say nothing of his solid silverware.

Lark. Agreed! When shall we try it?

Sligh. Will you join us, Esty?

Esty. Jack, I'm surprised at this proposition, but on second thought I've no right to be surprised. I suppose you think me bad enough for anything. But, thank God, I've never stolen yet.

Sligh. Stealing! Who talked of stealing? This is merely a question of nocturnal finance.

Esty. There's no use joking. I never got a penny that didn't belong to me, and I never will.

Sligh. Came pretty near it though, once.

Esty. I know it. But chance prevented it, and saved me.

Sligh. (*Sneeringly.*) Humph! If you consider yourself *saved* there's no use of argument.

Esty. None. I'm not the man I used to be. And I'm sorry to learn that you have not mended your ways in all these years.

Sligh. No preachin' now, if you please. All I want to know is whether you'll blow on us.

Esty. Perhaps I shall. If it was anybody but Old Greenback I would very quick. I think it would do him good to lose part of his money.

Lark. So you would turn traitor if you chose, Esty?

Esty. (*Jumps up in a violent passion.*) Dare you call me traitor? (*Siezes bottle, and is about to strike* LARK, *who draws a pistol.*)

Lark. (*Jumps up and cocks his pistol.*) I'm ready if that is your game.

Sligh. (*Rushes round table front of* LARK; *knocks pistol aside.*) What the deuce do you mean by such nonsense? Don't raise a row here, or the game's up.

Esty. No man shall call me traitor. I did not seek your confidence, and would scorn to betray a *friend*.

Sligh. That's all right, old boy. Don't blow if you can help it. But I think we'll not give him time to blow. Let's try the thing to-night. That will leave him no time to reflect, and ease his conscience too. What do you say, Lark?

Lark. All right. I'm ready any minute.

Sligh. Then we've no time to lose. We must get our gimcracks in order before midnight. (*Going L.*) Good evening, Esty Sorry you can't join us, but business is business. (*Aside.*) Wonder if he suspects who Old Greenback is? No, that can't be. (*Exeunt R.*)

Esty. Here's a pretty go. Let a man once step aside from the path of strict rectitude and he is open to the base proposals of every villain. Hanged if I don't see about this business a little further (*Exit L.*)

Enter MOLLIE *R.*

Mollie. Bloody murder! Can I iver again trust me sivin sinses? I'm overpowered intirely! My prisence of mind is clane gone. (*Enter* PAT *L, unobserved.*) Och, an' I think I'll be obliged to faint for a few minutes to rekiver mesilf. (*Moves towards a chair to sit down.* PAT *clasps her in his arms.*)

Mollie. (*Screams.*) Mercy on me, Pat, an' is it you? How you scart me! *Pat.* (*With his arm round her waist.*) Shure, Mollie, darlint, an' what ails ye? Have ye the diptheria? Musha, an' like as not ye's got the new disase that's come around so suddint. The doctor says that Misther Jones's wife has it awful bad. It's a—a—begorrah, what is it? —a cycloid attack, if ye knows what that manes. An' I'm no Latin scholar meself, but accordin' to the best of me larnin' it must be a disase of the heart.

Mollie. Oh! it's dreadful to think of, Pat.

Pat. Mollie, dear, I'm slightly afficted in the same way meself. Let me perscribe ye a dose, to betaken ivery avenin' till a cure is afficted. (*Draws her to him and kisses her.*)

Mollie. (*Gives him a ringing slap.*) What do ye mane, ye blunderbuss. Och, an' ye'll kape your medicine a long time for me, I'll warrant.

Pat. An' it's for you I'm kapin' it. (*Turns up the brandy bottle and takes a good swig*)

Mollie. Och! ye greeny, an' when I want a stickin' plaster on my mouth I'll be after tellin' you. But I've somethin dridful to tell ye, Pat.

Pat. Be jabers, an' I guessed as much.

Mollie. Ye knows that Dr. Esty and Jack Sligh?

Pat. Yis.

Mollie. Well, they came here and ordered a drop, an' had another bad lookin' chap with them. Whin I wint out they tould me to close the dures.

Pat. An' ye did as they tould ye?

Mollie. Yis. They looked so quare like that I jist put me ear to that bit of a crack by the dure, an' heerd ivery blissid worred they said.

Pat. An' wot did they say?

Mollie. They were plottin' murther an' robbery an' traison.

Pat. Begorrah, an' where is the traison and murther to take place?

Mollie. At yer master's.

Pat. The divil you say. An' whin does the performance begin?

Mollie This very night at midnight. The Docthor, good luck to him, said he'd take no part in such avil works.

Pat. Hoorah! Thin I'm good for the other two meself. I'll help meself to another drop to stiddy me narves. (*Takes a pull at the bottle.*) Mollie, I'm off, an' you'll plase excuse my abrupt haste. (*Going R.*)

Mollie. Don't get your head broken, Pat.

Pat. Niver a bit. (*Exit L.*)

Mollie. (*Taking tray with goblets, etc., R.*) He's a brave bye. I hope thim spalpeens wont get the better of him. (*Exit R.*)

CURTAIN.

ACT IV.

SCENE, *same as in Acts I. and II. Lights dim on stage. Enter*
PAT *with fowling piece, followed by* FRANK *with a revolver.*

Pat. Faith an' its nearly midnight. The dirty blaggards may come
ony minit. Begorrah, they'll not be expectin' to find us all ready for
entertainin' company. It was a bit of a surprise party they were plannin',
the rascals. Ha! ha! shure and it will be a complate surprise. (*Brand-
ishes his gun. Speaks to it.*) Be jabers, ye're a broth of a bye. Ye
can rache farther than ony shillalah.

Frank. Pat, keep still, or they'll hear us and escape.

Pat. Escape! I'd like to see them rogues run faster than buck
shot. Ha! ha!

Frank. Pat, this is serious business. Don't laugh. I fear something terrible is going to happen.

Pat. An' that's just my own opinion. I'm no prophet or something will happen to one of them chaps that will be mighty serious like
for him.

Frank. What would we done if Mollie hadn't overheard them?

Pat. Begorrah, they'd hilped themselves to the ould man's money
mighty aisy.

Frank. It would nearly kill him to lose a large sum of money. I
believe he'd almost go mad.

Pat. Mad! Arrah, thin, an' ye're right. He'd be madder than a
disappinted office seeker. His timper would kill him intirely. He'd
be a ravin' corpse in tin minutes.

Frank. Hark! They are trying the hall window.

Pat. Git behind that chair, an' I'll shilter behind this table. We'll
let them get well into the job first. (FRANK *gets behind arm chair L,*
PAT *behind table L C. Noise of prying open shutters outside L.*)
Aisy now, me bye.

Enter burglars SLIGH *and* LARK *L.*

Sligh. (*In a low tone.*) Good, so far. No trouble to get into this
old shell.

Lark. Where does he keep his money?

Sligh. In a bureau in the sitting room. He sleeps in the next
room back of that. The door's open. Come on. Be cautious. (*Start
toward R.*)

Pat. (*Rises.*) Be jabers, I'll give ye a caution. *Levels the gun
and fires. Gun snaps the cap but does not go off.**
SLIGH *seizes the gun and they struggle,* FRANK *rises and levels his
revolver at* LARK. *Fires and misses him.* LARK *draws and shoots*
FRANK, *who falls toward C with a yell of pain.* LARK *tries to
draw on* PAT, *but the rapid evolutions of the two make it impossible.*
LARK *seizes the gun with his left hand, and together they wrench it*

* In the burglary scene the action should be very rapid.

from PAT, *who is hurled back against the wall R by* SLIGH. *Enter* ESTY L. *He rushes to C.*

Sligh. (*Speaks very rapidly R C in rear.*) Lark, we're betrayed. They've raised the family. We can thank you for that, Esty. So you've found out who Old Greenback is at last? Fool! I should think you would like to get back some of the money he stole from you. Curse the luck.

Lark. (*Who is at R C in front, to* ESTY.) I've a notion to shoot you. (*Levels his pistol.* PAT *snatches up the pistol dropped by* FRANK *and levels at* LARK. SLIGH *strikes down his arm with the fowling piece. Enter* GREENBACK *R crying, "Seize them."* SLIGH *dashes towards L crying to* LARK *"Escape for your life."* LARK *rushes to door L followed by* SLIGH, *firing at* ESTY *as he passes.* PAT *fires at them and breaks* SLIGH'S *leg.*)

Sligh. (*Struggling to rise.*) Help, Doctor, my leg's broken.

Esty. (*Examining Frank's wound.*) This poor boy needs help first.

G. (*Excitedly.*) What does this mean?

Pat. It manes that your robbed, but divil the thing did they get.

Esty. (*Aside. Looking at* G.) Good heavens! It is George. (*Picks up* FRANK *and places him in an arm chair C. Opens his clothes. Examines wound. Takes a small case of instruments from his pocket and lays them on the table. Probes the wound lightly. Shakes his head, "It's no use."*)

G. (*Looks from one to another, bewildered.*) Robbed, did you say? Oh, I'm ruined, ruined.

Esty. (*Aside.*) Ruined if he knew it.

Enter MRS. G. *R.*

Mrs. G. Oh, Frank is killed. (*Bends over him. Speaks in an undertone to him.*)

Pat. Howly saints, it is this poor bye that's ruined. (*Holding* FRANK'S *hand. All gather round* FRANK.) Do ye feel much pain? Are ye much hurt?

Frank. (*In a weak voice.*) Very badly, I'm afraid, Pat.

MILLIE *rushes in R.*

Millie. What's the matter? Somebody's hurt. (*Screams.*) Oh mercy, it's Frank. (*Kneels by his chair R. Grasps his hands.*) Are you hurt much, Frank? Oh, you're not. I know you are not.

Frank. Millie, I'm badly hurt,

Millie. Don't say that, Frank. You must get well. You will, won't you?

G. (*Examines the wound.*) Don't be alarmed, Millie. He'll be all right in a few days. The wound is not deep, I think. There is little blood. The bullet must have glanced from a rib. I'm glad they didn't get the money. We were lucky, I think.

Mrs. G. For shame, Seth. Don't mention money at such a time as this.

Pat. What's the use of money when this poor bye's at death's dure?

Esty. (*Turns away. Aside.*) How can I break the awful truth to them.

G. Esty, how did you happen to come here just in nick of time?

Esty. I heard of the villain's plan, and came with officers, who are now at the door. I came at once, and found Pat and Frank engaged in a death struggle.

Pat. Officers! Then may be they've caught that villain. If Mollie hadn't tould me what she heard we wouldn't been here, an' Frank, poor bye, wouldn't bin mortally hurted.

G. Thank you, Mr. Esty, for your services, and you too, Pat and Frank.

Esty. You have nothing to thank us for.

Officer. (*Enters hurriedly L.*) We've got the villain. He's safe enough. (*Sees* FRANK.) What have we here? *

Esty. Murder!

Officer. Heavens, what a night's work!

Mrs. G. Mercy on us, Mr. Esty, you are as pale as a sheet. What can we be thinking of that we haven't sent for a doctor? We're all out of our wits. Pat, go for him at once.

Esty. It is useless. He cannot live. I am a surgeon. His case is peculiar. I wish to give a few words of explanation to Mr. and Mrs. George Walford.

G. (*Starting.*) Walford! Lost! Who are you man?

Esty. Do not be surprised. You will learn all soon enough. (*To* MILLIE, *who is still kneeling by* FRANK'S *chair*) Girl, arise. (*Lifts her. In great agitation.*) Others have closer claims on this poor sufferer. (*Smoothes* FRANK'S *brow.*)

Mrs. G. Others have claims! What do you mean?

Esty. Seth, I am your brother Will.

G. (*Starting violently.*) What! Heavens! I thought you dead.

Mrs. G. This anxiety is terrible! What mystery is this? You know something of Frank's parentage. Can it be that he is our son? Speak and give relief to a mother's aching heart.

Esty. He is your long lost Willie.

Mrs. G. (*Kneels by* FRANK *R of chair, and kisses him again and again.*) Oh my poor boy, to find you dying is the last agony in a long life of anguish. And such a meeting after years of intercourse. (*Covers her face in her hands.*)

G. Wife, this man is an impostor. We have every reason to believe that our son died years ago. Sir, substantiate your story.

Esty. (*Passes to* G., *L C.*) George, I could easily satisfy you that I am your brother, did circumstances require proof. Willie was not drowned, as you supposed. In revenge of my wrongs I hired a villain to abduct him from his home. To elude justice we were obliged to abandon him to strangers. I have suffered more than death because of it. The man whom I made my servile tool, to-night tried to rob your house. He is here to bear witness.

Sligh. It is true every word of it.

Esty. Do you still doubt?

---

* Should it be inconvenient to introduce the officer, for want of actors, Pat may step to the door L. and return, reporting Lark's capture. He may also prevent Sligh's escape, making an appropriate remark.

G. No. It is too horrible to admit a doubt. What an awful judgment. To think of my treatment of my own poor boy. (*Takes* FRANK's *hand, and falls on his knees at L of his chair.* GREENBACK *looks intently at* FRANK.) It can't be true. (*A pause.*) 'Tis a hideous dream. What evidence have you that this boy is the Willie you abandoned?

Esty. When we had him with us he fell one day and cut a gash back of his left ear. It healed and left a scar, sloping obliquely downward and backward.

Frank. Father, the scar is there. You will find it under my hair.

G. (*Finds scar.*) Doubt was anguish, but certainty is the torment of furies.

Mrs. G. Is there no ray of hope? All may yet be well.

Pat. Docthur, can't ye help the bye someway?

Esty. Frank, are you ready to go?

Frank. Yes. If I could but stay with father and mother a little longer I would be so happy.

G. Is there no hope?

Esty. None!

Sligh. (*Aside.*) Murder! and a rope for me. Oh for two sound legs! I'll try it. (*Tries to crawl out L.*)

Officer. (*Stopping* SLIGH.) Hold on, my boy. We need you.

G. And you, my brother, have done this. I thought myself a monster. What is the man who will steel an innocent babe? *Demon?*

Esty. Brother, dare I ask forgiveness of any but Him who forgives the vilest? Is there any reconciliation? (*Extends his hand.* GREENBACK *refuses it.*)

Mrs. G. Remember he had wrongs. Let the grave cover all thought of revenge.

Frank. (*Speaking slowly and with effort.*) For my sake, father, forgive him. He meant me no harm. (GREENBACK *takes* ESTY's hand in silence.)

Esty. He's going fast.

G. Willie darling, will you forgive me?

Frank. You were good to me, father, when nobody else was, and mother has been so kind. Kiss me, papa and mamma. (*They kiss him.*) Where's Millie?

Millie. Here I am, Frank. (*She kisses him.*)

G. The curse of Mammon is on us. Oh gold! when will thy power to blight and destroy be ended? My treasures are adders to sting me My punishment is just. (*Bends over* FRANK *in silence. All silent for a few moments. Rises and looks in* FRANK's *face.*) DEAD! (MILLIE *drops on her knees and leans her face on* FRANK's *body.*)

Arrangement of characters : a semicircle around FRANK's *body.*

MILLIE.

GREENBACK.   MRS. G.

    ESTY.   PAT *R.*

L OFFICERS, (if present.)

SLOW CURTAIN.

WANTED:
A CORRESPONDENT.

CHARACTERS.

Queergrain,   Addie Wild,
Mrs. Queergrain,   George Wild,
Puss Pearly,   Box,
Jack Spigot,   Dinah.

COSTUMES.

Any clothing suited to the social standing of the wearer. Jack stylish, and in the last act fastidiously dressed.

STAGE DIRECTIONS.

R means right, as the actor faces the audience; L, left; C, centre.

WANTED: A CORRESPONDENT.

ACT I.

SCENE, *Queergrain's library. A bookcase and writing desk C, in rear; pictures and statuary on the walls; sofa L; file of newspapers by bookcase; large easy chair, etc.** JACK, *seated in a careless attitude, reading " Personal" column of the " Times."*

Jack (*Reading.*) " Lady correspondent wanted. Address, Semper Fidelis, Dexter Station." Ha! ha! Semper Fidelis, you are ever faithful, eh? Your Latin evidently belongs to the brazen age. " Will the lady dressed in a light suit, who had linen cloak on her arm, crossed North Ferry about 3 o'clock, and noticed gent, please send her address to Pencil, this office?" Look out, Mr. Pencil, or you may need sharpening before you get through with that angel in a light suit. " Gentleman correspondent wanted. Address Samantha Ann, Box 345, Oakwood place." Oho! The fair sex is in the field, and competition is lively. Really I had forgotten this is leap year. This one is certainly a joke: " Wanted, correspondent by an elderly gentleman, with a view to matrimony." The old sinner ought to be ashamed of himself, sowing wild oats at his time of life. Botheration, there is no end to the trouble such business gets one into. It's a little fun and bushels of trouble. I wonder if Puss suspects the trick Addie and I have played on her, and what would she say if she knew of my inamorata incog.? Confound her incog. How do I know who she is? She might be my great-grandmother for all I know to the contrary. By the fates, I believe she is old and as ugly as a mud fence, for she persists in writing, and will not consent to an interview. How to dispose of her is the problem.

Enter PUSS. JACK *starts.*

Puss. What weighty problem demands your attention now, Jack?
Jack. Oh! nothing in particular.
Puss. Dear Jack, it takes you a long time to read the paper to-day. Is there any special news? Let me see! (*Peeps over his shoulder.*) I'll declare, you are reading the Personal column. What do you find there to interest you?

* If it is not convenient to place a bookcase on the stage, a bracket with books may be suspended on the wall, and a table take the place of the desk. Where the stage allows the use of a third door for the closet, or where there is a recess, or where a screen can be used for the purpose, make the exits and entrances as given in the text ; otherwise, let the exits and entrances all be at one side, and the closet at the other.

Jack. (*Confused.*) Oh, I was just looking at the markets.

Puss. Now, Jack, don't prevaricate, for you know I've caught you. The markets are on the inside of the paper. What do you say to that, my good fellow?

Jack. Well, if I should happen to find the Personal column in looking for the markets, and should glance over its contents, what's the harm. Personals are intended to be read, or why should they be printed, my dear?

Puss. And you men like to read them.

Jack. Don't women read them?

Puss. Why do you ask such an absurd question?

Jack. Why do you not answer my question? I am afraid women not only read them, but write some of them, too. Listen, dear Puss. (*Reads.*) "Wanted, gentleman correspondent by a jolly old maid. Money no objection. No widowers need apply." Here is another. "A strawberry blonde would like——"

Puss. Do stop. (*Snatches the paper.*) Never mind what she likes, you mean, teazing thing, you. You are just making up a lot of stories as you go.

Jack. Not as good as the originals, I assure you.

Puss. Jack, is it wrong to answer a "personal?"

Jack. Why do you ask? Have you any thought of engaging in such a tender affair? Let me see, which one is it? The elderly respectable gentleman? Remember, Puss, he says with a view to *matrimony.*

Puss. Jack, you ought to be ashamed to talk so, when you know we are engaged.

Jack. What made you ask me such a question, then?

Puss. It's a pity I can't ask a question without——

Jack. Being quizzed? Your remark suggested the question.

Puss. You are suspicious, and I hate suspicion.

Jack. Then answer my question and remove suspicion.

Puss. Mr. Spigot, I deny your right to question me so authoritatively. Besides, I asked you a question first, which you have not yet answered.

Jack. Of course it's wrong, Puss—decidedly wrong—it's wicked, especially——

Puss. For ladies.

Jack. I intended to say for those who have unusually nice views of propriety. But I will accept your amendment, and say for ladies.

Puss. How considerate, Mr. Spigot, to think of including the ladies at all, since you lords of creation usually deny them the right to take the initiative in anything, especially an affair of the heart.

Jack. Pooh! Women may do anything they can do well, for all I care.

Puss. I believe you said such a correspondence was decidedly wrong—in fact wicked?

Jack. I used those words, I believe.

Puss. (*Aside.*) I'll remember them. They will prove an extinguisher.

Jack. I asked *you* a question, Puss.

Puss. I've quite forgotten what it was, Jack.

Jack. The poorest memory is the one that chooses to forget. Why did you ask me if it is wrong to reply to a personal?

Puss. (*With a toss of the head.*) My memory is so poor that I have forgotten why.

Jack. In other words, you refuse to answer.

Puss. As I denied your right to question.

Jack. But you questioned me.

Puss. That was a fair question.

Jack. You are stubborn.

Puss. You are exacting.

Jack. Because I asked a reasonable question?

Puss. You are suspicious.

Jack. You catechise me about what portions of the paper I have been reading. Isn't that suspicion too, Miss Lynx-eye?

Puss. Oh, dear! To think that you could ever call me names!

Jack. (*Rises.*) I'm afraid we'll never get along together, Miss Pearly.

Puss. I grant you full release, Mr. Spigot. (*Turns away.*)

Jack. (*Aside.*) I guess she'll come round. (*With important air.*) She won't hold out long when *I* say the word.

Puss. (*Aside.*) An exposure may cure his folly, but mine is as bad. (*In a penitent tone.*) Dear Jack! (*He turns away.*) Will you hear a word?

Jack. (*Coolly.*) Several will be required in apology.

Puss. (*Aside.*) I'll make up, and get even. (*Aloud.*) Will you forgive me?

Jack. I will, but the conditions are a kiss. (*Kisses her. She screams as* QUEERGRAIN *enters L.*)

Q. Ahem! ahem! Beg pardon, Jack and Puss. I didn't know you were here. No harm done, I hope?

Jack. None, that I am aware of.

Q. I will take a turn on the piazza.

Puss. Never mind, Pa. I am going up stairs. (*Exit R.*)

Jack. And I shall take a peep around the stables. (*Exit L.*)

Q. They are, evidently very happy. I wonder if ten years of married life will make any difference in their happiness? If it does not they will prove a lucky exception to the average matrimonial experience. Hum! Mrs. Queergrain and myself were once in bliss. Now we are in—hot water. Mrs. Queergrain always misunderstands me. Well, she is not entirely to blame. Society is to blame. She merely puts too rigid an interpretation on its requirements. Society says that married people must give up, more or less, all their intimate friends of the opposite sex, no matter how pure and mutually improving that friendship may have been. Society demands that marriage should impose restraints which effectually smother such friendship. Marriage offers love instead, but when that love is a delusion what then? What then? Bow to the tyrant, says Mrs. Queergrain; defy him, say I. But business must be attended to. Let me see. I will write a note to Miss Wild, asking her to call this evening. We must finish that library list before Saturday, or the deuce will be to pay. (*Seats himself and writes.*) At eight? Yes, that will do. Mrs. Q. will be at the mite society this evening. Wouldn't she raise old Nick if she knew this? (*Rings for* Box.) The poet should have said, instead of "Hell hath no fury like a woman scorned," "Hell hath no fury like a jealous woman." (*Enter* Box *R.*) Here, Box, deliver this note at once. Don't fail.

Box. Shall I wait for the answer?

Q. No, it requires no answer. (*Exit R.*)

Box. (*Looks at note.*) Another note to that woman. (*Enter* Mrs. Q. *R.*) Queergrain is a brick. But I musn't go out in this coat. I'll run up to my room and change it. (*Lays note on table. Exit R.*)

Mrs. Q. What is this? Husband mails no letters at this time of day. (*Picks up note.*) Oh, dear! oh, dear! Can I believe my eyes? A note to a woman. Oh, dear! I shall die. I'm fainting. I will call Puss. (*Goes towards door.*) No, I'll see first what is in this delicate epistle. (*Opens note. Reads.*)

MISS ADDIE,—

We will resume our work this evening, if it suits your convenience. Drop in here instead of going home. The family will be absent, and we shall have nothing to disturb us. Come at eight.

Yours,   MACK QUEERGRAIN.

Oh, the wretch! the false, perfidious wretch! To think that he would deceive me so. Calls her his Miss "Addie," and says, "We shall have nothing to disturb us." Well, they may be disturbed. I will at once confront him with his scandalous conduct, and then leave him forever. What shall I do? I'll warrant she is some despicable creature that he has picked up. Ha! I know what I'll do. I will send this precious missive of affection, and take care to be at home when they "resume their work." What can that mean? I shall see to-night. (*Seals note and places it on table.*) Hark! he is coming again. He must not know I've seen that. (*Enter* Box *R.*) Box, are you going down town?

Box. Yes, ma'am. What did you wish?

Mrs. Q. Nothing, I believe. Oh, I forgot. Tell Flint to send up my scissors that were left to be ground.

Box. (*Pockets note. Aside.*) I wonder what Queergrain is up to now anyway. (*Exit L.*)

Mrs. Q. So Box mistrusts him too. And I am not unjust in my suspicions, as some of my friends would have me believe. Men all need watching, and you can't go much amiss when you suspect them of mischief.

Enter DINAH *with note, L.*

Dinah. Mrs. Queergrain, here is a letter for Mr. Queergrain. It was lying in the hall, where it has been dropped by the postman.

Mrs. Q. (*Takes letter. Aside.*) A lady's hand. I'll take care of this myself. (*Aloud.*) Dinah, has a lady called here alone lately?

Dinah. Yes; there was Miss Myrtle, last week.

Mrs. Q. Yes, I know. I saw her. I mean when I was out.

Dinah. Yes; there was the female book agent. She called again.

Mrs. Q. I saw that old thing too. I mean a *young* lady.

Dinah. Missa, I know nothing about no young ladies but them that called on Miss Puss. (*Aside*) Shan't tell all I know.

Mrs. Q. And there were no others called?

Dinah. I vows 'pon honoh, Missa, that I admitted no young lady into this house. (*Aside.*) That's true, too, for Massa admitted her. (*Exit* DINAH *R.*)

Mrs. Q. (*Tears open note hastily.*) I'll soon see what she has to say. (*Reads.*)

MR. QUEERGRAIN:

   Dear Sir—As I have not seen you to-day, I take this means of enquiring when we shall meet again. Can you stop a few minutes this evening on your way home?

         Yours,   ADDIE WILD.

(*Angrily crushes note and drops into a chair hysterically.*) Mercy! oh dear! oh dear! You brazen wretch. How dare you write to my husband asking when you will meet him again? So you have met before, and often too, I know. I am the most miserable of women. I wish I was dead, if it was not that I want to live to expose their sly plans, and shame them with discovery.

Enter PUSS *R.*

Puss. Ma, have you seen Jack within half an hour? Why how agitated you are. Has anything happened?

Mrs. Q. The bolt has fallen at last.

Puss. The night lock will keep burglars out.

Mrs. Q. How can you be so dull? You know I refer to Mr. Queergrain. His guilty secret is out at last. My dear, we are undone. Our peace has flown forever.

Puss. Oh! is that all? I thought something serious had happened.

Mrs. Q. Poor child! you do not realize the family humiliation. I wish you could give a serious thought to your own welfare and the happiness of your poor mother. My own child has no sympathy for me. Oh dear!

Puss. Ma, I know you are wronging Pa. Because his views are peculiar in many ways I don't see why you should think of him as you do. He may be wrong sometimes, but then he is the kindest of men.

Mrs. Q. He is kind enough to *some people*, I know. But will that kindness soothe the outraged feelings of a betrayed wife? Oh, he is altogether too kind.

Puss. Ma, will you learn nothing by experience? This terrible blow has already fallen a dozen times. The family has been a dozen times undone, and yet we thrive and succeed in maintaining a very genteel position in the community.

Mrs. Q. This time I have the proofs. There is no longer any room to doubt. My suspicions were not so unjustifiable after all. Read that and be convinced.

Puss. (*Reads the note. Aside.*) I'll declare it's Addie Wild.

(*Aloud.*) That is conclusive. It is too true. (*Aside.*) Some of Addie's tricks. (*Aloud.*) To-night, at eight. (*Aside.*) Won't there be fun. Jack's hour too.

Mrs. Q. You can't trust the men. Jack is a good boy, Puss, but he is a little wild. You had better watch him.

Puss. Just what I have thought, Ma. In fact, I suspect he is up to some mischief, and to-night at eight I hope I shall be able to inform myself positively as to his guilt or innocence

Mrs. Q. At eight? Where?

Puss. In the library.

Mrs. Q. The very time and place where an injured and long-suffering wife will heap con'usion on the head of a recreant husband.

Puss. (*Aside.*) For his complete vindication. (*Aloud.*) I shall cure Jack effectually.

Mrs. Q. Have you any proof?

Puss. I have.

Mrs. Q. Then administer a telling rebuke. Let the lesson sink deeply while there is yet time.

Puss. That I will. It will be a good joke. (*Aside.*) A serious one, may be, if he should discover the identity of his unknown fair one to-night. (*Aloud.*) Hark, Ma! Some one is coming.

Enter Q. *and* JACK, *L.*

Jack. Puss, where is Box?

Puss. How should I know where the servants are? I've not seen him.

Q. I sent him on an errand down town a few minutes ago.

Mrs. Q. (*Aside.*) Audacious!

Puss. What did you want with him, Jack?

Jack. I only wanted him to run an errand to the tailor's. But no matter, I'll send a boy.

Puss. (*Aside.*) He is going to bite. (*Aloud.*) Getting a new suit, Jack?

Jack. Yes.

Puss. Light or *dark?*

Jack. (*Hesitates.*) Dark, of course.

Puss. Oh, of course. I need not have asked that. (*Aside.*) Your suit will come to grief, or I'm mistaken.

Q. Mrs. Queergrain, you remember The Woman's Home Philanthropic Society holds its monthly meeting this evening; you will attend, of course?

Mrs. Q. It's quite a walk to Mrs. Quiggles. Could you accompany us there? The gentlemen sometimes attend.

Q. I fear it will be impossible for me to go. I am very busy at present.

Mrs. Q. Oh, I dare say you are busy. You always are when it comes to going anywhere with *your wife.*

Q. Nonsense, my dear! You know I am always willing to accompany you when it is necessary. I see no particular necessity of my going this evening.

Mrs. Q. Always willing, but never ready! I see no particular necessity of your staying at home.

Q. My dear, I have just told you I am very busy.

Mrs. Q. Men always have some excuse for neglecting their wives.

Q. My dear, why do you talk so? You know it is but a step, and you have often gone alone.

Mrs. Q. Often gone alone!' No need to tell me that. Everybody knows that. I *have to go alone.*

Puss. Ma, you know we can go alone very well this evening. (*Whispers aside.*)

Q. Wife, don't be unreasonable.

Mrs. Q. I knew it would come to that. I might have expected to be abused.

Puss. Ma, don't say that. We can go alone quite well. (*Aside.*) Remember our plans.

Q. I will go too if it is really necessary, though I can't see why I should attend the meetings of a Woman's society.

Mrs. Q. No, you need not go, Mr. Queergrain.

Q. Perhaps Jack will be kind enough to see the ladies to the society and call for them at the close of the meeting.

Jack. Really I should be happy to do so, but I do not know how I am to manage it this time. This is club night, and I have a special engagement.

Puss. (*Aside.*) In a special club. (*Aloud.*) We will excuse you, gentlemen. We can manage quite well without you, indeed. (*Aside.*) Ma, we will give them plenty of time. (*Aloud.*) As there is some extra work before the society, we shall be rather late in getting back.

Jack. All right, Puss. Sometimes we are late at the club.

Puss. And will be to-night, I suppose.

Mrs. Q. The gentlemen will be so occupied that they will be oblivious to the flight of time. (*Exeunt* MRS. Q. *and* PUSS *R.*)

Jack. (*Whistles or sings.*) "Should auld acquaintance be forgot," etc.

Q. I'll wager Burns wrote that after marriage. I think matrimony tries auld acquaintance about as severely as anything else does.

Jack. Mr. Queergrain, I think you are a little hard on the state of matrimony, considering you are an honored member of the order Benedict. I don't believe married people scold any more than single people, or that they are any more exacting or disagreeable generally.

Q. Perhaps they are not. But then many people seem to think that marriage gives them the right to scold and suspect and make themselves and everybody around them miserable.

Jack. Well, I had not thought of any such right. It doesn't exist. (*Aside.*) If Puss had that right now, wouldn't I catch it?

Q. What is the difference whether it exists or not. If a person believes he has a certain right, that thing is right for him, no matter what others think.

Jack. You will have to abandon that theory. You can prove anything right in that way. After all, marriage does confer the right of the parties to correct each other's failings. In fact, that is one of its sacred obligations.

Q. For Heaven's sake, Jack, don't apply that principle too soon nor too strongly, or there will be an explosion. But I don't think you will have need to do so, for Puss is a good sensible girl.

Jack. She is a splendid girl. (*Aside.*) I wish though she hadn't begun that correspondence. (*Exit R.*)

Q. Jack reasons well for a boy. But his logic's lame, or I'm a dunderhead.

Knocking heard L, Q. opens door.   Enter ADDIE.

Addie. Good morning, Mr. Queergrain. You wouldn't come to see me, so I came to you.

Q. Take a seat, Miss Wild. But why do you say that I would not come to you?

Addie. You did not come anyway. I supposed you would stop on your way up town at noon to-day.

Q. I did not know you wished to see me.

Addie. Didn't you get my note?

Q. I received no note from you, but I sent one to-day, asking you to stop this evening, so that we could finish that list of books.

Addie. I got your note, but can't imagine what became of mine.

Q. The stupid post office people have mislaid it, or sent it nobody knows where. Mine I sent by the coachman. We can finish that list to-night, can't we?

Addie. I don't know. The library must be kept open until nine, and it will be too late after that.

Q. I will send a clerk round to take your place. Young Lester is just the one.

Addie. That will do if people do not interrupt us too much. Evening is a bad time for work at the library.

Q. Pshaw! we will work here.

Addie. Will Puss be at home?

Q. No; Mrs. Queergrain and Puss will both be at the Philanthropic Society, and we shall have everything to ourselves.

Addie. Couldn't we finish the list to-morrow?

Q. I shall be absent from town to-morrow. That list must be sent to the bookseller before the close of the month. I will send Lester to the library at eight. I shall have the catalogues all here ready to begin work at once. (PUSS *and* MRS. Q. *heard talking outside R.*)

Addie. Oh dear! I thought Puss and Mrs. Queergrain were not at home this afternoon. What shall I do! That might reveal everything. I mustn't be seen here. I'll go. (*Starts towards closet door.*)

Q. Plague take it, what does she mean? They'll see you.

Addie. (*Opens closet door L.*) Oh dear! that's the closet.

Q. If you *must*, be quick. I'll get rid of them. (*Pushes her into the closet and closes the door.*) I'm slow, but I see it all at last. Deuced slow I was to take a hint. This would be a pretty mess for the scandel-mongers. This is the result of being too liberal.

Enter MRS. Q. *and* PUSS *R.*

Mrs. Q. What! alone, Mr. Queergrain? Oh, you were only soliloquizing aloud. Are you arguing politics with some imaginary opponent? I caught the word liberal just now.

Q. (*Nervously eyeing the closet door.*) I was only thinking that people are sometimes too liberal.

Mrs. Q. I venture the opinion that very few people have the failing of too great liberality, though all may think themselves generous.

Puss. Ma, please don't begin to philosophize with Pa. He would not quit till tea time. Would you, Pa?

Q. (*Aside.*) She seems in a good humor. I'll try it. (*Aloud.*) Wife, what do you say to a walk? It is a beautiful afternoon.

Mrs. Q. A walk! (*Aside.*) The first for a year! (*Aloud.*) Oh, I should be glad to take a short walk before tea.

Puss. May I go, Pa?

Q. Certainly, child. Let us be off at once. (*Exit Q. R., followed by the ladies.*)

Mrs. Q. I can't understand it. He never thinks of such a thing as a walk usually.

Puss. Come on, Ma. Pa is waiting. (*Exeunt.*)

Addie. (*Appears from closet.*) I've made a dunce of myself for a trifle. What made me run the risk of being discovered in such a situation? And then, what will Mr. Queergrain think? That is the worst of it. I must explain to-night.

Enter JACK *R.*

Jack. Hello, Addie! What in the world are you doing here alone?

Addie. I just came in for a few minutes to see Mr. Queergrain about some library business, and was about to go as you came in.

Jack. Then you didn't see him.

Addie. Yes, I did.

Jack. But he and Mrs. Queergrain and Puss are out taking a walk. They didn't go out and leave you alone, surely?

Addie. That is exactly what they did. I did not wish to accompany them.

Jack. And you didn't take your leave. Waiting for me, eh? Why how did you get that cobweb on your shoulder? I declare, you're blushing. What's the matter?

Addie. Oh, you are entirely too inquisitive, Jack.

Jack. But there is some mystery about this, Addie. What is it? You must tell. You look guilty.

Addie. Well, Jack, if you must know I'll tell you, but you mustn't tell it for the world. You are my confidant, you know. I didn't wish Puss to know just yet that you and I are old acquaintances. It might spoil our plans. So I just hid in the closet till Mr. Queergrain took the ladies out for a walk.

Jack. Ha! ha! ha! Hid in the closet! Well, that beats me. Just think of a young lady calling on her friends, and then hiding in the closet to avoid seeing some of them. Romantic, decidedly! I'm glad Puss didn't find it out though. Ha! ha!

Addie. Hark! Some one's coming. (Puss *heard outside, talking to* Mrs. Q. *R.*)

Jack. Hang it, there's Puss back. I wish you had gone at once. She is going up stairs and will be down in a minute. Couldn't you go into the closet again till I dispose of her? Another time won't make much difference.

Addie. It ain't just proper, but then as it's all a joke I'll run the risk. (*Enters closet*)

Puss. Why! are you here alone, Jack? I thought you were out calling.

Jack. I've been back some time. I'm tired staying in doors. Don't you want to take a walk?

Puss. A *walk!* Gracious me! I've been walking to-day till I'm nearly tired to death.

Jack. Oh, you have been walking. (*Aside.*) What a fool I was to forget that

Puss. Jack, what do you think? Pa and Ma were taking a stroll; something that does not happen often since Pa has been so busy. It will do them both good. Ma worries too much sometimes. But I was so surprised that Pa should take a walk this time of day. He never did it before.

Jack. Yes, it is singular. (*Aside.*) I think, though, I could explain it. (*Aloud.*) I have a dull, disagreeable feeling just now. What will shake it off?

Puss. Sit down here and we will have a pleasant chat. That will wear off your dullness.

Jack. No, I'm tired of the house. I need a breath of cool air. Suppose we go out into the garden. I never tire of the beauties of nature.

Puss. I forgot that. Once you get to talking all your dullness will vanish. You must chase it away. You know I pride myself on your mirthful disposition and wit. If you distinguish yourself again, as you did last evening, I shall call you Monsieur Bon Mot. May I not?

Jack. Call me anything you choose, so it isn't bad.

Puss. But you are dull, Jack. What is the matter? Haven't you got over our little passage at arms this morning? I thought that was all made up.

Jack. It was, I assure you.

Puss. What is the matter, then? I never knew you to act so. Have you a skeleton in the closet?

Jack. There is nothing the matter. I don't *usually* keep skeletons in my closet. (*Aside.*) I hope to the Lord this one will not tarry long. (*Aloud.*) But let's go to the garden.

Puss. And I will make you a bouquet just like the one you wore the first time we met. That will put you in good spirits, won't it, dear Jack.

Jack. Yes, darling, that will set me all right again. (*Aside.*) If that girl don't smother in the closet. (*Exeunt R.*)

ADDIE *appears from closet.*

Addie. That hateful closet! A pretty fool I've made of my-self to help Jack play a joke on Puss. Jack thinks that's the reason, but Puss is so jealous that it isn't safe to have her think that we're acquainted. Well, Jack is a thoughtless young butterfly, among the fair sex. Ha! the sly rogue to entrap Puss into a correspond-ence in order to balance his own delinquencies! My part in this little game was easy enough, viz.: to furnish one male corres-pondent, with all modern improvements, such as small talk; soft nothings of speech, *very soft;* sentiment of the mildest and most approved pattern; a taste for the opera, and a wonderful power of criticism therein; orthodox in all things, with opinions in none; penmanship faultless; spelling architecturally correct, though some latitude is allowed on that point; above all, a handsome face (cabinet size $8 per dozen); good clothes and plenty of pocket money. Ha! ha! if my brother George can't fill the bill, it's his affair, not mine, for all responsibility of third parties terminates at a very early stage in such proceedings. I more than half sus-pect Puss is playing a similar game on Jack. Poor goose, he boasts of his last conquest and suspects nothing. Puss is a deep one. They'll both learn a lesson that will do them good. Mr. Queergrain didn't understand my hiding in the closet. That must be explained. (*Exit L.*)

ACT II.

Scene—*Same as Act I.*

Jack. What odd privileges leap-year bestows! A young lady coolly sends a delicate note saying that she will call at eight o'clock, if I am not engaged. I am always at home for the ladies, and at home *with* them, too. It's lucky that Puss is away. I always was a fortunate chap. There is nothing improper about this. The girls took their admired fortunates to the leap-year party. I am in for some fun. She is in love with me. That photo did the business. All the girls acknowledge that Jack Spigot is a heart-smasher. (*Struts foppishly.*) I hope her heart is not entirely used up. Pshaw! She is not the kind to break her heart so easily. I wonder if she is pretty? If she isn't, I'll freeze her with polite-ness. If she is pretty?' A little flirtation, that's all. I must put the finishing touches to my toilet. (*Exit R. Enter Q. L.*)

Q. How shocking to think that Addie suspected me of improper motives and was willing to meet me under such cir-cumstances! That closet was a revelation. Perhaps, after all, Mrs. Queergrain was right. She mustn't know of this. Hang it, I believe the marriage harness fits none too closely, after all, and that the social harness ought to fit a great deal closer. I'm deceived in the rising generation. (*Petulantly.*) Addie flirts secretly. Jack flirts publicly. Puss flirts *in the style.* The servants flirt in the kitchen, and they all flirt abominably. (*Knocking L. Opens the door. Enter* Addie.)

Addie. Good evening, Mr. Queergrain. (*Q. bows.*)

Q. Take a seat. (*Places chair.*) You are very punctual in your engagements.

Addie. Punctuality is one of the cardinal virtues. As you are ready, I presume we can begin at once. I hope we shall accomplish a large amount of work to night.

Q. I hope we may be able to finish this work entirely. I am heartily sick of it.

Addie. Before we begin, I wish to make an explanation in regard to something which—(*Footsteps heard outside R.*)

Q. Hark! (*Listens.*) Some one is coming. Who can it be! Jack has gone to the club, and the ladies are gone to the society. I thought the servants had all gone to the dance. (*Opens door and peeps out R.*) Good Lord! Whoever it is is lighting a lamp. Miss Wild, please step into the closet. No one must see you here.

Addie. I will not hide like a convicted culprit again in that hateful closet. I am innocent of any wrong intentions, and——

Q. Innocent! and so am I. But I've been indiscreet. I've done wrong. There'll be a scene, and people will talk. Do not compromise yourself and me by appearances. Go, please.

Addie. Oh, dear! (*Enters closet L. Q. closes door and steps behind his writing desk.*)

Enter Box R.

Box. Why here is a lamp burning. They forgot that, I suppose. She is not here yet. Susan is a sensible, dear girl. She prefers staying at home with me to going over to the Hall and dancing all night with all the young sprigs in town. But where can she be so long. Ah! she is coming at last. I can tell her step long before her fairy form appears. I'll pretend I am not here, and surprise her. (*Turns down one lamp and blows the other out. Drops behind large chair.*)

Enter MRS. QUEERGRAIN R. disguised as chambermaid, veiled.

Box. (*Springing up.*) Aha! my charmer! Got a veil on, eh! Thought you would fool me. I'll pay you for that trick. (*Pulls off MRS. Q.'s veil, and kisses her before he discovers his mistake. Both recoil in amazement.*)

Box. What the——

Mrs. Q. What do you mean, Box, by such scandalous conduct?

Box. I didn't mean it at all. I didn't know it was you. I beg pardon, I do, I—I—

Q. (*Stepping forward suddenly.*) You had better beg mine too. Such conduct is inexcusable.

Box. Really, Mr. Queergrain, I meant no harm. I thought it was Susan, seeing that she had *her* dress on.

Q. I don't see that you are excusable to enter my library and conduct yourself in such a manner with Susan even. I do not wish my servants to act so unbecomingly. Mrs. Queergrain, perhaps you will not object to explaining why you appear here in such an unbecoming attire?

Mrs. Q. I can explain that when you explain why you are here at all. You led me to believe you had an engagement down town.

Q. I didn't say I had an engagement down town.

Mrs. Q. You said you were crowded with work, and you never work here.

Q. Madam, I can explain that satisfactorily in due time.

Mrs. Q. In due time! Now is the time, or never. I am ready now to explain anything that may need explanation. (*They stand and gaze at each other.*)

Enter Puss R.

Puss. Why, Pa, are you here. I thought you and Jack had engagements. (*Aside*) Addie hasn't come after all. (*Aloud.*) Pa, what tableau are you and Ma representing? It's decidedly good, ha! ha! Now I have it! King Cophetua and the beggar maid. Pa has a regal look, and Ma is not a bad beggar maid in her present attire. A misunderstanding again, I suppose? What is it, Ma?

Mrs. Q. I will not speak first.

Q. Nor will I.

Puss. Then I will speak. I can clear up this mystery, I think. But you must all follow my instructions. First of all, we must go into the parlor for a few minutes.

Q. Into the parlor! What for?

Puss. Never mind what for. Only obey instructions and all will be clear in a few minutes. Come. We'll be back in a few minutes.

Q. I'd like to know what she is going to do. (*Exeunt R*, Puss last.*)

Box. (*Passing out. Aside.*) If I get out of this scrape, you shan't catch me surprising anybody again. That was a surprise, sure

Puss. (*Aside.*) I wonder if she will be ready soon. Hark! There's a timid knock at the door. And Jack's coming down stairs to answer it. Good! good! Everything works like a charm. I hope he hasn't heard us. (*Exit R.*)

Enter L JACK *and* DINAH, *latter heavily veiled and disguised.*

Jack. Let me take your hat and coat (*stammers*)—I meant your bonnet and shawl. (*She takes her shawl off, and hands it to him.*) Your hat and——. Hang it, I meant your things. Excuse me, I am not accustomed to receive lady callers. Take a seat. (*Points to chair.*)

Dinah. (*Speaks with a lisp.*) You are quite excusable. (*Seats herself on sofa L.*) Of course it seems a little odd for a lady to call on a gentleman in this way. Leap year does not come often. I don't feel at all at home myself.

Jack. (*Seating himself on chair opposite her.*) That's so. I wish it did, though. I beg your pardon, I forgot to take your hat. Let me take that, Miss Flyer.

Dinah. Thank you, it is hardly worth while for me to take off my hat.

Jack. You need not be in such a hurry. We must get acquainted.

Dinah. I shouldn't like to remain long, for the folks might return before I left.

Jack. Pshaw! They will not be back for an hour or more. Mr. Queergrain never gets in till ten or after, and Mrs. Queergrain will stay at the society until it adjourns, and that is nearly ten.

Dinah. I shan't remain long. I intended merely to make a short call.

Jack. Very well, let it be short, if that is the inevitable, but please don't be formal about it.

Dinah. That's my sentiment. I never did like formality. So let's get acquainted. I've been wishing ever since we began this very pleasant correspondence to meet you.

Jack. Indeed! (*Aside.*) I thought so. (*Aloud.*) I certainly can say that I was very desirous of the same pleasure. We might just as well have met sooner, and so have tasted this happiness often. I presume, though, you are an advocate of self-denial.

Dinah. To confess the truth, I hardly knew whether it would be right to receive a call from an entire stranger.

Jack. So you concluded to call on me. I appreciate your delicacy, and think more of you for it. (*Aside.*) Over the left.

Dinah. Please, Mr. Spigot, don't say that.

Jack. What?

Dinah. That you think more of me.

Jack. Well, if you don't wish me to say that, I will take that back and say that you have done the proper thing. (*Aside.*) In a horn.

Dinah. Thank you, Mr. Spigot, I'm so glad to know that you think so.

Jack. Of course there can be nothing improper in our meeting, and if the thing itself is right the place can't make much difference. I have longed to see your face ever since I first looked on your photo.

Dinah. You are inclined to flattery, Mr. Spigot.

Jack. It's the truth, anyway. (*Aside.*) Why don't she take off that abominable veil. (*Aloud.*) Miss Flyer, hadn't you better take off your hat?

Dinah. No; I must make a short call.

Jack. (*Aside.*) Deuced slow to take a hint. (*Aloud.*) You don't mean to say that you are going to keep that veil over your face till you leave, and not let me see your face at all?

Dinah. I'll be your inamorata incognita, the mysterious Lady of the Veil.

Jack. (*Aside.*) A beauty! I will see her face. (*Aloud.*) Madam, your Sir Knight wishes to see the beautiful face of the Lady of the Veil. He is dying for one of her smiles.

Dinah. You have my photo., and if you wish to see my face you must call on me.

Jack. (*Aside.*) Ugly, I'll bet. A scheme to trap me. (*Aloud. winningly.*) Miss Flyer, your photo. can't smile. Besides, I wish to verify it before I continue our acquaintance further. Will you give me the opportunity to gaze on your beautiful countenance?

Dinah. Mr. Spigot, I have the best of reasons for refusing your request. When we meet again all will be made clear.

Jack. When we meet again! I'm going to solve this riddle now.

(Seats himself beside her on the sofa. Produces photo. Looks at it.) What splendid eyes! and what delicately molded lips! Miss Flyer may I sip the nectar of those ruby lips? *(Advances.)*

Dinah. *(Rises.)* What do you mean, sir?

Jack. The plain English of it is, may I kiss you?

Dinah. Kiss me! How dare you!

Jack. I am always ready to dare and to do when there is no more sacrifice involved than on the present occasion. *(Seizes her and attempts to lift her veil. She screams.* PUSS *and others enter R.)* What the—— Confusion!

Puss. Goodness alive! what's the matter?

Q. This is a night of surprises.

Mrs. Q. *(Severely.)* Mr. Spigot, it devolves on you as a gentleman to explain your conduct.

Puss. We are ready for explanations, Jack.

Enter BOX *L, showing in* GEO. WILD. *Announces, "A gentleman who wishes to see* MISS PEARLY." MR. Q. *beckons* BOX *to remain.* GEO. *stops by* JACK L., *faces* PUSS, *who is in R. C.* MR. *and* MRS. Q. *between them.*

Geo. Good evening, Miss Pearly.

Puss. *(Surprised.)* What! How did you come here? You assume a great deal. I said Thursday evening.

Jack. Thursday! You knew I should be gone then. It's your turn to explain. Why don't you introduce the gentleman?

Geo. I will attempt——*(*JACK *beckons him to keep quiet.)*

Q. *(Aside.)* I hope she's not in there yet. *(Glances at closet.)*

Mrs. Q. Puss, you promised to clear up this mystery, but it only increases. Stop your nonsense, and tell us what it means.

Puss. Ma, don't ask. I can't explain. Where's Addie! *(Looks around bewildered. Door of closet opens and* ADDIE *steps out beside* GEO.)

Mrs. Q. *(Hysterically.)* Merciful heavens! my worst fears are realized. I am undone! Oh! oh! oh! Mr. Queergrain, how came she there?

Puss. Oh, Addie! I'm so glad you are here. Ma, this young lady is Miss Addie Wild, an intimate friend of Pa's and mine.

Mrs. Q. Then why is she in the closet? and why are you at home to-night, Mr. Queergrain?

Q. Mrs. Queergrain, I thought that the child of my most intimate friend, and a schoolmate of Puss's, could visit here safely at all times. We made an engagement this morning to meet and finish the library list this evening.

Mrs. Q. Yes, but this secrecy—the closet, Mr. Queergrain?

Addie. Mrs. Queergrain, that was all my fault. Mr. Queergrain, to-day I did not shrink from meeting your wife, as I fear you supposed. I blush to think that I should give the slightest ground for such a thought. It was only Puss I wished to avoid.

Puss. Only me! I declare!

Mrs. Q. So you avoided her once before, to-day, and avoided me just now. Queer conduct for a lady!

Addie. Mr. Spigot and I were carrying out a little ruse which we had projected. You need not stare, Puss. We did not wish Puss to know just yet that Jack was an old friend of mine, lest she might suspect something and spoil it all if she saw us together.

Mrs. Q. And all this trouble comes from a boy's-and-girl's trick.

Q. It's all my fault. I pushed her in. I thought she was —— It's all right.

Mrs. Q. If it's right to try to decieve me, then it *is* all right.

Q. Only a mistake all around! No harm done, that is if you can explain satisfactorily that little matter between you and Box, my dear.

Mrs. Q. The blundering blockhead!

Puss. We have all learned a lesson by experience. Mr. Danby, (*To* GEO.) I shall introduce you to the company.

Geo. Not by that name, please.

Addie. Ha! ha! Brother George, I will introduce you to Mr. and Mrs. Queergrain. (*They bow.*)

Q. (*Shaking hands.*) Well, well! more surprises! George, I shouldn't have known you after your long absence.

Puss. Gracious, George, it can't be you.

Geo. But it is.

Jack. Puss, your unknown correspondent. Confess, my pouting delinquent. We know all about it.

Mrs. Q. My daughter, you shock me terribly. To think that my child would do such a thing. I've lost confidence in human nature. What *will* mankind come to?

Jack. To a pretty woman when she advertises for a correspondent.

Puss. It's mean as can be. George, I shan't like you a bit for helping them.

Geo. It was only a joke, Puss.

Jack. Another *lesson* learned, Puss.

Puss. How did you find out I advertised for a correspondent?

Jack. Easy enough. Don't throw the draft of your next advertisement into the coal scuttle.

Puss. You're too provoking for any good. But I'll forgive you, Jack. I think I'm even with you. Did you ever lose a letter?

Jack. Yes.

Puss. And found a correspondent. Furnished to order. Ha! ha!

Q. Call it a draw game.

Mrs. Q. I'm horrified!

Jack. (*To* PUSS.) Then who is this lady? I don't recognize her.

Mrs. Q. (*Gazes at* DINAH *who attempts to run off R and is prevented by* MRS. Q. No; since you have done such an unlady-like action, stay and bear its consequences. How dare you run away?

Puss. Ma, let the poor girl go. She' ssuffered enough. (*Beckons* DINAH *to go.*)

Jack. Leave this to me. (*To* DINAH.) I beg your pardon, madam; who are you? (Q. *glances at* DINAH, *who is seated on sofa, and nods significantly at* MRS Q.)

Puss. Wait a minute, Jack; will you forgive her and me? Remember it must be an unconditional pardon; no reservations.

Addie. Don't be hard-hearted, Jack.

Jack. I guess I can afford to grant full absolution.

Mrs. Q. Let this be a warning, a dreadful warning. But I'll know who she is.

Q. My dear, I think we have learned that true love endures no tests.

Mrs. Q. And no unshared secrets!

Jack. (*Aside.*) She can't resist *me*. I'm too much for 'em generally. (*Aloud. To* DINAH.) Madam we await your pleasure. Excuse my curiosity, but I'm anxious to have the pleasure of your acquaintance. (*Steps back towards* DINAH, *who is in rear L. A pause.*)

Mrs. Q. *I'll* make her acquaintance. (*Advances toward* DINAH.)

Puss. Please don't, ma.

Mrs. Q. I *will.* (*Jerks off* DINAH'S *veil. Latter hesitates a moment, then runs off R. All laugh.*)

Jack. A tric, confound it !

Puss. Another *lesson*, Jack !

QUICK CURTAIN.

A FAMILY STRIKE.

CHARACTERS.

———

BLITZEN,   GUS GALLIVANT,
MRS BLITZEN,   WILKS BLITZEN,
JULIA BLITZEN,   MARY, SERVANT,

COSTUMES.

———

Any clothing suited to the social standing of the wearer.   Gus stylish, and fastidiously dressed.

STAGE DIRECTIONS.

———

R means right as the actor faces the audience; L, left; C, centre.

A FAMILY STRIKE.

SCENE, MR. BLITZEN'S *parlor elegantly furnished. Julia discovered seated reading a note.*

Julia. Oh day of days! Can I believe it that this delightful Tuesday, October 9th, is the day I have awaited in such suspense? Yes it's to-day. (*Looking again at the note.*) He says Tuesday. Oh I do wish this day could be as long as the last long month has been since I parted from dear Gus at the Springs. But it will not. How provoking! that our joys must be so few and fleeting! It will be as short as those delicious evenings we spent together driving and waltzing. How they flew on the wings of—of—yes of love for I loved him from the very first. Wasn't it romantic to think that Gus should be the one to find my card case and return it to me? Of course we had to exchange cards after *that*, and then I couldn't think of being so rude as not to bow to him on the promenade the next time we met, and—well—(*Sighs*) Now he visits the city with his uncle. Ah! I wish he had come without that respected relative, for somehow I never could get acquainted with *him*. Indeed his *overpoweringly* benevolent look seemed always saying " I pity that giddy young thing." I'll have him understand I don't long for pity. I despise it. But I'll try and love him for Gus's sake.

Enter MRS. B. R.

Mrs. B. Julia, when do you expect Mr. Gallivant?
Julia. At three. They come on the noon train.
Mrs. B. And his uncle will call with him I suppose?
Julia. I believe so. I wish he wouldn't. He wants to get acquainted with the family. So Gus says. He's a self-appointed investigation committee. Oh dear! What if his decision should be unfavorable!
Mrs. B. Don't fret my dear! I guarantee he'll find few more genteel families than this, if Mr. B. behaves himself, and *I'll take care of him.* But my dear, we've not yet got our dresses for Mrs. Newfangle's party, we must try strategy on Mr. Blitzen this time. I'll send at once and tell Mrs. Gauzeall not to present her bill till we decide about the new dresses; it *might* influence Mr. Blitzen, you know. (*Ringing of door bell heard.*)

Julia. Why who can that be? (*Looks out.*) Oh dear I believe it is Mr. Shekel, and Gus is not along! (*Excitedly.*) There's some mistake. His note said at three. What shall we do?

Mrs. B. Keep cool and receive him as if he were expected. It's some eccentricity of his. But he'll not catch Mrs. Blitzen napping I think. (*Goes to door L.*)

Enter WILKS BLITZEN.

Wilks. Mrs. Blitzen, I presume.

Mrs. B. (*Bowing.*) We were not expecting you so soon, but our pleasure is all the greater as you can be with us longer.

Wilks. Oh the pleasure is mutual. (*Aside.*) Not expecting me. Shouldn't wonder, nobody told them I was coming.

Mrs. B. This is my daughter Julia. I presume you remember her.

Wilks. (*Turns to Julia.*) Yes, I remember Julia quite well. How are you Julia? I suppose you remember your uncle, although it is quite a long time since we met. (*Offers her his hand.*)

Julia. I remember you quite well, though it is some time since we met. (*Aside.*) I'll declare, he acts strangely. Calls himself "uncle" and me Julia. Its evident that he's agreed. (*Aloud.*) I'm so glad you're come.

Mrs. B. And we sincerely hope you will enjoy your visit.

Wilks. Thank you. I shall, I'm sure. But first, I want to see Mr. Blitzen about some baggage, and then I'm ready to visit.

Mrs. B. I'm very sorry! He's just stepped over to the next street, but will be back in a minute.

Wilks. Then I'll go out and meet him. I want to surprise him.

Mrs. B. But you may not be able to find him. I'll send for him.

Wilks. No, I saw him, I think, as I came in. I shall have no difficulty if I wait at the corner. It will be a surprise to hail him on the street. (*Exit L.*)

Mrs. B. I should say it would surprise anybody. Why, how familiar he seems. No reserve at all. Is Gus any thing like his uncle?

Julia. I didn't use to think so. It's remarkable! He seems so sociable now. I guess I was mistaken in him. The fact is, I never saw him more than three or four times, and never spoke over a dozen words to him.

Mrs. B. It's very evident that he has made up his mind that everything is all right.

Julia. Well, I hope so, ma. I'd die if he should separate dear Gus and me. (*Exit R.*)

Mrs. B. Nonsense! What sentimental notions girls get into their heads' to furnish amusement to them when they think of it in after years.

Enter SERVANT L.

Servant. Mrs. Blitzen, there's a gentlemen at the door enquiring for Miss Blitzen.

Mrs. B. Is he young or old, Mary?

Servant. He is youngish like, and tall. Looks like he might be a clerk.

Mrs. B. Then tell him Miss Blitzen can not see him to-day. (*Exit servant L.*)

Mrs. B. These duns are a frightful bore. Why can't people wait?

Enter SERVANT L.

Servant. He says he must come in—that he had an appointment.

Mrs. B. Then tell him to come in. I'll soon dispose of him. (*Exit servant L. Returns showing in Gus.*)

Mrs. B. (*Frigidly.*) Did you wish to see me, sir?

Gus. (*Hesitating.*) Well, yes, madam; though I called to see Miss Blitzen.

Mrs. B. She is not in sir. Besides *I* attend to all such affairs.

Gus. (*Aside.*) The deuce you do! (*Aloud.*) Madam, there must be some mistake!

Mrs. B. (*Stiffly.*) None at all, sir.

Gus. But Miss Julia knows that I intended to call to-day.

Mrs. B. Sir, I told you *I* attend to those matters.

Gus. Those matters! (*Aside.*) Thunder! I wonder if they have many such affairs.

Mrs. B. You must come to-morrow. (*Aside.*) It will never do for Mr Blitzen to see that bill for those silks.

Gus. Hang it! (*Aside.*) This is deuced queer conduct for one's intended mother-in-law. I'll try again. (*Aloud.*) Madam, there must be something——

Mrs. B. Nothing of the kind. Young man, I said you could call to-morrow. (*Aside*) I wish he'd go. Mr. Blitzen may come at any moment.

Gus. (*Aside.*) By George she can't play that on me. (*Aloud.*) Madam, may I see *you* this afternoon? *You*, I presume, are Mrs. Blitzen. Can I have an interview with *you*.

Mrs. B. (*Desperately.*) Yes yes. (*Aside.*) Anything to get rid of him. Go! Go at once. Don't let Mr. Blitzen see you.

Gus. (*Aside.*) Oh *that's* it. The old man's been cutting up about it. (*Aloud.*) Very well, madam, I'll call this afternoon.

Mrs. B. Good day.

Gus. Good day. (*Bows and exits L. Mrs. B. exit R.*)

Enter BLITZEN R, *seats himself, picks up paper.*

Blitzen. (*Reading.*) ELMIRA, July 25. All trains are stopped on the Erie road. The strikers are in force, and threaten violence at Hornellsville. The Brooklyn troops are moving west cautiously. Strikers are tearing up the track in advance of the train. CHICAGO, July 25. Everything is quiet here so far, but serious trouble is threatened. 400 regulars arrived to-day.

LONDON, July 24, 2 P. M. The American strikes and riots are creating a profound sensation throughout Europe. Creating a sensation! (*Drops paper.*) Of course they will. Capital was uneasy enough before. Now it's insane. Blow it! I believe I'd sell my "Centrals" at 75 and turn them into 4 per cents. Hanged if it don't look as if a man with money wasn't safe now-a-days. He's taxed to death; bled for all sorts of sham enterprises; called mean and lacking in public spirit if he don't subscribe freely; and then dubbed a "big-bug" or an "old aristocrat" for his pains. "Big-bug." That means he is a conspicuous prey for every ravenous old gobbler that comes along in the shape of a public enterprise. Hang enterprise! (*Enter Wilks L.*) Give me the old fashioned stage coach. It never struck.

Wilks. And the highwayman declared a monthly dividend of 100 per cent plus your valuables. Tut! tut! man you never saw a stage coach.

Blitzen. Who the deuce are you? Wilks Blitzen, by Jove! Why, brother, how are you? (*Cordially shakes hands.*) When did you come? Have a seat. (*Gives Wilks easy chair.*) Give an account of yourself, old fellow.

Wilks. Well, I am here on a visit of several days.

Blitzen. Good! Wife along?

Wilks. No.

Blitzen. Good again! We'll enjoy ourselves.

Wilks. What do you mean? I enjoy myself with my wife better than in anybody else's society.

Blitzen. Fudge! (*Aside.*) Wait till you get a second wife.

Wilks. I beg your pardon, Walter. Really I had forgotten that I had not seen you since your marriage. Allow me to congratulate you. She seems a very pleasant lady

Blitzen. Ah, thank you! (*Aside.*) I need consolation worse. (*Aloud.*) So you've met my wife? But where in the world, pray?

Wilks. Here, in this room. I just stepped out to meet you, but missed you entirely. Your wife and daughter gave me such a cordial reception, that I am surprised you are not happy with two such charming women.

Blitzen. Wilks, happiness is a grand humbug.

Wilks. Ha! ha! Not much, it ain't. There are no blanks drawn in life's lottery. If you don't draw an opera-house, you may draw an elephant.

Blitzen. An elephant! Now you've hit it. An elephant, whose trunk is a confounded Saratoga, filled with flummery and nonsense.

Wilks. Walter, don't talk about those things. How's Julia?

Blitzen. Ah, that's the trouble. (*Sadly.*) I could stand the other, but Julia, sweet girl! She is following in the wake of her worthy step-mother. It's dress, and balls, and parties, and receptions, and style till my very head is turned. I hear nothing else. Lord bless me, I dont know the names of the things on my dinner table any more. We talk French entirely. We *parley voo*. Devil take the *parley*. (*Voice heard outside R, calling, Mr. Blitzen! Mr. Blitzen!*) Hear that! They're calling me. I'm their slave! I'm liable to duty any hour of the day or night. They want money; or they want to consult about some useless article they've set their mind on; or they're diving into some infernal expense.

Wilks. Keep cool Walter. Keep cool.

Blitzen. (*Jumping up excitedly.*) It's true. I'm a ruined man. If this thing keeps up, I'll go into bankruptcy. (*Voices heard again, louder than before.*) I wish *I* could *strike*. It would do me good.

Wilks. I wish you could, too. Strike a bonanza, for instance, in our Colorado mine. Have you had any news from our investments in the mines?

Blitzen. Not a line. But I shall hear by to-day's mail, and I feel confident it will be good news. Our superintendent felt sure we should strike a rich lead.

Wilks. And that will be a *strike* of the right kind. It's not half so risky as the one you contemplated a few moments ago.

Blitzen. Why didn't you bring John along? I should like to see my nephew again.

Wilks. That reminds me that he stopped to greet an old chum at the corner store, and has forgotten to come. They'll talk all day, unless something's done. I'll run down and hurry him up.

Blitzen. Do, and don't forget to hurry yourself up, too. We'll have you some dinner in a few minutes.

Wilks. I shall not be gone long. Don't inaugurate that strike. Try moral suasion. Call out your reserves. (*Exit L.*)

Blitzen. Try the reserves! That's a good idea. There's a good deal of unadulterated cussedness stored up in Walt. Blitzen, and I'll see what that will effect. If a crisis must be precinated, I hope it will be a ten strike.

Enter a SERVANT *with a note which* BLITZEN *reads.*

MR. BLITZEN. *Dear Sir:* Let us respectfully call your attention to the enclosed bill. The account has been running over one month, and you will excuse our presenting it now, as times are so very close, etc., etc.

Another bill from that confounded milliner! I paid a large one a few weeks ago, so this can't be very heavy. (*Unfolds a preposterously long bill. Reads items.*) One hat, with pompon aigrettes, $50. *Fifty dollars for a hat!* What on earth is a pompon aigrette? 12 yds. torchon lace, @ $10 per yd., $120. One Jabot, $25. One *Jabbit!* Humph! I'd like to know where they wear that? One collar, Swiss medallions, $15. Blow me, if there isn't one article I know the name of. Fifteen dollars. That keeps me in collars five years. I won't pay it! *I'll not.* They can't come that any more. I won't be bankrupted by fashion and milliners! The milliners may go to Halifax. There's need of a *strike* right here at home. I'll strike, too. If the iron ain't hot, I'll make it hot. (*Brings down his fist with a tremendous thump on the table.*)

Enter JULIA BLITZEN. R.

Julia. Pa, did you hear ma call? (*No answer.*) It is only three weeks till Mrs. Newfangle's party, and you know we must go. We shall be expected.

Blitzen. (*Savagely.*) Well, who said you couldn't go?

Julia. Why, Pa! What ails you, to-day?

Blitzen. (*Excitedly.*) Parties ail me! Fashion ails me! Milliner's and dressmaker's bills ail me! Flummery ails me! What in time else do you want to attack me, for Heaven's sake?

Julia. Pa! Pa! You surprise me. You are not well. Don't make yourself uneasy. You are nervous.

Blitzen. Nervous? I'm not nervous. But it would shock the nervous system of a mummy to attend all these parties and doings. I'm not going.

Julia. But the Newfangles will be offended if we absent ourselves.

Blitzen. Go! Go! If you want to.

Julia. Pa, ma and I will be so sorry to go without you. You remember you promised to go; and besides, I was to have a new dress specially for that occasion. Remember that, pa.

Blitzen. Wear one of the dresses you've got.

Julia. Why pa, I'm shocked! At this, the most select reception of the season, all the ladies will appear in *new* dresses, prepared specially for the occasion.

Blitzen. Your mother called a dress new till she'd had it a year

Enter MRS. B. R.

Julia. Ma, he refuses to get my new dress. I can't go.

Mrs. B. Then, of course, he will refuse mine, too. Oh dear, you want us to be shabby and unworthy of you.

Blitzen. Good gracious! Has it come to this pass, that silks and laces are necessary to make a man's family respectable and worthy of him? If it has, I'll leave the country at once.

Mrs. B Of course not to make us unworthy of you. I meant our friends. What will they say?

Blitzen. Let them say what they please. I don't see any thing especially worthy about the Newfangles. Newfangle got his money by swindling in army contracts.

Mrs. B. Don't speak so, dear. Mrs. Newfangle is such a nice woman. Think of her, she'll be so grieved. Can't we have the dresses? It's only a trifle, you know?

Blitzen. If she gets mad over that, let her get mad, that's all.

Mrs. B. But it's such a small matter, compared with our circumstances.

Blitzen. Only a trifle Look at that. (*Seizes bill from the table and presents it to Mrs. B.*) Do you call that a trifle? I'll be ruined by trifles.

Julia. (*Aside to Mrs. B.*) How unfortunate that it should come in just now.

Mrs. B. Mr. Blitzen, possibly you may remember that when we were engaged, I spoke of the social position we were to occupy. You know I'm fond of society. That was understood, wasn't it?

Blitzen. Never fully understood till the present moment.

Mrs. B. You wished some one to bring your daughter out.

Blitzen. And you've done it, with a vengance.

Mrs. B. Yes; I've made an accomplished lady of her. (*B. groans.*) I had some money, too. You may remember that?

Blitzen. I do. (*Aside.*) She's spent three times the amount. (*Aloud.*) But I tell you I can't afford it. Times have changed. I have an expensive lawsuit on hand.

Mrs. B. Which you and Mr. Noodle will win. Mr. Noodle is positive But, my dear, let us not talk about the lawsuit now. You know Mr. Gallivant is coming to-day.

Blitzen. Don't mention that Gallivant, never again. I forever hear his name. Julia is eternally raving about Gallivant! Gallivant!

Julia. Oh pa, you are prejudiced against poor Augustus.

Blitzen. As I am against monkeys, and other like pests.

Mrs B. Mr. Blitzen you are worrying over some trouble. Now I have it! It's the strike. That will soon be settled. It can't effect your securities.

Blitzen. The *strike!* You've guessed it, at last. I say it will effect us. It must. In fact *I've struck.*

Mrs. B. You've struck? What do you mean?

Blitzen. I mean, I've taken the most decided step of my life. I can't stand this eternal worry. *I've struck to end it.*

Mrs. B. Mercy on us! He's struck! He's ended it! Julia ,dear, he's compromised in the lawsuit, as he has often threatened,and ruined us. (*Wringing her hands.*) We're ruined.

Julia. Oh pa! How could you have the heart to do such a thing, and ruin your family? And poor Gus! His uncle may object if you should fail to establish the justice of your claim in the case. Oh dear! (*Wringing her hands.*) I'm undone.

Blitzen. Oh! So I've raised a deuce of a breeze!

Mrs. B. Heartless! (*Sobbing.*)

Julia. Cruel, cruel, parent! (*They turn to R and L sobbing.*)

Blitzen. That was a ten strike for a chance shot. (*Aside.*) I'll play that as long as it will win. They've worried me enough.

Enter WILKS L.

Wilks. (*Pauses. Aside.*) Here's a time of it. (*To Blitzen.*) You failed to take my advice, and you see the result.

Mrs. B. Dear me, and you, too, advised him against this fatal step.

Wilks. I did madam.

Mrs. B. But he will hear no advice. Rash man. It is suicidal. (*To Wilks.*) Of course we know *your* conclusion.

Julia. And it is cruel to others who are innocent.

Wilkes. (*Aside.*) What the nation has the conclusion of a man who has spent ten years among the savages of Colorado, to do with it?

Blitzen. (*Aside.*) Yes, to Gus—one of Darwin's links. (*Aloud.*) You mean young Gallivant I suppose. If his uncle can't take care of him, he had better send him to an asylum.

Mrs. B. Mr. Blitzen! How shockingly rude.

Enter GUS L. JULIA *rushes into his arms, he kisses her.*

Gus. Dear Julia, we arrived one train sooner than I expected.

Blitzen. (*Mistakes Gus for his nephew.*)   Why, how are you my boy.   You are always welcome in this house.   (*Shakes hands cordially.*)

Gus.   I'm quite well, thank you.   How are you, sir?

Blitzen.   First rate, first rate, my boy!

Gus. (*Aside to Julia.*)   Ah dearest Julia, your father has relented. He must have found out something favorable to me.   But your mother?

Julia. (*Aside.*)   Pa surprises me.   (*Aloud.*)   Let me introduce you to ma, Mr. Gallivant.

Gus.   Happy to meet you, Mrs Blitzen.   (*They bow and shake hands.*)

Mrs. B.   I am glad to welcome you here.   (*Aside.*)   Dear me! What a stupid blunder I made to-day.

Blitzen. (*To Wilks.*)   How fond the young folks are of each other.   She calls him her *gallant* just as she used to do, wife.   I'm glad they have not forgotten old times.

Julia. (*Aside.*)   What *does* pa mean?

Wilks.   It seems they are mindful of former meetings.   (*Aside.*) Another mistake.   I'll wait for developements.

Gus. (*Aloud.*)   My dear sir, I shall never forget those days. (*Aside to Julia.*)   He has consented then.

Julia. (*Aside to Gus.*)   He must have been impressed by your appearance.   (*Aloud*)   Pa, it is strange— (*Hesitating.*)   I mean—

Blitzen.   Strange!   What's strange, Julia?

Mrs. B.   Your conduct and actions, Mr. Blitzen.

Blitzen.   Nothing strange about it, if you refer to what passed a few minutes ago,   *I've struck,* that's all.   As I'm the head of this family, the family has struck.

Mrs. B.   Then you mean to say, you've ruined us!

Wilks.   No, made your fortune.

Mrs. B. (*Starting hopefully.*)   Ah, indeed!   Then you consent?

Wilks.   Madam, I dont understand you.   I have consented to nothing, I assure you.   (*To Blitzen.*)   Good.   We'll pile up the dust.

Blitzen.   That we will.

Mrs. B.   What can he mean by piling up the dust?   (*To Gus.*) Will you please explain what your uncle means by his strange conduct?   He and Mr. Blitzen seem to understand each other, but for the life of me I can't fathom their meaning.

Gus.   I was not aware that uncle had yet conferred with Mr. Blitzen.

Blitzen.   We have, though, and its all right.   He objected, but that made no difference.   He'll come round sometime to see things as I do.

Gus.   The deuce he did!

Wilks.   His uncle!   What has he to do with silver mining? Didn't you get news from Colorado?

Blitzen.   No.

Wilks.   Then we are not millionaires?

Blitzen.   Not that I know of.

Wilks.   You said we had *struck.*

Blitzen.   I said *I* had struck.

Wilks.   Concern it, why did you raise a fellow's hopes only to dash them to the ground!   I thought you were talking of silver mines.

Mrs. B. Silver mines! Strikes! (*Glances around.*) Objections and agreements! Mr. Blitzen, are you crazy?

Blitzen. Not a bit of it. I never was saner in my life.

Gus. I doubt that, if you say you have consulted with my uncle, for he was at his hotel half an hour ago, and I am confident he never saw you in his life.

Blitzen. (*Astonished.*) Never saw me? Why, who are you, anyway? Wilks, isn't this your son John?

Wilks. I never saw him in my life!

Blitzen. You haven't. Then who are you? (*To Gus.*)

Gus. I am Augustus Gallivant. I came here to see your daughter Julia.

Blitzen. The blazes you say! (*Dances around frantically.*) What have I done? I've actually shaken hands with that fellow, called him nephew, and played the dunce generally.

Mrs. B. You are right, M. B., when you say *played the dunce*. That's the only pertinent sentiment you've given utterance to in the last half hour.

Julia. Dear pa, what did you mean when you said you had made an agreement with dear Gus's uncle?

Blitzen. Mean? I said no such thing.

Mrs. B. And did you mean nothing in regard to compromising the lawsuit?

Blitzen. I compromised no lawsuit.

Mrs. B. Then, pray, what did you mean?

Blitzen. I meant that I'll stand no more of this confounded expense for toggery and nonsense that's of no use under the sun to anybody.

Mrs. B. And all this fuss is about *two new dresses*.

Blitzen. Exactly.

Mrs. B. And you have raised all this disturbance about paltry matter of expense for the clothing of your wife and daughter?

Blitzen. There was a last straw that broke—

Mrs. B. Mr. Blitzen!

Julia. Pa!

Blitzen. Yes, that broke Mr. Blitzen.

Enter SERVANT *with telegram.* MR. B. *opens it and reads, shouts "hurrah," grasps* WILKS *by the hand.*

Blitzen. (*Reads aloud.*) "Have struck a bonanza. Blitzen Brothers control the mine."

Wilks. Good! Good!

Mrs. B. We were always lucky.

Julia. That's just splendid! Isn't it, Gus?

Gus. Allow me to congratulate you on your good luck, Mr. Blitzen.

Blitzen. Thank you. I think I owe you an apology, Mr. Gallivant. I have not given you a fair chance by judging you, unheard.

Julia. Pa can't help but like you, Gus. Can you pa?

Blitzen. Well I'm about of your mind, Julia. I waive all objections, and consent.

Julia. ⎫
Gus. ⎭ Oh thank you !

Blitzen. No thanks necessary. (*Aside.*) I'll save money by it in the end. Mrs. Blitzen, you may consider this strike ended unconditionally.

Mrs. B. Happy to do so, but you must come down handsomely by way of forfeits. Don't say no. It's settled.

Blitzen. All right, my dear. I'll run this family as long as I can on a silver mine, and then—

Wilks. You will strike again.

Blitzen. No, lease a gold mine.

CURTAIN.

THE SPARKLING CUP.

CHARACTERS.

LEDGER, wealthy business man.

JOHN HEARTSEASE, " The drunkard."

TRUSTHAM, Temperance reformer.

STOUGHTON, Proprietor of the " Shades."

WISHALL.

CHARLES WINSLOW, Express agent.

PEWTERMUGG.

CANTWELL, Temperance reformer.

BILLY STOUGHTON.

WALTER WESTON.

GUZZLE.

HANS GIPFEL, Hartsease's gardener.

MRS. HEARTSEASE, ⎫
⎬ Engaged in temperance work.
MRS. WINSLOW, ⎭

SUSIE HEARTSEASE.

KATRINA GIPFEL.

A policeman, FREDDIE STOUGHTON, a beggar girl, Loafers, etc.

COSTUMES.

Any clothing suited to the station of the wearer.

STAGE EXPLANATIONS.

R, means right for the actor as he faces the audience;   L, left;
C, center.

THE SPARKLING CUP.

ACT I.

SCENE I. *A room in* HEARTSEASE'S *house, elegantly furnished ; pictures, etc. ; sofa* R *; chairs* R *and* L *; table* C, *around which are seated at dinner* MR. *and* MRS. HEARTSEASE, LEDGER WISHALL, WINSLOW, *and* SUSIE.

Ledger. Dear me, daughter (*To* MRS. H.), how time flies! Here we are celebrating your thirty-seventh birthday, and I begin to realize that I am an old man. Well, I've seen a goodly share of this world's joys, and some of its trials too; but I've had a little the best of it, and I'm good for a round score of years yet.

Mrs. H. Certainly, father. You must not think of calling yourself old yet.

H. Father, don't mention such disagreeable subjects. Bring naught but light hearts to such occasions as this.

Winslow. We can with unfeigned pleasure be light-hearted to-day.

Ledger. Quite true, sir! Quite true. I don't know what put such disagreeable thoughts into my head, unless it was the remembrance of the jovial parties that used to meet on your birthday, Hattie. Those were fine old times, but their familiar faces are gone. There! I'm at it again. John, I'll thank you for another glass of that wine. May be that will infuse a little more geniality into my lazy blood.

Mrs. H. Dear father, you are always good company, without wine to cheer you. For years you never tasted it, and were then a kind father and a genial friend. You were amiable and——

Ledger. Hold! daughter, hold! The virtues I possessed must have been more numerous than the evils let loose by Pandora. Am I depreciating? If so, let me have good cheer, for wine gives life to sociability, just as the October forests show their most gorgeous colors under the gilding of the sun's magic rays. I'm in the October of life. So wine for me, if you please.

H. Katrina fill Mr. Ledger's glass.

Mrs. H. But, father——

H. A little for the stomach's sake will hurt no one, wife.

---

* Although this play is more effective when appropriate scenery is used, yet amateurs may put it on the boards with very little troub e or expense. A small bar is *necessary*. To change the parlor scene into a street scene, merely remove all the furniture and the pictures, etc.

(KATRINA *fills* LEDGER'S *glass*.) Winslow, this is the royal juice of the grape, from the sunny hillsides of France. Take a little.

Winslow. No, thank you. I never drink any kind of liquors.

Ledger. Signed the pledge, eh, and warm up before breakfast with hydrant water? How exhilirating these cold mornings! Have a glass just to honor this occasion.

Winslow. No, thank you.

Susie. Grandpa, "He that placeth a temptation before another is guilty if that other fall."

Ledger. Of course, if Winslow is afraid we'll not insist.

Mrs. H. Mr. Winslow is not weak in refusing, but strong. I admire his courage.

Susie. So do I. (*Glances at* WINSLOW.)

Winslow. With such allies I shall certainly withstand all temptations.

Wishall. My best wishes for the man who can utter a good honest *no*.

Susie. And mine, too.

Ledger. Of course we know, Susie, where your best wishes go. But I'm surprised at you, Hattie. You'll be a crusader next, I believe.

Mrs. H. I wish I were one now.

Ledger. Ha! ha! Who would have thought it, that my daughter would count the glasses of wine that her guests drink? And even wishes to stand at saloon doors and count those other people drink. Here's to many returns of this day (*Drinks.* WISHALL *and* H. *drink*.) Well, now, that's a good joke. Ha! ha! Don't you say so, John?

H. Hattie is in earnest. She furnishes the mathematics of life, and I dispense the humor and poetry.

Ledger. It's a joke, John, I swear it's a joke. There's a deal of humor about my daughter. She takes it after her father. I'll leave that to Wishall. What do you say, Wishall?

W. Sir, I've always thought there was much humor in you.

Ledger. Ah, I told you so.

Mrs. H. My jest is earnest, father.

Susie. Grandpa, humor may be of several kinds.

Ledger. Such as jolly humor, genial humor, affectionate humor, dry humor, and sarcastic humor.

W. And a deuce of a humor.

Ledger. Your addition to the list was evidently suggested by the pangs of conscience. Ha! ha!

W. A jest, like a dream, images the heart. So the speeches and features of our friends are but kaleidoscopes in which are phases of ourselves. We see the ever varying patterns, and unskilled, think them things of beauty; but the heart, sometimes more skilful than the eye, discerns what the creature self would gladly hide, and pierces to the motive, and behold the shuffling beads and bits of broken glass. Thus the thoughts and actions of our fellow men reveal us to ourselves perchance embellished, and perchance distorted; plodding the old familiar paths or threading the mazes of a new delight, or startling us in the toils of a master passion. Your allusion to my conscience is but the echo of your own.

Ledger. Which means, I take it, that *my* old familiar path is bad humor. I admit that I have some mettle at times, in fact, I'm proud of it. It was in our family. To some men, it is not best to be too civil. They grow presumptuous on it.

W. Indeed! And some men cherish it as the dearest part of their daily creed never to be civil to *certain* of their friends.

H. Civility is a good stock in trade in my opinion.

Winslow. And the market is never glutted.

Ledger. Some men complain of a want of civility in others, when the real difficulty exists in their own peevish sensitiveness. Mr. Wishall, you are entirely too thin-skinned (*Looks at* WISHALL.)

W. But the quills of a social porcupine, or rather an unsocial one, may pierce the thickest skin, Mr Ledger.

Ledger. Social porcupine! Truly an elegant figure. I'll leave it to the company who is the social porcupine on this occasion, yourself or myself, Mr. Wishall.

Mrs. H. Father! gentlemen! Let not all this pleasantry be misunderstood.

H. (*To* WISHALL.) It's all a jest, of course.

Susie. Grandpa will have his say always. But we don't mind him. Mr. Winslow, which do you like best, serious folks or funny people.

Winslow. I like to see the two combined, so that the serious vein may be just deep enough to furnish soil to support occasionally an excellent jest.

Ledger. A jest, did you say? (*Pours out more wine and drinks.*) Yes: "We'll all be gay and happy." Come, John, give us a song. (*Attempts to rise, and staggers back into his seat.*)

Mrs. H. Not at the table! Father, you are ill.

Ledger. Ill! who says I'm ill. Never felt better in my life. Well, we can't sing here; I forgot that. John, we'll smoke if we can't sing. (*Attempts to take cigar from his case and drops the case.* MRS. H. *whispers to* H.)

H. Father, come to the library, and we'll take a smoke. (*Picks up case, and offers his arm to* LEDGER.)

Ledger. Yes, certainly! come Winslow, and you, too, Wishall. I'm of a forgiving nature, come on. I wish we had a drop of that glorious old Bourbon that I sampled for Tipple & Co. as I came up this morning; glorious it was, I tell you. (*Exeunt R,* H. *and* LEDGER, *latter staggering and leaning heavily on* H.)

Wishall. (*Aside, following*) Must I endure all the ill-natured taunts of this drunkard? (*Exit R. All rise from the table.*)

Mrs. H. Misery! misery! must my father become a confirmed drunkard?

Susie. Oh, mother! don't call Grandpa a drunkard! It's terrible to say that of him.

Mrs. H. Child, I know it is terrible, but alas! day by day conviction grows upon me. (*Servant shows in* TRUSTHAM, *L.*) His habit ot drinking grows upon him while he imagines himself safe. He would scorn to think that Marcus Ledger, the proud and prosperous merchant, could fall to the level of a common drunkard, and yet I fear the worst.

Trustham. Pardon my intrusion, Mrs. Heartsease.

Mrs H. Don't speak of intrusion. I need the counsel of yourself and your fellow-workers.

Trustham Mrs. Heartsease, I heartily sympathize with you. I see every day the sad effects of rum. Its fascination is more potent for its slaves than the fabled charm of the serpent over its helpless victim. If you would save your father and husband remove the wine from your table. " Enter not into temptation."

Mrs. H. My husband! May angels guard him!

Susie. Mercy, mother! what danger threatens papa? What is it, Mr. Trustham?

Winslow. Be calm, Susie. It's nothing.

Trustham. Under the Providence of God we'll avert all danger, my child. Mrs. Heartsease, are you willing to make this trifling sacrifice, and remove the tempter far from you? By so doing you will array yourself on the side of temperance and morality.

Mrs. H. Oh, I'll do anything, anything you ask, so you may save my loved ones.

Trustham. God alone can do that. But you must work. Here is a notice of the temperance meeting this afternoon. (*Hands her notice.*) Come, and, if possible, bring your husband and father. Be strong in the right.

Mrs. H. (*Rings for* KATRINA, *who appears R.*) My influence must be exerted for or against temperance. I can no longer remain neutral. I will cast my lot with the temperance reformers.

Katrina. Moost I take away te table oond dings?

Mrs. H. Yes; remove the things at once. (KATRINA *busies herself about table. Picks up goblet with wine in it and drinks the wine.*) Katrina, we will have no more wine on the table.

Katrina. No more wine on te table! Vat you say? Where will we trink him? In te kitchen?

Mrs H. Katrina, we will drink no more wine at all. It is wrong to encourage intemperance.

Katrina. No wine at alls! Vat an itee? Nopody efer got intemperance by trinkin goot wine oond peer. Pad wiskey gits peoples dair intemperance. (*Laughs heartily*) Vat an itee! Vat peoples te Americans bin! (*Laughs.*) Hans will never work in te garten all tay mit no wine or peer. He would get te sunhstrike.

Mrs. H. But wine and beer lead to brandy and whiskey. It is safest not to make the beginning.

Katrina. Oond vat *will* us trink, eh? Shpring wasser ?

Mrs. H. Yes, pure water supplies man's every want.

Katrina. So I moost carry vasser, noting but vasser from te poomp to make dair tea oond coffee, oond to trink raw. Vat an itee! We all ties mit a bad cold, trinken so mooch cold vasser. (*Busies herself at table.*)

Mrs H. Don't fear, Katrina; we shall be all the better for it. (*Exit R.*

Winslow. Yes; water is the great life giver in all nature.

Susie. I believe Ma is right about wine drinking. But I never thought of it before. Then pure cold water is so refreshing. Wine always makes my head ache. I wish Pa and Grandpa would sign the pledge. (*Exit* KATRINA.)

Winslow. It is their duty, I think, and for your sake, Susie, I hope they will.

Susie. (*Blushing, drops her eyes.*) I hope they will sign it for their own sakes.

Winslow. Yes; they owe it to society. Their influence will aid others, and encourage them to take a decided stand. *I* feel that I need every good influence, and every possible safeguard.

Susie. *You,* Charles! You, who are above temptation?

Winslow. No one is above temptation, Susie. To-day I feel an additional safeguard to my footsteps. When I think of the course *you* have taken it will nerve *me* up to walk more determinedly in the only safe path, the path of purity and honor.

Susie. I'm glad that my influence can assist anyone. But come to the parlor, Charles. (*Rises and leads to R.*)

Winslow. I'm very sorry, Susie, to be obliged to hurry off on this occasion.

Susie. What do you mean?

Winslow. I have pressing business at the office, which I must see to personally.

Susie. You said nothing about it before.

Winslow. I didn't know it till this morning.

Susie. Well, it's too bad anyway!

Winslow. I must be there at four. (*Looks at watch.*) Adieu.

Susie. Good day. (*Goes to door L.*) Next time you must not hurry yourself away like this. (*Exit* WINSLOW *L*, SUSIE *R*.)

CURTAIN.

SCENE II. *Parlor in* HEARTSEASE'S *house, elegantly furnished; table C. Discovered* SUSIE *seated on sofa R.* PEWTERMUGG *seated by table C*

Susie. Yes, the cause is gaining every day. There will be a temperance mass-meeting to-morrow.

P. I hope it will continue pleasant weather for the meeting. I see you are very much interested in the subject of temperance.

Susie. I am. I do not see how any intelligent person who has given the subject a thought can fail to be interested.

P. I've thought much lately upon the subject myself, and my heart is with the advocates of temperance. It pleases me to think that *my friends* are on the right side. I am very glad, Miss Susie, that you and your mother have taken sides with the temperance workers. (*Passes to sofa and seats himself beside her*)

Susie. (*Quickly.*) We should not look at it as a matter of *friendship*, but as one of *duty*.

P But friendship and *love* strew duty's path with down. Love is a subtle force, but it wields a mighty power.

Susie. So you would call the temperance reform movement a work of love?

P. Well, yes. But let us talk no more of temperance at present. Miss Heart-ease, I wish to say something to you which I have long contemplated saying.

Susie. (*Rising quickly.*) Please don't. If it is a secret I shall tell it. You know it is said a woman cannot keep a secret.

P. (*Rises.*) You misunderstand me. What I have to say is a secret, I admit. Nevertheless it is something which you can hear only from me.

Susie. Please let it pass. My curiosity is dull this evening.

P. But it is a matter of moment, and I must speak.

Susie. It is quite unnecessary.

P. Then some other time I will tell you. I'm in no hurry. Come to think of it, I have an appointment down town. I will call again. (*Passing to L.*)

Susie. But in your rounds of temperance work don't come to me with *secrets*.

P. Good evening.

Susie. Good evening. (*Exit P, L.*) Well, he is a dunce to speak of *love* in that way. If it was not that he is quite respectable, and really a good meaning fellow, I'd cut his acquaintance on short notice. But if he can take a hint he will not mention that subject again. (*Exit R.*)

CURTAIN.

ACT II.

SCENE I. LEDGER'S *counting-room*. WISHALL *seated by a desk writing. Enter* LEDGER.

Ledger. Mr. Wishall, are those monthly statements finished?

W. Yes, sir, and sent by this morning's mail.

Ledger. Have the clerks made out the bills of those goods to be shipped to-day?

W. They are hard at work at them, sir. They will be ready in due time.

Ledger. All right! All right! Nothing like promptitude in business. I made my fortune by it.

W. Certainly, sir. A *business* man must attend to business.

Ledger. It is the only ladder to success for the beginner.

W. Yes, and attention to business is the only security for the old established house.

Ledger. Well, that is true in the main. Of course much depends on the kind of subordinates one has. Now I do not give as much attention to my business as formerly because I can leave everything with *you* and depend upon its being done. You have grown up in the business and understand it from beginning to end as well as a boy understands his mother's pantry.

W. A business should be managed by its owners.

Ledger. I suppose then that I should attend to this business myself, or admit you as a partner, eh?.

W. You do not doubt my capability?

Ledger. No; but why should I admit you as partner into a lucrative business which I have built up myself? An interest is worth money.

W. I might ask who owns the ground on which these warehouses stand?

Ledger. Well, I believe half of it is yours; or will be, at the expiration of my lease, twenty years from now. Your share is made valuable by the improvements I have put upon it. Besides I pay you a handsome salary, and you should be satisfied.

W. You hold the land rent free and reap a golden harvest. Was it equity to obtain the valuable property at a nominal rate by taking advantage of father's necessities?

Ledger. Your father gave the lease to satisfy an honest debt. The land was valueless then. If I make money out of it whose business is it?

W. But did not father expect that I would be made partner in your business, and that some benefit would accrue to me as a recompense for the sacrifice which he made?

Ledger. Oh, my dear sir, men often have extravagant expectations. Have a little patience, and wait.

W. (*More decidedly.*) Mr. Ledger, I've waited now twenty years. In twenty years more I shall be an old man. Then riches will do me little good. I ask, is that justice?

Ledger. (*More decidedly.*) Wishall, you could have left me at any time and made your fortune elsewhere. I have not detained you. But your insatiable ambition will not let you rest satisfied. You have been promoted step by step to the highest position in the house. Still you are not satisfied. If you were partner you would wish to be the chief. No, sir, no partnership yet. You have hinted often enough about that matter. Let this be the end of it. When I am ready I will speak.

W. But don't I deserve it? You know that I have abilities above the average. Have I not really performed the work of a partner?

Ledger.   Sir, I think you rate your abilities at their full value. Per-haps you do not appreciate mine?

W.   Mr. Ledger, you are aware that lately you have neglected business.

Ledger.   (*Warmly.*) 'Because I paid you for attending to it.

W.   (*Warmly.*   But sometimes you have not been *able* to attend to it.

Ledger.   (*Jumps up excitedly.*)   I understand your insinuation, sir.   It is not gentlemanly in you to refer to that subject.   If I take more wine occasionally than you think is proper for me, that is *my* busi-ness; and if I neglect business at times, *that* is my affair, not yours.

W.   (*Angrily.*)   I claim it is not entirely your own affair.   Others have the right —

Ledger.   (*In a passion.*)   Stop, sir!   I won't be insulted.   Let me never again hear of wine or partnerships, or we part at once. Never again, if you please.   (*Exit, angrily, L.*)

W.   Wine is an unwelcome subject to him.   Well it may be, for it has soured his temper, dulled his sense of honor, and will soon ruin his fine business, and make him a burden to himself and his friends. (*Goes to work at his desk.*)

Enter PEWTERMUGG L.

P.   Good day, Wishall.   Hard at work I see.   What a busy old hive this is.   No drones here.

W.   Well, I should say not.   Take a seat.   And the workers find little honey among the gall.

P.   Ah, you poor scribblers do have a tough time of it.   I couldn't stand it.   Wishall, why don't you go into business on your own ac-count?   You have a head for business that would make your fortune.

W.   Well, I had thought of it, but in fact I hoped to do better by remaining here.

P.   Yes; I understand Mr. Ledger can't spare you; and then his habits of late will soon compel him to relinquish business.   Then you will become partner and the head of the house.

W.   Hold on Pewtermugg.   Don't catch your bird till you've made the cage.   Ledger intends to be chief here while he lives, fit or unfit.

P.   But it is only a question of time.   (*Leaning toward W.*)   Did you know that he had another attack of apoplexy the day after Mrs. Heartsease's birthday dinner?

W.   (*Starting.*)   No!   (*Rises and paces the floor.*)   is it possible!

P.   His physician says he is liable to have another any time, and that he can't survive many of them.

W.   Horrible!   Horrible!   (*Soliloquizing.*)   He may drop off at any time, and then what means have I of obtaining my just dues?   But I'll have them.

P.   The assets will certainly be very large.   You are needlessly alarmed, Mr. Wishall.

W.   (*Recovering himself.*)   What was I saying?   Something about the estate, I believe.

P. Yes; and I remarked you need have no fears. He will leave a large fortune.

W. Very large. There are heavy claims, but a large fortune will remain for Mr. and Mrs. Heartsease.

P. Excuse me, Wishall. You are solicitous about the management of the business after his death ?

W. Whether I am or not is my own affair, Mr. Pewtermugg.

P. I beg pardon. I meant no offence. I have heard it rumored that Heartsease is a silent partner.

W. And suppose he is ?

P. He would probably become the head of the firm.

W. And Charlie Winslow his partner, if I can tell meal from bran.

P. Do you really think so ? Why do you come to such a conclusion?

W. Susie will materially assist in bringing such a state of affairs to pass.

P. Well, I think you are a little off in your reckoning there.

W. You are off in your reckoning. Any one could see that the girl likes him, and he'd be a dunce for not loving as fine a girl as Susie.

P. Don't be too sure. Time will tell. But we must keep Winslow from getting in here if we can.

GUZZLE *appears L. He stops at door.*

W. I don't see that I can do anything honorable in that direction, and as for you I think it is none of your business.

P. But it is my business. I tell you I'll put Winslow in the background there. (GUZZLE *gives a knowing shake of the head and comes forward.*)

Guzzle. How d'ye do? Hope I don't intrusion!

W. Not at all, Guzzle!

P. How are the folks up at Heartsease's, Guzzle?

Guzzle. I guess that's about what I came in to ask you, Wishall.

W. What! Don't you live there now?

Guzzle. Well, no. I've found a higher sphere.

W. What's the matter? Any trouble? Have you struck for higher wages?

Guzzle. Well, you see they had lots of wine the day of the party up there, and it was some new kind.

P. Old, you mean.

Guzzle. And all-fired strong. The fact is I took a little too much. Mrs. Heartsease didn't like that, an' got to talkin' temperance next day. That riled me, to hear her talkin' that sort of doctrine when her husband hadn't got over *his* drunk yet. I talked back a little, an' that riled Heartsease. He said he wa'nt goin' to have no such feller 'round there sassin his wife, an' told me my resignation would be acceptable. The short of it is I don't chore there any more.

P. So Heartsease was drunk, too.

Guzzle. Yes ; and he's too good a man for that. It's a darned pity. I sometimes think I could sign the pledge when I see him reeling as if he'd the blind staggers.

W. I'm sorry. You had better go back.

P. But what is your higher sphere, Guzzle?

Guzzle. I'm assistant to an architect.

W. Eh?

Guzzle. I carry bricks to the third story, and the architect—lays them. You see I'm rising every day; ha! ha! But how are they up at Heartsease's?

W. All well.

Guzzle. Glad to hear it. That's an almighty nice family. (*Exit L.*)

P. (*Going.*) Wishall, remember what we've spoken of to-day. We will talk it over again. It's too bad to see the way Ledger is rushing to ruin. Heartsease is on the same road. His habits will soon unfit him for business, and that may be to your interests. I'm sorry for Heartsease, too. Guzzle is right. He is too good for such a fate. Now if it were that Winslow, hang him! But he is too cold-blooded to be led very far, though I've seen him take an occasional glass.

W. That's nothing to his discredit I take a little myself sometimes.

P. Oh, of course, in a *respectable* way. So do I, though my influence has always been on the side of temperance.

W. Ha! ha! ha! Talk of influence. Influence always leaves precept to follow example.

P. Has Winslow an appetite for drink?

W. If he has I hope he will throttle it forever.

P. Suppose it should be for our interest to invite him to join us occasionally in a social glass.

W. Our *interest!* Mr. Pewtermugg, two things I will never do. Never will I weaken any soul's faith, or poach on the purity of a human heart.

P. Oh, of course not. That would be dishonorable. But if he should indulge in a little youthful folly it's his own matter I suppose. Good day (*Going L.*)

W. Good day. (*Exit P. L.*)

CURTAIN.

SCENE II. STOUGHTON'S *saloon, "The Shades." Seated* BILLY *and* GUZZLE *at cards by a table R. Two Loafers by another table, R playing checkers* STOUGHTON *behind the bar. Enter Loafer who staggers up to the bar.*

Stoughton. (*In a surly tone.*) Well, what do you want now?

Loafer. Old rye.

Stoughton. Get out; you've had enough to-day.

Loafer. Nate Stoughton, you did not speak to me so when I wore broadcloth and had plenty of money. Then it was, "How do you do, Mr. Thirston? Billy, wait on Mr. Thirston. Be quick; the gentleman's waiting!"

Stoughton. Go to the devil!

Loafer. Thank you; I will not visit you till you are at home.

Stoughton. Get out, before I kick you out! (*Turns and arranges bottles.*)

Billy. (*Jumps up.*) Euchred, by Jingo!

Guzzle. No; euchred by Guzzle. Set em up?

Billy. What 'll you have? (*Advancing to bar.*)

Guzzle. A little red-eye.

Loafer. I'll take some of that, too.

Billy. I heard father tell you to go, some time ago.

Loafer. And I'll go, when I get my dram.

Billy. See here, old "Nubs," I think you had better go at once. Travel, now—lively!

Loafer. I won't do it. (*Squares in attitude of defense.*)

Billy. Oh, go. (BILLY *hustles him rapidly out L, scuffling as they go.* PEWTERMUGG *enters L.*) There! I guess you'll go now. We don't want such low fellows as you here. (*Exit Loafer.*)

P. Good evening, Mr. Stoughton.

Stoughton. Good evening, Mr. Pewtermugg! Glad to see you.

P. What a trial it must be to have such fellows around.

Stoughton. Yes; they give a *respectable* place like mine a bad name.

Billy. Dad's too easy on 'em. It takes me to settle their coffee. (*Goes behind bar to mix drinks.*)

Stoughton. (*Laughing.*) Billy knows how to quiet a rowdy. I'm glad of it, son. It helps me a great deal.

Guzzle. And if such a man is *very* drunk, Billy ain't afraid to tackle him.

Billy. Come, Guzzle; none of your dry jokes.

Guzzle. Hurry up the drinks, then, if you don't want any more dry jokes.

P. It is those low fellows who cause all this evil of intemperance, anyway. They know no bounds to their depraved appetites.

Stoughton. Aye, that's it, exactly. They have gone to such excesses in drinking that many people, now-a-days, are actually ashamed to take a glass of beer in a saloon. It used to be that a man could take his bitters whenever he pleased. Now it is changed, and my business is nearly ruined. In fact, these low drunkards, with the aid of a few canting temperance fanatics, have made drinking *almost disreputable.*

Enter WALTER WESTON, L.

Walter. Hello! Stoughton. How are you, pard? (*To* GUZZLE.) Whose treat now, Billy?

Billy. Mine, Walter,—I'll be generous. Shall I mix another?

Walter. Well, yes, seeing it's you.

Billy. What'll you have?

Walter. Crusaders' terror.

Guzzle. Hurry up, Billy; I'm as dry as a hen in a meal-barrel.

Billy. Well, here's confusion to the crusaders. (*They drink.*)

P. I've always been a temperate man, and I advocate temperance principles, but *I* will drink when I please, if I choose, and stop when I please; and people may *say* what they please about it. I'll not sign away my liberty.

Stoughton. Ah! I like to see a man of spirit, who don't carefully weigh every trifle before he dares to give his opinion on a subject.

Enter HEARTSEASE, *L slightly intoxicated.*

H. Good evening, gen'lmen.

Stoughton. How are you? I hav'n't seen you for some time.

Guzzle. By Ginger! He's on another tear.

H. A cocktail, Stoughton.

P. I thought you had sworn off, Heartsease.

H. Well, I did sort of promise those blue ribbon fellows. Hav'n't touched a drop for a week, but I met a jolly old chum down town to-night, and we just took a glass for old times, you know. Have something, Pewtermugg?

P. (*Pretends to hesitate.*) Well, yes, seeing it's you. But I seldom drink anything stronger than pale ale.

Guzzle. (*Aside.*) Unless you're behind the door.

H. Take something, Stoughton. (*They fill and drink. Notices* GUZZLE.) Why! here you are, Guzzle. I'm glad to see you. (*Business shaking hands.*) Mrs. Heartsease wants you to come back and work for us.

Guzzle. I'd like first-rate to oblige Mrs. Heartsease, but I'm afeerd, since you've took to cold water up there, that we wouldn't never git along together. My stomach's kinder weak, and cold water goes agin it.

H. 'S that so? Excuse me—won't you take something now?

Guzzle. Don't care if I do.

H. Come, boys—all of you. We don't meet often. (*All come forward; in their haste one of the loafers knocks the other and the checkers over the floor.*)

1st Loafer. (*On the floor.*) What the devil are you doing? (*Business in getting up.*)

2d Loafer. Never mind the checkers; I'm dry.

H. Here's to your health, boys! Give it bumpers! I guess the temperance folks won't let me have another spree.

Stoughton. "Enjoy the present," is my motto. (*The intoxicated Loafer elbows* PEWTERMUGG.)

P. (*Disdainfully.*) Stand back, fellow. (*Aside.*) Catch me drinking with that crowd. (*All drink but* P., *who slily throws his liquor into a spittoon.*)

H. That's jolly-hic, boys; j-hic-olly!

Enter TRUSTHAM, *L.*

Trustham. On my life! John Heartsease!

H. Dick Trustham! How-hic-are you, old boy?-hic. G-hic-lad to see you. Give us a shake of that old p-hic-paw. (*Business shaking hands.*)

Trustham. John Heartsease, this is indeed painful.

H. Painful! Sick, eh?-hic. Try a little of Stoughton's pain-killer. (*Others all laugh*)

1st Loafer. I don't want no lectur. Buck, let's go. (*Exit Loafers, L.*)

Trustham. Heartsease, think of your family. Spare them. Think of that wife who is now awaiting you at home.

H. Waiting for me!-hic. I guess not! She's at-temp-hic-temperance meeting, and they don't go home till mor-hic-mornin'. Its jolly, boys! It's jol-hic-jolly!

Trustham. Mr. Pewtermugg, will you escort him home? I am shocked at this. I can't go with him, as I have an engagement.

P. Mr. Heartease! Heartsease! Come, let's go home.

H. Is it mornin'? Yes, we'll all go home in the mornin'. C'mon, boys! (*He falls over a spittoon. P. and T. assist him to rise. Exeunt P., and H. L, H. staggering, and leaning on P's arm.*)

Trustham. How easily man may degrade himself below the brutes, when appetite is his master. Mr. Stoughton, I wish to post a notice here.

Stoughton. (*Ironically.*) Certainly you may. What queer ideas of right you temperance people have! You come in here with the Bible in one hand, and a tract in the other, preaching charity and good will to men, while your errand is to destroy your neighbor's business and ruin him.

Trustham. Mr. Stoughton, it is not against you that we wage war, but against the nefarious traffic you are engaged in.

Stoughton. Who is hurt when you take the bread from my family?

Trustham. Think of the families whose bread has gone over your bar.

Stoughton. I don't ask 'em to buy, and I pay a license to sell.

Trustham. No government can make right what God has made wrong

Stoughton. Well, I don't propose to argue with you. I never wrote tracts nor lectured. (*Steps behind the bar.*)

Trustham. (*Turning to the boys.*) Young men, you are all cordially invited to our meeting.

Guzzle. I cal'clate we'll be there. We attend meetin's reg'lar.

Trustham. Mr. Weston, will you come? Think of that mother who is daily praying for you.

Walter. I believe I think of her about as often as any one does. She's the best mother in the city.

Guzzle. You're right there, unless it's Mrs. Heartsease. If I had such a mother, I b'lieve I'd quit drinkin' jest for her sake. But, then, I cal'clate I'm a fixture here for some time.

Trustham. Mr. Weston, think what your mother suffers. Don't break her heart.

Billy. Hearts will stand a good deal of stretchin', and I s'pose Mrs. Weston's is like other people's, pretty tough.

Walter. (*Warmly.*) See here, Billy, you and I are friends; but I don't allow anybody to make such remarks about my mother.

Billy. It seems to me you're mighty techy!

Guzzle. Keep cool, boys.

Trustham. Will you go to the meeting, to-morrow evening?

Walter. May be if everything is lovely. But I don't *sign*, understand. I don't see such a terrible harm in an occasional *smile*. Governor says it never hurt him.

Trustham. And yet it may be destruction to you. "Enter not into temptation."

Stoughton. Trustham, isn't it enough for you to come in here, sticking up your bills, without meddling with my customers? I prefer that you do your talking somewhere else.

Trustham. Certainly, if you prefer it, I will not talk here. Good evening, gentlemen. (*Exit L.*)

All. Good evening.

Walter. Come, boys, let's take a look round town.

Billy. All right. (*Exeunt L. Stoughton behind bar, arranging glasses, etc.*)

CURTAIN.

SCENE III. HEARTSEASE'S *house. Present, seated*, HEARTSEASE, L *of table;* MRS. H., *R of table;* SUSIE *on sofa, R;* TRUSTHAM *L;* HANS *and* KATRINA *standing L.*

Trustham. Mrs. Heartsease, this is indeed encouraging. Five hundred signers to the pledge in one week!

Mrs. H. And then you have met with so much encouragement and sympathy from those who have heretofore stood aloof. I wish I could take a more active part in the work.

Trustham. Mrs. Heartsease, there is much that you can do. Encourage the fallen ones socially. In that direction lies the secret of our strength. Make them think they are worth saving, and then it will be easier to save them. They need sympathy and kindness more than lectures and advice, though they will need these. Mr. Heartsease, I always carry a pledge-book with me. Will you not sign to day? (*Rises and places book on the table.*)

Mrs. H. Do, husband! Please, do not longer delay. At this time there should be no room for doubt. (*With tears.*) Remember poor father's last words. Shall that terrible death-bed scene be forgotten in a few weeks? *He* saw, alas too late, the evils of intemperance.

Trustham. It will strengthen your resolutions, and prove a guardian, should temptations assail you.

Susie. Yes, father; I have signed, and you are left alone.

H. Where my family goes, I go. (*Signs.*)

Mrs. H. Thank God! saved at last!

Trustham. Be ever vigilant. Even pledges have failed in the hour of need.

Susie. Father will never break his pledge, I know. His honor is sacred.

Hans. (*Aside.*) Vell, I dond know; somedimes dot bledge-baper tears pooty easy. (*Aloud.*) Is dair wine put down in dot bledge?

Trustham. It includes all intoxicating liquors.

Hans. Schnapps?

Trustham. Yes.

Hans. Oond *cider?*

Trustham. Yes, sir.

Hans. Oond *gin?*

Trustham. Certainly!

Hans. Oond *lager?*

Trustham. Certainly, sir. *All* alcoholic beverages.

Hans. Gott in himmel! I signs no bledges. I coot sign a *prandy* oond *wisky* bledges, shoost to blease dem demperace beoples. Dunder und hagelvetter!—vat coot a man drink, mit his pretzels? Oond no vinegar on his sauerkraut, maype? Katrina, don'd you sign no bledges.

Katrina. We don'd need no bledges to keep demperance, ven de wine is dook from de table off.

Hans. Wine from de table avay! So! Oond I bin feelin bad ofer since Ach! himmel! Man nefer hear of de like of dot in a shentleman's house in faterland. Say, Meester Heartease, moost I hoe, oond trim de vines in de garten all tay, oond trink vasser?

Mrs. H. We can't encourage intemperate habits, Mr Gipfel, in our servants. They should save their money, and preserve their health.

Hans. Oond vat is helts eef a man must be always *dry?* Mine lager cost me ten cent in de forenoons day, oond ten cent in de after day, if you dakes de wine away. Zwanzig cent I pays efery tay. Ist dot de vay to encourage a poor mans? Dot brakes me alltogedder oop. (*Exeunt* HANS, *R, and* KATRINA *L.*)

Trustham. This man foolishly spends for lager twenty cents a day, no inconsiderable item for a poor man.

Mrs. H. And gets for it nothing in return.

Trustham. Nay, worse than nothing; for even this seemingly harmless lager dulls the intellect, deranges the stomach, bloats the body, deadens the senses, and makes the hapless devotee play the clown to every caprice of a perverted appetite.

H. Too true. Alas! too true. (*Exit* H. *and* T., *L.* MRS. H. *and* SUSIE, *R.*)

CURTAIN.

ACT III.

SCENE I. *A street. Enter, meeting* WISHALL *L,* PEWTERMUGG *R.*

P. Good evening, Wishall. This is lucky. I've been looking for you.

W. Well, what is it? I'm in a hurry just now.

P. Oh, don't be in a hurry. It is only a little matter of business.

W. Blow it, I've no time now to talk business. (*Attempts to pass* P.)

P. (*Crossing before him.*) Wait a minute. You remember our conversation some time ago in regard to Winslow?

W. I do, and I gave you my answer. I'll be no party to such baseness.

P. Have you met him in a convivial way?

W. Yes; but not in the way you suggested, and I never will.

P. Don't make any rash assertions, for you may change your mind. You are aware that the firm of Ledger & Heartsease paid out several large sums of money to various parties the day before Ledger's death, and *the day of his death.*

W. Well, what of it, Mr. Pewtermugg?

P. We shall see soon enough. Give me a little time. One check of $5,000 was paid to you, I believe.

W. (*Starting.*) How did you find that out?

P. That you will learn in due time. You received the money?

W. I did.

P. For what did Mr. Ledger pay you so large a sum at once?

W. (*With dignity.*) That is my business, sir!

P. It *may* be the business of some one else too.

W. Ledger *owed* me, of course, Pewtermugg.

P. Yes; in justice, but not in law.

W. (*Warmly.*) What do you mean sir?

P. Keep cool! Keep cool! You see I know considerably more about some things than you give me credit for.

W. (*Starting.*) What! (*Recovering.*) Yes, by impertinent meddling!

P. It is better for us to be *friends*, Wishall, so keep cool. You know my brother is cashier in the Merchants' National Bank, and what he knows of course I'm not entirely ignorant of.

W. (*Greatly agitated.*) Stop! For heaven's sake say no more.

P. We might as well have a clear understanding. I refer to that check.

W. Does the Bank suspect anything?

P. *Suspect!* They know all. Through the intercession of a friend the matter is hushed up and the check paid.

W. I'm a ruined man! Oh that fatal step! Why did I not trust to the generosity and justice of the new firm.

P. Hush, man! It is a clear case of forgery, but you are not ruined. As I said a friend has made everything right.

W. Thank God for that! Pewtermugg, give me your hand. (*They shake hands.*) I can not express my gratitude to you for this. (*Enter* GUZZLE *unobserved L.*) But I did not know you had so much ready money. You must have wronged yourself in doing this. I'll make it right with you.

P. Oh, I—don't mention it—I—Yes, I have a little money. Shall we be friends?

W. (*Hesitating.*) Yes.

P. *Good!* You have influence with Winslow. If he should form intemperate habits, Heartsease will soon see that he is not the man for a partner, or son-in-law either. Heartsease has already badly crippled his business. You are a necessity there, and he knows it. He must soon admit you as partner. When I am a member of his family of course I will stand next in succession.

W. Yes, if there's anything left by that time.

P. You must look out for that. Keep an eye on Winslow, (*Going L.*) and be jovial in his company. (*Exit L. Exit W. R.*)

Guzzle. Oho! What's old Pewterpot up to now, I wonder? Settin' up some job on Winslow I'll bet. Darn my socks if Winslow aint the best of the two, by a long chalk, if he does take a dram now and then without goin' behind the door to drink it, as Pewterface does. I guess I'll jest keep an eye on this ere job. (*Exit R.*)

SCENE II. *A street. Enter* HEARTSEASE *R*, CANTWELL *L*, *meeting.*

H. Good evening, Mr. Cantwell.

C. Good evening, Mr. Heartsease. How do you do?

H. Quite well, thank you. How are you progressing in the temperance work? All goes well, I hope?

C. (*In a tone of canting piety.*) With God's grace, it does. This is the Lord's work, and I have never before felt the burden of serving Him so light as at present. It is blessed to give good counsel, and strengthen the doubting one. I really believe I shall take a short trip, delivering lectures in the neighboring villages, if the committee can see the way clear toward paying my expenses. They have it under advisement now. Really, it would be a nice little trip for me.

H. And you expect the Lord to advance cash to meet current expenses, while you are tilling his vineyard?

C. Certainly, if I *donate* my time. The Scriptures say the "Laborer is worthy of his hire."

H. Let's look at that passage in a business point of view.

C. The *Bible* is the only safe guide in business or out of it.

H. But you will at least allow a man to interpret the Scripture in a business-like way.

C. (*Somewhat petulant.*) Bother to interpretation! Plain English is not hard to interpret. The good Book says, "The laborer is worthy of his hire," and that is enough for me.

H. Very good. It also says, "He that hath pity upon the poor lendeth to the Lord." Now, Mr. Cantwell, you will admit that drunkards are mostly *poor* men.

C. Yourself, for instance!

H. (*Sarcastically.*) *Myself!* So you set me down as a *drunkard!*

C. Oh, not now, certainly. I do not for a moment doubt the sincerity of your reform. I beg your pardon. I meant no offense.

H. Then don't use offensive language. If you are going to bring up everybody to *your* stiff-necked notions of propriety you will find that your work as a reformer will be a miserable failure.

C. Really, Mr. Heartsease, I beg pardon. I do not wish *every* man to conform *at once* to my ideas. I am willing to go *down* to them, and *counsel* with them, and *comfort* them.

H. Counsel and comfort are sweet to a starving man! How

much did you subscribe to the Library Association fund?

C. (*Suddenly drops his canting tone.*) Ahem! ahem! Well, as soon as that is really set on a secure basis, I will help it liberally.

H. As soon as its success is assured you are willing to help. I'm sorry I could not give it five times the amount I did subscribe, for I think it will prove one of the most effective agents in the temperance work.

C. Mr. Heartsease, I certainly am willing to help any laudable enterprise, or any person who really needs help, and is worthy of it. (*Resumes canting tone.*) I am only the steward of what the Lord has placed in my hands.

H. I am glad you have said so, for I happen to need a small loan myself.

C. (*Feigns surprise.*) *You* need a loan! a *rich* man like you!

H. Rich men are sometimes embarrassed.

C. Do you speak seriously?

H. Seriously.

C. How much do you need?

H. I need four or five thousand dollars. One thousand, with some collections I hope to make, would pull me through.

C. Really, I keep very little money deposited on call. I have made some investments. Now, Shaver would let you have it in a minute. He keeps money for such purposes.

H. Oh, I see; with your endorsement. Thank you. That will do as well as the cash.

C. (*Quickly.*) No! no! you misunderstood me. I made a solemn vow years ago that I would never endorse for any man.

H. Then I advise you to keep your vow. (*Turns toward L.*) Good evening.

C. Good evening, Mr. Heartsease. (*Exit R.*)

H. I knew before I asked him that he would refuse. If it is so hard for a man of means and good social position to reform, what must it be for the poor miserable outcast! Many of my old and tried friends treat me coolly because of the stand I have taken, and because my wife is an active temperance worker. Most of my new friends look on me much as they would on some dangerous wild beast they had just captured. It's well enough to use soothing words, backed by formidable quotations, but don't get too near the dangerous beast. Without help, I must go to the wall. I can't stave this off much longer, the way they are pushing me now. (*Starts toward L.*)

Enter PEWTERMUGG *L, meeting* H.

P. Good evening, Mr. Heartsease.

H. Good evening. Mr. Pewtermugg. Glad to meet you.

P. And I'm glad to meet you. How's Susie?

H. Quite well. Pewtermugg, I'm in a hurry. I must raise some money before ten to-morrow. Do you think I could arrange it with your brother?

P. How much do you need?

H. I *must* have a thousand.

P. You know I have a little money. I believe I could let you have that amount for a few days.

H. Hello! You're the man I want. When can I have it?

P. I'll give you a check now, and you can get it cashed in the morning. Let's go into the "Shades," across the street, and I'll write it out.

H. I'd rather not go in there. I've signed the pledge.

P. Tut, man! We're not going in to drink.

H. I know, but some of my old chums will be sure to be there.

P. What of that? You are not afraid of them. Set them an example of total abstinence. Can't you trust yourself?

H. I guess I can. I must learn to resist temptation.

P. You're right there. Come! (*Aside.*) This loan will bind him to me. I'll secure an interest in the business, and then the girl is mine. (*Exeunt L.*)

CURTAIN.

SCENE III. *Interior of the "Shades." Seated by table R* WALTER WESTON *and* GUZZLE *at cards.* LOAFERS *R and L,* BILLY *behind the bar.*

Enter L, WISHALL *and* WINSLOW, *latter slightly intoxicated.*

Winslow. (*Advancing to bar.*) What'll you have, Wishall?

W. I'm not particular.

Winslow. I *am.* I want something that will invigorate the system this cold evening. We'll take a little "death on the doorstep."

W. No; not for me. I'll take a julep.

Winslow. Of coure you want something mild. *You* have to look after your palpitation a little, old boy. I don't. I've a clear conscience, a light heart, a thirsty throat, and——

Guzzle. (*Aside.*) And an empty head.

Winslow. But here goes. There's no time for long stories. (*They drink*)

Enter L, HEARTSEASE *and* PEWTERMUGG.

Winslow. Hello, old pard! (*Shakes H.'s hand. Staggers slightly.*) How are you? I haven't seen you for a long time. (*P. writes at the bar.*)

H. That's so. Why don't you come up sometimes? We should be glad to see you.

Winslow. Confound it! I—— Fact is, I'm too deuced busy. Have a smile?

H. No; I've signed the pledge!

Winslow. Bully for you, old boy.

H. Winslow, hadn't you better go home?

P. (Aside.) He'll soon be a confirmed drunkard! Then for my plans.

Winslow. Home! Did you say? (*Tries to sing "Home, sweet home;" fails.*)

Billy. See here, we can't have this racket in here. Winslow, you'd better go home. They're crusadin' to-night, an' I want it quiet.

Winslow. Zat so? Let em crusade! Say, Jack, old boy, smile, won't you? (*Noisily*) Set em up, Billy. Set em up.

P. (*Hands H. check he has written on the counter.*) Here's your check, Heartsease. Why what ails you, man?

H. I don t feel well. The smell of the liquors has affected me. My God! why did I risk myself in here! What will wife say? I'm sick, help me home! (*Sinks into a chair.*)

Winslow. I say John, old boy, you don't feel well. This is glorious brandy. It will revive you. Your pledge says nothing about medicine. (*Puts glass to H.'s lips. He drinks.*)

Wishall. Winslow, for shame, desist.

Walter. I say, Winslow, that's too bad. You've ruined that man.

P. He hasn't violated his pledge yet. He's sick.

Guzzle. I cac'late he *will* break that pledge of his'n in two minutes, more or less, when that tiger's milk touches bottom. I've felt jes' so, and it always takes more of the same stuff to set a feller right. Cut for deal.

H. (*Looking wildly around.*) Where am I? I remember now. What ails me? My veins are bursting. Brandy! Give me brandy? That will ease my pain. (*Rushes to counter and gulps down a glassful.*) There! now I feel better. Glorious brandy! Ah, it lifts a man from the dull earth to soar among the fleecy clouds.

Guzzle. To fall into the gutter kerchunk when he lights!

H. I'm better now. Great God, my pledge! My honor! Oh, it will kill Hattie! I'm ruined!

Wishall. His words are prophetic.

Winslow. You're all right, old boy!

H. I'm ruined; give me drink. (*Billy pours out another glass of brandy.*)

P. (*Aside.*) The fool will ruin himself, and spoil my plans. You've had enough, Heartsease. Let's go home. (*Attempts to prevent him from drinking.*)

H. I must have it. (*Seizes the glass and swallows its contents. Rushes out R, followed by P. and* WINSLOW.)

Wishall. Another man gone to ruin! He's too noble by far for such a wretched fate. He is the very soul of honor, and when he realizes that he has broken his pledge I fear the consequences will be terrible. Curse the fates that throttle men with the demon of drink. And I've stood by and seen these men dragged to ruin. Nay, worse, I have drawn them into the pit by my presence and example, arrant coward that I am. It would take the tongue of a Cicero to heap upon me the scorn of honest men did they know me. The reckoning for this must be terrible. (*Exit L.*)

Guzzle. I guess it won't though; nothing but a splitting headache and a curtain lecture.

Billy. Yes; you can bet on the lecture when that old woman of his'n finds it out. She's a reg'lar old stump speaker.

Guzzle. Billy Soughton, there haint no nicer woman in the town than Mrs. Heartsease, nor a better man than John Heartsease.

Walter. That's so.

Guzzle. She's helped me out of many a scrape, and the fellow who runs her down to my face has to be a better man than me, that's all.

Billy. Humph! didn't you talk about her?

Guzzle. That's my business, not yours.

Billy. And it's *my* business what *I* say. My tongue's my own.

Guzzle. And the darndest, meanest piece of property ever a man owned.

Billy. Guzzle, you're drunk.

Guzzle. (*Jumps up, and advances toward the bar.*) See here, young man, if you know when your pulse is steady, you'll just close that slit under your proboscis, or I'll close it quicker than a steel trap.

Billy. If you're too drunk to behave, get out.

Walter. (*Rises, and advances to bar.*) Boys, this has gone far enough.

Enter STOUGHTON *R.*

Stoughton. What's all this row? (*To Walter.*) Get quiet. Put away those cards. The crusaders are coming.

Walter. Not if I know it, I don't. I won't act hypocrite for anybody.

Stoughton. Devil take the luck! I wish they would stay at home and attend to their own business.

Enter L MRS. H. *and* MRS. WINSLOW.

Mrs. H. Mr. Stoughton, we have come to visit your place on our rounds.

Stoughton. Very well.

Mrs. W. Have you any objection to our leaving some tracts on your tables? We have done so at other places.

Stoughton. I guess there'll be no objection.

Mrs. W. As secretary of the County Bible Society, I wish to leave some copies of the Bible in your place.

Billy. Oh, yes; Charlie will need them.

Stoughton. Boy, remember you are talking to ladies.

Mrs. H. Mr. Stoughton, I particularly wish you to read this tract on the "Evils of Intemperance."

Stoughton. I know enough of them already.

Mrs. H. I daresay; but read the views of others; and you, too, Mr. Guzzle. (*Gives him a tract.*)

Guzzle. Thank you, Mrs. Heartsease.

Mrs. H. Mr. Guzzle, you are degrading your manhood in

resorting to such places; and you, too, Mr. Weston. Come to our meeting, and sign the pledge, won't you? (*Gives him a tract.*) Your father has signed.

Walter. Hello! The governor's surrendered at last! That will do for him, but boys like fun.

Mrs. H. Seek other amusements. I wish I had time to talk to you, boys.

Billy. Better go home and talk to your drunk husband.

Stoughton. Billy, confound you. Keep a civil tongue!

Mrs. H. (*Greatly agitated.*) Oh, what is the matter? Something dreadful!

Billy. He went home drunk to-night, was all.

Mrs. H. Merciful Father! must I drain again this cup of shame and bitterness!

Mrs. W. Don't despair! There must be some mistake. Let us still hope.

Billy. No mistake at all, Mrs. Winslow. Your son Charles can tell you all about it. He was in the same boat.

Mrs. W. Alas, my son! Has he yielded again, despite a mother's warning!

Mrs. H. Some traitor has betrayed my husband. He never would voluntarily break his pledge. We must go to them at once. (*Exeunt L.*)

Billy. I guess that puts an end to their preachin' and singin' for a few hours.

Guzzle. (*With anger.*) Bill Stoughton, you're a low, dirty skunk, and if ever you talk about them ladies agin, and I hear it, I'll tan your skunk skin for you. Mind that.

Loafer. Go it greasers! You're a trump, Guzzle.

Guzzle. Darn me if I wouldn't sign that pledge now, just to help them women along.

Billy. You're a healthy specimen to talk about signin' the pledge. You be.

Guzzle. I cac'late I *am* healthy. Want to heft me? Sing out if you do.

Stoughton. Mr. Guzzle, I don't wish any disturbance here. I don't ai ow such talk about any member of my family in my presence.

Guzzle. Come on, Walter. (*Going L.*) I can't stay here for fear I'll be tempted to slap that consarned mean puppy. Let him insult a woman! It's safe to do that I calc'late. (*Exeunt WALTER and GUZZLE L. Scene changes.*)

SCENE IV. *A street. Enter PEWTERMUGG, L, with an old express pouch under his arm.*

P. So Winslow has signed the pledge, and reformed. Well, I suppose his reformation will last about as long as Heartsease's did. But Winslow can't shake off the bad odor of his late revels all at once, I assure him. (*Enter GUZZLE, unobserved, L.*) The old adage,

"Give a dog a bad name, and you might as well hang him," will hold good in his case, I guess. His gaming will not help him in case of trouble. The Express Company know of his weakness, and will spot him at once. I took care that they should not remain in ignorance. I've worked up a case for them. This is a glorious night for the trial of my plan. Wishall the coward, wouldn't join me, but his tongue is tied on that little check business of his. To-morrow I shall be in possession of $25,000, and Winslow will be in a felon's cell. Then Miss Susie may prate about her heart's being another's, and John Heartsease, the bankrupt, may go to the devil. Susie will be welcome to her jail-bird. He'll have plenty of time and good quarters, to reform in. Now for revenge, and fortune at the same time. It's a bold strike, and the stakes are fortunes and reputations. But I've never failed yet. Heartsease and Winslow have snubbed me like a dog, but I'll be even with them yet. If I scent danger, a turn in Europe will be good for my health. Ha! ha! (*Exit R.*)

Guzzle. (*Coming to C.*) Well! *Jerusalem Crickets!* If that don't beat snake-fightin', as we used to say, down where I was raised. What the tarnation is oid Pewterpot up to? Darn me! if he don't run his ugly mug into something too hot for pewter, I'll treat. (*Exit R.*)

CURTAIN.

ACT IV.

SCENE I. *Interior of the "Shades." Card-playing at table, R; at L, seated around a table, WALTER, HANS and HEARTSEASE at cards. At left of bar a large placard, containing in large letters, "$5,000 Reward!—Robbery of the American Express Co."*

Walter. (*Throwing down cards.*) Ha! ha! It's your treat, Hans! Hurry up! Dutchy, my mouth waters for one of Billy's famous cocktails.

Hans. My dreat? How ist dot? I don'd understhand him.

Walter. Set 'em up, Sauerkraut, and no music!

Billy. That's all fair, Hans; you lost.

H. And don't be so confounded slow making up your mind, Old Kraut Tub!

Hans. Vell, vat you hafs, shentlemens?

Walter. Old bourbon!

H. I'll take brandy, straight. That cuts the red wood every time.

Hans. Ein glass lager. (*All laugh.*)

Walter. Try Saratoga water, Hans. That's good for a weak stomach.

Hans. Ach! you fellows tink you are long-headed; but I am tick trou de eyes.

Billy. Through the skull, you mean.

Hans. Yaw! yaw! trou de eyes. De prandy burns oop te stomachs oud, oond der lager keeps der indernal arrangemendts cool.

Walter. Dutchy, let's have a song.

Hans. I sings no songs.

H. Come, Hans, a song hic for auld-hic lang syne.

Hans. I nefer trinks dot! Vat ist dot?

Enter GUZZLE, *L.*

Walter. Hello, Guzzle! where have you been? I've not seen you for two whole hours.

Guzzle. I've had a little private cipherin' to do to-day.

Walter. Got something on the string?

Guzzle. Yes!

H. Boys, let's take something. (*Fumbles in his vest pocket.*) I've just five dollars left, but that will last till my friends ante again. Jolly good friends I have-hic. There's Dick Trustham-hic. He gave me this. Jolly old boy, Dick is. Come!

Walter. My motto is never refuse wine in Paris.

Guzzle. Nor whiskey in Cork!

Loafer. (*Looking up from cards.*) The divil ye say! Bad luck to ye.

H. What'll you have, boys? (*Beckons to Loafers in R.*) Come on, and be social. (*All rush up eagerly, and drink.*)

Walter. Heartsease, give us a song.

H. By Jove! I will. Why didn't I think of that sooner? (*Sings in a boisterous manner.*)

> " When I was single I made the money jingle,
>   And the world went so easy with me then, O then."

Billy. See here, Jack Heartsease, if you are going to make a night of it, go somewhere else, and don't disturb a decent neighborhood.

Walter. Ha! ha! Let's drink to the virtues that flourish under the roof of the " Shades."

1st Loafer. See here! That point is mine.

2d Loafer. No it ain't—the last trick was mine!

1st Loafer. You 'nigged!

2d Loafer. You're a liar!

1st Loafer. You're a cheating blackguard! (*They begin to fight.*)

Walter. Go it, plug-uglies?

Billy. Look here! you knock-kneed mule-drivers! I won't have this row. (*Separates them.*)

Enter CANTWELL, *L.*

C. What a shocking sight for the eyes of an enlightened generation!

Guzzle. Of vipers! Won't you take something?

C. Young men, "Wine is a mocker, strong drink is raging." " Flee from the wrath to come." I come to you on a mission of mercy, in the name of temperance.

Walter. A lamb among wolves! (*All laugh.*)

C. Young men, this levity is indeed dreadful among those who are hanging on the brink of such a fearful precipice. Listen to the voice of truth, and follow the light of reason.

Billy. Old man, give us a rest on your preachin'. I guess the light of *your* reason is nothin' but a tallow dip in a tin lantern.

C. Alas! are the sacrifices of myself and Mr. Trustham in your behalf all in vain?

Guzzle. Don't mention your efforts in the same breath with Dick Trustham's. His are at a premium, but your pesky old paper is protested long ago. You like scripture,—I'll give you a text. "Woe unto you Scribes and Pharisees, hypocrites! for ye devour widows' houses, and for a pretense make long prayers." You know the rest. Hadn't you better lower your rents before you talk temperance? Reform like charity begins at home.

C. (*Groans.*) Oh, Lord, "They are a perverse generation." Pity these poor blind worms.

Walter. Deacon, we've heard that about the worms before.

Billy. Don't worry the poor reptiles and cast up their blindness. They were made blind on purpose so they could'nt see the sins of a perverse generation. Tell us about the wolf in sheep's clothing. This is an experience meetin'.

C. (*Groans.*) Ripe for destruction! (*Exit L.*)

Enter PEWTERMUGG, *L.*

P. Heard the news, boys?

H. News? Yes-hic; the 'Spress Co-hic-ompany was robbed last night.

P. Fudge! Do you call that news? They've found out who did it!

H. Hic-I knew that at first.

P. What! Who did you think it was?

H. The thief, of course! Gimme 'nother c'nundrum.

P. Pah! dolt!

Walter. Who was it, Pewtermugg?

P. Charlie Winslow!

All. Charlie Winslow!

H. It's too bad. Charlie was a brick at readin' tracts, after he signed.

Walter. I don't believe it. Winslow was proud of his honor.

P. And honor requires a man to pay stakes lost.

Billy. I'm not surprised. Winslow gambled freely. I wouldn't trust him.

P. Nor I.

Guzzle. Bill Stoughton, you're a liar and a coward. But it's jest like your sneakin' natur', to strike a man when he's down or drunk.

Billy. (*Blustering.*) What's that you say?

Guzzle. Oh, don't bluster! I said you lied, and I'll prove it, if you want me to.

Billy. Look out, Guzzle! Don't aggravate me, or you'll rue it. I've seen him gamble, and I'll leave it to Weston. He seen him.

P. I've seen him lose.

Walter. I never saw him lose very heavily.

Guzzle. There! Billy Stoughton, I told you you lied. You are always stickin' in your short spoons where they don't belong.

Billy. Do you call me a liar?

Guzzle. Don't fizz over like a pop-bottle. Of course I did.

Enter STOUGHTON, *leading* FREDDIE, L.

Stoughton. Boys I won't have this row. I keep a respectable house.

Guzzle. The devil prides himself on respectability. Nothin' *low* about him.

Stoughton. What do you mean? Is that an insult?

Guzzle. No, no. I was only givin' the devil his due. That's all.

H. Why! here's Freddie. How are you-hic, bub? Your visits here are like hic-angels'.

Stoughton. Yes; his mother don't allow him to come to the saloon. She's afraid it will spoil him. One of her notions, you know. I humor her in it, for Freddie's *her* boy, and Billy's mine.

P. That accounts for their difference in taste.

Loafer. Here, Freddie, have a drop of my toddy.

Freddie. Thank you, sir; but mamma says I mustn't taste strong drink.

P. Better take her advice, sonny.

Loafer. Niver a bit will it hurt ye.

Guzzle. Curse the man that will tempt a child with whiskey!

Loafer. Faith! an' it's yersilf that's badly fuddled, or ye wouldn't make sich an uncivil spache.

Guzzle. Would you have him like yourself and myself—objects of contempt to decent people? I'd a darnation sight rather bury him, if he was my boy.

Walter. Why! what ails you, Guzzle? Blow me! if you don't make a good temperance lecturer. You need something to steady your nerves. Set 'em up, Billy. Come, Heartsease, and Pewtermugg.

Guzzle. Guess I will. Maybe it will help to smother the devilment I feel in me to-night, bigger'n a dray-mule. Gimme red-eye.

H. Sheet iron lockjaw!

P. A little whiskey-sour!

Walter. I'll take brandy straight. Here's to the genial proprietor of the "Shades!" (*They drink,* H.'s *hand trembles so that he cannot bring the glass to his mouth. He takes his handkerchief, holds one end in the right hand, puts the other round his neck, draws up the glass, and drinks.*)

Billy. There's a trick worth knowin'! Sleight-of-hand!

Walter. Necessity is the mother of invention.

H. I don't feel just right. My nerves ain't steady-hic. I felt so once before. It's almighty queer.

Loafer. (*Aside.*) Snakes in his boots!

Guzzle. Let me take you home.

P. Better take care of yourself first.

Guzzle. Oh! I can take care of myself, and some other people I know, too.

Enter LITTLE GIRL, *who sings.*

SONG.—Air, "The Beggar Girl."[*]

Over the pavements, and in at each door,
  Hungry and barefoot I wander forlorn'
My father is dead, and my mother is poor,
  And she grieves for the days that will never return.

Pity, kind gentlemen, friends of humanity,
  Cold blows the wind and the storm rages on ;
  Give me some alms for my mother for charity;
  Give me some alms, and then I will be gone.

Call me not vagabond ; wine the defiler,
  Darkened the home that was happy and bright,
Poor father! he followed the artful beguiler.
  Lonely and weary I'm begging to-night.
    Pity, kind gentlemen, etc.

Think, while you revel so careless and free,
  Secure from the wind, and well clothed and fed;
Should fortune so change it, how hard it would be
  To beg at a door for a morsel of bread.
    Pity, kind gentlemen, etc.

Freddie. Little girl, let me pass round and collect for you. Papa, mayn't I put in the quarter Ma gave me to buy candy? (*Drops quarter into his hat, and starts around the room.*)

Stoughton. A penny is quite enough, my son. Don't be extravagant, even in your alms.

Freddie. But she needs it, Papa—she's so poor. I'll do without candy. (*A few throw in pennies, which* FREDDIE *hands to her.*)

Little Girl. Thank you so much ! You'r so good.

Billy. Her old daddy will have plenty of punch to-night.

Little Girl. Please, sir, my father is dead.

Billy. We've heard that story before, you little reprobate. Now get out.

Walter. Let her stay, Billy.

Billy. (*Comes from behind the bar, and pushes her toward door, L.*) Get out !—this is no tramps' lodging-house.

Stoughton. She'll go directly, Billy.

Billy. She'll go now. If I've got to keep bar here, I'll keep it quiet. If you don't like that, old boss, just keep your own bar. (*Pushes her toward door.*)

Guzzle. Touch that girl again, and I'll knock you into Jamaica, you white livered coward, you! (*Steps before Billy.*)

Freddie. (*Rushes between Billy and the Little Girl.*) Please don't, Billy.

Billy. Guzzle, we'll soon see who's boss here—you or me ! (*Seizes bottle from counter, and attempts to strike* GUZZLE. *Latter wards off blow, and strikes Billy, who staggers, and wildly strikes at* GUZZLE, *but hits* FREDDIE *with the bottle.* FREDDIE *falls, crying,* "BILLY, I'm killed—don't hit her! ")

---

[*] Adapted from "The Beggar Girl," by permission of the publishers, Messrs. Oliver Ditson & Co.

Stoughton. (*Rushing forward.*) Rash boy! What have you done?

Billy. It wasn't my fault. I didn't see him.

Stoughton. (*Kneels on the floor, C; draws* FREDDIE'S *head upon his knees.*) Speak, darling! Are you hurt? My God!—he has ceased to breathe! He is dead! *Killed by his own brother!* Heaven pity his mother! Oh! wife was it for this that we reared children—to fall by each other's hands? (*Rises, and lays the body carefully upon the floor.*) My sins cry out against me! Oh, God! why have you struck him, instead of me? I deserved it. (*Wrings his hands.*) Oh, this is too hard to bear!

Guzzie. The fruits of Rum! God forgive me, and I'll never drink another drop!

CURTAIN.

SCENE II. *Room in* HEARTSEASE'S *house. Windows in flat, L and R; furniture scanty and mean, indicating great poverty; sofa R; table C; chairs R and L;* MRS. H. *and* SUSIE *sitting by table sewing.*

Mrs. H. Oh, when will your father return? Will nothing restore him to his senses? Alcohol has maddened him, and nightly he adds to the burden of shame which has blasted his once fair name, and sunk us into the lowest depths of poverty. Verily, strong drink is a demon which possesses the soul and enslaves the body of its victims.

Susie. Dear mother, is there no hope for father?

Mrs. H. Alas! I see none. His business has passed into other hands, his property scarcely sufficed to meet the demands of his creditors. Everything went wrong, after your grandfather's death. Had it not been for Mr. Wishall's good management, we should not have even this house—robbed, as it is, of all that makes home pleasant, and shared by those who were formerly our servants.

Susie. (*At window, L, looking out.*) I cannot hear him yet.

Mrs. H. He is later than usual, to-night. I fear something has happened. To-night he is reveling on the generosity of Mr. Trustham. I fear our few remaining friends will be obliged to abandon us to our fate. But I shall never cease to labor in the cause of temperance.

Enter KATRINA, L.

Katrina. Ist Meester Heartsease home yet?

Mrs. H. No. Why do you ask?

Katrina. Hans has peen home more as an hour. I'll ask him if he saw your huspand. (*Exit L.*)

Mrs. H. Oh! that I could persuade him to turn from his ways. Arguments that I daily use upon others, avail naught with him. His only answer is, "My honor's gone, and a man without honor is not worth saving."

Enter H. *L; he stares around the room, then advances toward C.*

H. (*Staring at Mrs. H.*) Are you ready, Hattie? I've kept you waiting, have I? Forgive me, won't you? But get your bonnet and shawl. We must go.

Mrs. H. Go where?

Susie. What ails you, father?

H. Hurry up! They're pursuing us.

Mrs. H. Lord help us! He has the delirium! There's nobody pursuing you, John.

Susie. Be quiet, father! No one shall harm you.

H. There! I told you they would get me! (*Glares under sofa, R.*) See that fire! (*Points.*) *See it!* SEE! There's a firey serpent in it! He's come for me! His master's coming, too! They're coming! See! (*Points.*) See that demon! His head is a ball of fire! His arms are large snakes! (*Retreats a step.*) Save me, wife! Susie help me! They've got me! (*Drops on the floor, and writhes in agonies.*) Take them off! They're strangling me! (*Clutches at his throat, as if pulling off a foe.*) (MRS. H. *at door, L, calls,* "MR. GIPFEL!")

HANS *and* KATRINA *rush in, L.*

Hans. Mine Gott! Schnakes in his poots!

Susie. Help him, Mr. Gipfel!

Hans. Ach! He gets himself better pooty quick! (H. *sits upright on the floor*)

Mrs. H. There, you're better, John!

Susie. Poor father! We will protect you. They are gone now.

SLOW CURTAIN.

ACT V.

SCENE I. *Room in* H.'S *house, same as in last scene of Act IV; seated,* MRS. HEARTSEASE, *R of table;* TRUSTHAM, *L of table;* HEARTSEASE *standing before Trustham, C.*

H. Mr. Trustham, I can never express my gratitude for what you have done for me.

Trustham. Pooh, John Heartsease! I have done very little, and that was my duty. Thank your wife for your return to reason.

H. Yes, dear wife, I do indeed owe it to you that I am still alive, and within reach of hope. I never can repay the devotion that you and Susie have lavished upon me.

Mrs. H. My reward is great, a husband saved.

H. Wife, daughter, I've been your unkindest enemy. I've made you beggars. I've ruined my prospects, and alienated my friends. But, thank God! my best friends, a loving wife and a dear daughter,

are still spared to me. Mr. Trustham, let me at least thank you for
your untiring interest in my behalf, even when I heaped insult upon
you. (*Takes* TRUSTHAM'S *hand, weeps*) I have even wasted, for
drink, money which you gave my dear wife to buy our bread. Can
you forgive me?

Trustham. It's all forgiven. Try to forget that, and let your mind
dwell on the future. There is much in store for you yet.

H. I will do as you ask. Last night's horrid delirium has aroused
me to a sense of my awful danger. If that terrible scene is ever
repeated, I am lost forever. Ugh! It makes me shudder to think of it.

Mrs. H. Husband, will you pledge yourself again?

H. Yes, dear wife; to-night I will publicly sign the pledge, and
take a stand for sobriety again. I know, alas! my weakness, now, and
I also know who are my friends. I trust I may stand firm this time.

Trustham. I trust you may. Friends are ready to assist you.
shall meet you at the temperance rooms this evening. (*Exit L.*)

Mrs. H. Oh, husband! my joy is greater than I dared to hope.

Susie. Father, I'm so glad!

H. I have most reason to be happy, for what joy is greater than
seeing the happiness of loved ones! (*Clasps them in his arms;
soft music,* "*Home, Sweet Home.*")

SLOW CURTAIN.

SCENE II. *Temperance reading-room; long reading-table, R, with
books and papers; files of papers on walls; President's stand rear;
small table front of it, with ink, pens. etc.; appropriate temperance mottoes on the walls; standing round small table, as
curtain rises,* MRS. H., SUSIE, H., TRUSTHAM, *and* PEWTERMUGG.

P. So you have concluded to lead a new life, I hear, Mr
Heartsease.

H. I am determined to try, and will sign the pledge this evening.

P. That's right! I'm glad to see the good work go on. We
need it. God speed it!

Enter WINSLOW *and* MRS. WINSLOW.

H. Mrs. Winslow, I shall redeem my promise.

Mrs. W. Heaven be praised for that! It lightens somewhat my
own great grief.

Susie. Mr. Winslow, I'm so glad to see you (*Offers him
her hand.*)

Winslow. Thank you. To hear *you* say so, is joy to one in despair.

Trustham. Cheer up, Charles; all may yet be well. You have
good friends.

P. Can I do anything? I'm willing to try.

Susie. Thank you, Mr. Pewtermugg! Thank you.

Winslow. I don't see how you can do anything. You did not see
anybody take the express pouch last night. It's a dark case for me. I
presume I shall be arrested before morning.

P. (*Aside.*) Ha! you're in the toils to stay.

Mrs. H. To think that my boy should be accused of robbery! Oh, the disgrace!

H. It is a sad affair, but let us hope for the best!

Trustham. Mr. Heartsease, you may now inscribe your name in this book. I will read the pledge. (*Reads.*) " I do solemnly promise to abstain from all use of all intoxicating liquors all the rest of my life. Lord help me."

P. Mr. Trustham, I have never signed this *new* pledge. I will do so now. I wish to contribute my mite of influence toward the good cause.

Trustham. Certainly, Mr. Pewtermugg. By all means, sign it.

Mrs. W. (*As P. is about to sign, enter* POLICEMAN, *followed by* GUZZLE, WISHALL, *and* HANS. MRS. WINSLOW *lays her hand on the* POLICEMAN'S *arm, entreatingly.*) You have come to arrest him. Please have mercy. Do not blast his fair name. I plead not for myself. He is young, and has all his life before him.

Officer. Madam, I must do my duty.

Guzzle. Mrs. Winslow, I reckon you've made a slight mistake. *This* is the chap the policeman's lookin' for. (*Points to* P.) Well, I swow! What's he up to now? 'Taint no use, old boy! I calc'late they'll put you where there'll be no temptation to drink anything stronger than Adam's ale. Reckon they'll keep you *tight* enough, without whiskey.

P. (*Greatly agitated.*) What do you mean, fellow?

Officer. It means that you are charged with robbing the American Express Company of $25,000.

P. (*Pretending coolness.*) This is all gammon! I suppose you are at the bottom of it, Wishall. Remember, I can play at that too, on a little account of yours.

Wishall. I suppose you refer to my business relations with the late Mr. Ledger. I shall settle that with his partner. John Heartsease, I owe you $5,000. Pardon an erring man!

P. Fool! what do you mean? Put yourself behind a grating, if you choose.

H. Mr. Wishall, I understand it all. Mr Ledger informed me that he intended to pay you the amount you name. He died before doing so. A check purporting to be drawn by him was presented by you for payment, and proved, on close examination, to be a forgery. I declined to push the matter, because you had, by years of faithful labor, earned far more than that paltry sum. It is yours, and you are welcome to it, though your course was so wrong that I could not admit you as a partner, as I intended doing.

W. (*With feeling.*) And he is the *friend* who concealed my crime, instead of yourself, base wretch!

P. Wishall, are you not equally a base wretch, in betraying what you acceded to? Traitor!

W. I revealed nothing. Should I reveal one-tenth part of your villainy the world would stand amazed.

P. (*Draws a pistol.*) Then you will *never* reveal it. (OFFICER *and* GUZZLE *seize him and handcuff him; women scream.*)

Hans. Py himmel! dot bistol might shoot himself off pooty quick.

Guzzle. (*To P.*) Now Boss, I guess we're even! I'll not let Wishall have all the credit of this little job. I've had a crow to pick with you ever since you turned my father and mother out of one of your shanties into the winter's storm. You struck me, because I said you were mean. It ain't always safe to strike a boy, because you can.

P. What's that to do with the present?

Guzzle. Oh, I havn't finished yet! Maybe you would like to know how I found out that you hired a boy to steal an old express pouch from the office? An' p'raps, you'd like to know why I followed you up to the depot, that dark night, when the night express came in? I wa'n't far away when you jumped into the express wagon along with Charlie Winslow, and gave him a nice Havana, to pass away time, an' then threw out the sack in the dark, and slipped your old stuffed one in on the seat beside Charlie. You're darned cute, Mr. Pewtermugg; but, remember that Guzzle's head has something in it, beside the effects of forty-rod whiskey!

Officer. Come. Mr. Pewtermugg, I must escort you to prison.

P. Better death, than such disgrace! Ruined forever! (*Exeunt L.*)

Mrs. H. Can this be true, or is it a dream? Mr. Pewtermugg was a man of such exemplary morals and excellent habits, that his fall has made me distrustful of—I had almost said, all mankind.

Trustham. After all, I always half-suspected him to be a sly, canting hypocrite.

Mrs. W. Oh, Charles, what a narrow escape you have had!

Winslow. And it seems I am indebted to Guzzle for deliverance.

Susie. Mr. Guzzle, we will never forget that service!

Guzzle. To serve you, Miss Susie, is reward enough, without thanks.

W. Winslow, forgive me for being an accomplice in the plot for your ruin, for I was an accomplice, in not warning you and advising you to beware of the allurements of wine, and the villainies of Pewtermugg.

W. I forgive you! I was most to blame. I thank God, I have escaped destruction! I shudder at the dark plot, which my imprudence has made possible. Never again will I taste intoxicating liquors! (*Signs the pledge.*)

Hans. Meester Trustham, I p'lieve I signs dot bledge! Dese Yankee trinks make me feel so schtupid, oond, would you p'lieves it? Last night I dreamed of schnakes, oond I told Katrina dees morgens dot I signs dot bledge eef she would. (*Signs.*) We'll trink frish vasser for a shpell.

Enter *L*, WALTER WESTON *and* STOUGHTON.

Stoughton. I've come to sign the pledge.

Trustham. Nobly said! Stoughton, you're too much of a man for such a vile traffic.

Stoughton An accursed traffic! It has ruined my family. One of my poor boys lies to-day in his coffin, and the other, alas! is worse off. Rum was the destroyer. I'll never sell another drop, or encourage a human being to partake of the cruel poison. (*Signs the pledge.*) Walter, take my advice—stop in time. (*Exit L.*)

Trustham. There is the pledge for all. Who else will sign?

Walter. Guzzle, I'll sign it if you will. I think we've drank enough. If murder and villainy follow wine, I will not follow it in their company.

Trustham. There is no fitter time to turn to the right.

Guzzle. I've made up my mind to sign the pledge, Walter, and I'm glad you have, too. (WALTER *and* GUZZLE *sign.*) I guess this crowd has sowed about enough wild oats to get up a reputation. I'm goin' to be a man, or sell out my canoe and quit . (*All sign*)

Mrs. H. Guzzle give me your hand ! (*They shake hands.*)

H. (*Signs.*) Would that this stroke of the pen were a release from the memories of the past ! Let us stand united against the tempter in the future, and strive to rescue the perishing.

MUSIC—SLOW CURTAIN.

THE ASSESSOR.

CHARACTERS.

MR. TAXSHIRK,

MRS. TAXSHIRK,

BUB TAXSHIRK,

SARAH JANE TAXSHIRK,.

THE TAX ASSESSOR..

COSTUMES.

Taxshirk and his family, substantial country dress; Assessor in plain business suit.

THE ASSESSOR.

SCENE. *Room in a Farmer's House. Enter farmer Taxshirk and the Assessor.*

Taxshirk. Take a seat mister. Let me see—what might your name be?

Assessor. My name is Dooley—John Dooley.

Taxshirk. Waal now I guess yeou aint no relation to the Dooleys down by Binkley's Corners, be yeou?

Assessor. Slightly related, I believe. Old Jack Dooley down by the corners is a second cousin of my father's.

Taxshirk. Then you're a son of Sim Dooley—long Sim, we called him.

Assessor. Exactly—the same.

Taxshirk. Waal dew tell! Heow is Sim.

Assessor. Oh, he's all right and good for many a year yet.

Taxshirk. I swow. Who'd a thought it. I'd like to see Sim again. Many a rastle Sim and I have had. He was about the best rastler in the kyounty. I held a pretty even whiffletree with him though, and we could never quite settle which was the best man.

Assessor. I've heard father speak often of his wrestling.

Taxshirk. Sim was a' most like a brother to me. We used to go to spellin' school together. I remember as well as yesterday the first time your father went sparkin' of your mother, Maria Briggs.

Assessor. Ah, you have a good memory I see, Mr. Taxshirk.

Taxshirk. Your father moved aout to this state the same spring I did. It's nigh onto thirty year I guess. I tell yeou, Mr. Dooley, your father and I were two of the poorest men that ever came west. Sallie and me had nothing in the house but three plates, three knives and forks, and two cups and sassers. We 'd a straw bed and coverled, and all the extra clothes that we had, that wan't on our backs, you could 'a put in your overcoat pocket. Dang my boots if you couldn't. (*Laughs.*)

Assessor. I've heard father say, often, that those were trying times.

Taxshirk. Waal they were, *I tell yeou.* We carried corn on critter back thirty mile to mill. It took plump three days to go to mill and back. I suppose your father has picked up considerable sence then?

Assessor. He can't reasonably complain. I see by the looks of your farm and your stock, that you are pretty well off for this world, too.

Taxshirk. I guess I had'nt ought to complain. Speakin' of stock, yeou don't see no finer, I kalkilate, than ourn. I've got the best kyows in the kyounty.

Assessor. Do you keep much stock, Mr. Taxshirk?

Taxshirk. Waal yes I guess so. We've about as much as Bub and myself can tend. We've eleven kyows, an' seven head of horses, an' I guess close rubbin' onto four hundred head of sheep. Milkin' the kyows, and tendin' to the butter an' cheese is a sight of work.

Enter MRS. TAXSHIRK *and* BUB.

Taxshirk. Sallie this is Mr. Dooley, Sim Dooley's boy. (*Mrs. T. shakes hands with him.*)

Mrs. T. Goodness me! Sim Dooley's boy. I haint seen your pap for ten year, or sich a matter. How is he?

Assessor. He is well.

Taxshirk. I am sorry Sim moved down into the other kyounty. We never see him nowadays. If I might inquire, are you married?

Assessor. I am.

Taxshirk. Where do you live?

Assessor. I moved up into this township last spring.

Mrs. T. I do say. Why, we never heerd tell of it.

Bub. Why, mother, didn't you hear about that Dooley feller that moved into Snook's old house?

Taxshirk. Yes, you heard of it, Sallie. You've forgot. Bub told us, yeou know.

Mrs. T. I 'spose I heerd it, but my memory ain't as good as it was twenty or thirty year ago. Bub remembers everything.

Taxshirk. Bub, have you turned the kyows to pasture?

Bub. Sairy Jane's doin' that.

Taxshirk. Bub, how much milk did old Brindle give when she was fresh?

Bub. Two wooden pails-full.

Mrs. T. Old Crumpley's just as good a cow any day.

Taxshirk. I guess if anything, she's a leetle better for butter, but I 'spose there ain't a tuppence difference between them. I wouldn't take a fifty dollar greenback of any man's money for either of them.

Enter SARAH JANE.

Sarah J. Pap, all five of the big colts jumped into the cow pasture, and the little ones are tryin' to git in too.

Taxshirk. That's the way it goes. Them colts will pester the life out of me. Bub, we must repair that fence after plantin'.

Assessor. Mr. Taxshirk, as time is precious, perhaps I had better state my business.

Taxshirk. Out with it, then! I guessed when I saw you comin' you was some city feller with patent-rights or somethin' of the kind. But I guess Sim Dooley's boy wouldn't go round swindlin' his neighbors with patent rights.

Mrs. T. Maybe he 's got sewin' machines.

Assessor. No, ma'am; I am——

Bub. He's the feller with oil chromos, I'll bet.

Assessor. You are mistaken! I am not a peddler.

Serah J. Mother, if he's the book agent that's round, I want a book full of battles like the one Sis Jones's pap bougnt for her.

Taxshirk. I guess we don't want any books these hard times.

Mrs T. The last one we bought, the kiver come off in less than six weeks, before the children was through readin' it. An' they ain't hard on books, either. The feller he came round again sellin' picters, an' he actually wouldn't take it back.

Assessor. Madam, I am not a book agent, I am happy to say: I am the township assessor.

Taxshirk. (*Jumps up excitedly.*) How 's that, Mr. Dooley? Sol Willams was elected, accordin' to my count.

Assessor. But he appointed me as his deputy. That's how it is.

Taxshirk. (*Gruffly.*) Wa'al, if *that's* your business, why didn't you say so. I want to git to my work.

Assessor. (*Produces blanks for the returns*) We will proceed then at once. It is, perhaps, unnecessary to read the explanation to you in full. I will read you the affidavit sometimes required. (*Reads rapidly.*) I do solemnly swear that I will enumerate to the best of my knowledge and belief all my properties of every kind whatsoever, as hereinafter mentioned, viz: chattels, moneys, loans, bonds, securities, &c., &c.

Taxshirk. (*Testily.*) Hold on, I say! I wouldn't give a straw for the man whose word isn't as good as his oath. I'll not swear, I guess.

Assessor. Very well! We'll proceed without the oath. How many milch cows have you?

Taxshirk. Seven!

Assessor. Excuse me, Mr. Taxshirk, but I understood a few minutes ago that you had eleven milch cows.

Taxshirk. Botheration! Four of them are dry!

Assessor. Exactly! (*Writes.*) Eleven milch cows, and four of them dry. (*Laughs.*)

Serah J. No that ain't right. There's eleven milch cows and four dry cows.

Taxshirk. Sairy Jane, go into the kitchen. Learn to hold your tongue when older folks than you be are talkin'! (*Exit SARAH JANE.*)

Assessor. Exactly! (*Reads.*) Eleven milch cows, four dry cows; worth, say $30 apiece. Is that right?

Taxshirk. (*Gruffly*) I kalkilate it is

Mrs. T. Mr. Dooley, you've no idea what a loss it was for them four cows to go dry. It made a big hole in the cheese.

The mules knocked down the fence and let the keows into the corn, an' four of them never got over the gorge an' we had to put them dry.

Taxshirk. Sallie, hadn't you better see to the kitchen. (*Aside.*) Confound it, women can't keep their tongues. (*Exit* Mrs. T)

Assessor. Mules! Ah, mules are unruly animals. How many mules, Mr. Taxshirk?

Taxshirk. Only seven!

Assessor. Worth say $50 apiece.

Taxshirk. (*Snappishly.*) They're not worth it. Mule meat is cheap and mean.

Assessor. You have very fine stock, Mr. Taxshirk, and doubt-less your mules are no exception, but we will compromise at $40 per head. How many horses?

Taxshirk. Nine! Worth about $50 per head on the *everage* I kalkylate.

Assessor. Cheap horseflesh! Any for sale at those figures? I want a good span of horses.

Bub. Why, Pap, you was offered $300 for Selim last week.

Taxshirk. Bub, can't I teach you not to meddle when I'm talkin'.

Bub. (*Angrily.*) You'd forget you had a head if it wan't for me.

Taxshirk. Clear out you young scamp and no talkin' back! The 'Sessor an' me can tend to this business. Git to haulin' rails to mend that fence. (*Exit* Bub.)

Assessor. We'll say $75 per head for the horses all 'round. Will that do?

Taxshirk. (*Hesitating.*) Wa'al I guess so.

Assessor. You said four hundred sheep, I believe. Say one dollar per head. Anything else?

Taxshirk. Ten hogs, worth a matter of $15.

Assessor. Well pork is cheap. (*Writes.*) Is that all the live stock?

Taxshirk. All I think of.

Assessor. Your daughter mentioned some colts; five large and five small, I believe.

Taxshirk. Well, by jingo, my memory is getting bad! I clean forgot them. (*Laughs.*) Put in the ten at $150.

Assessor. Call it $200. (*Writes.*) What is the value of your household furniture and appurtenances?

Taxshirk. We're not very stylish here, as you see. We've nothin' but cheers and tables an' bedstids, and sich like. I guess the hul kit is worth about $300, countin' the new bureau in the best room.

Assessor. What is the value of your farm implements?

Taxshirk. About $100, or sich a matter.

Enter SARAH JANE.

Sarah J. Mother wants to know what time it is by Bub's watch. The clock 's stopped.

Assessor. Oh, yes; one watch. (*Writes.*)

Taxshirk. (*Angrily.*) Confound that clock, I'll smash it into flinders the next time it stops! Sairy Jane, go long and don't bother me.

Enter BUB.

Bub. Pap, shall I take the horses or the oxen to haul the rails?

Assessor. Oxen! Quite true, we forgot them. How many yoke?

Taxshirk. (*In a rage.*) One yoke; put it down! Bub, you're an ass. Mr. 'Sessor, put *that* down too. One taxable ass. (*To* BUB.) You young imp! when I send you out why don't you stay out till you're sent for? Go! (*Exit* BUB. *Sounds of piano heard in adjoining room.*)

Taxshirk. (*Aside.*) I wish that piano was in China.

Assessor. I was not aware that your daughter could play If there's anything I like it's music. What is your instrument worth?

Taxshirk. So you're going to tax that too, be you? It's nuthin' but ornament and nonsense, and ought to go in free.

Assessor. Couldn't do it. The directions are explicit. Read them. (*Hands paper to* T.)

Taxshirk. I paid $500 for it, but it ain't *worth* anything. It's all a piece of tomfoolery.

Assessor. Really, Mr. Taxshirk, hadn't you better call in your family to assist you in listing your property? Your memory is so very bad.

Taxshirk. No, confound it. Thanks to your meddlin' an' pryin' round, you've got it all. (*A pause.* ASSESSOR *writing in his book. In loud key.*) I say, you've got it all. (ASSESSOR *continues writing. Still louder.*) Confound you, man, why don't you go? Are you waiting for more live stock to grow, so you can 'sess it?

Assessor. Not at all! not at all! Thank you, Mr. Taxshirk, for the very full returns I've got. Good day! (*Exit.*)

CURTAIN.

TWO GHOSTS IN WHITE.

CHARACTERS.

Miss Praxis, Principal of young ladies' boarding school.

Mrs. Gushover, Visitor.

Miss Sourtop, Matron.

Belle,
Julia,
Annie,
Nettie,
} School girls.

Bridget, Chambermaid.

COSTUMES.

Any clothing suited to the social standing of the character.

SITUATIONS.

R, means right for the actor as he faces the audience; L, left, C, center.

TWO GHOSTS IN WHITE.

SCENE,— *Girls' room in female boarding school; entrance L; closet door R; bedroom door L C in flat; sofa R C; study table C; chairs, books and articles pertaining to studies.*

Annie. We'll have just a jolly time, Jule. Fred and Will said they would bring their chums, two splendid fellows, for Belle and Nettie.

Julia. Won't that be nice! But how did you manage it this time? Sourtop has eyes all over her head.

Annie. Yes; just like a potato. (*Laughs.*) You see my gold pencil has a hollow space inside big enough for a tiny note. Well I lost the pencil, by accident, of course, under a seat, while doing penance in the shape of the morning walk in the park. Fred, by accident too, found it after we had gone. What did he do but come boldly up to the seminary and deliver it to Miss Praxis herself. She scolded my negligence a little, that was all.

Julia. Ha! ha! I should never have thought of that. Will they bring a ladder?

Annie. No, you big goose! That isn't safe any more. You know the new kitchen runs out under the old oak, and Fred says that is just the thing. From the roof of the kitchen they can easily get onto the roof of the wing, and then the lightning rod will take them directly to Belle's window.

Julia. Oh, dear! I'm afraid they'll fall!

Annie. Ha! ha! you're afraid Will may get hurt!

Julia. I wasn't thinking of Will at all.

Annie. Oh, certainly not! you never think of him. There's not the slightest danger. Didn't they say the last time they were here, that they always climb the lightning rod to their room when they're out of the college late? It will be just gay! Ma sent me cake and fruit, and Fred will bring oysters and pickles. Wouldn't Sourtop tear her hair if she'd find it out?

Julia. Let's go and see if Belle and Nettie will be sure to be here

Annie. Oh! of course they'll come. (*Exeunt L.*)

Enter L, MISS PRAXIS AND MRS. GUSHOVER.

Miss P. Mrs. Gushover, this is a fair specimen of the rooms in our boarding halls, as you will see by comparing it with those of your daughter.

Mrs. G. Indeed, Miss Praxis, I think your arrangements are all perfection. I do, really, and I'm glad to find it so. I've worried a great deal this year about my darling Belle. I've told Mr. Gushover again and again that we must spare no pains to edicate our child. Says I to him, says I, Gushover we can't be too particular about the edication of our chiid. Says I, riches takes wings, (Mr. Gushover is one of the solidest men in our town) but knowledge don't.

Miss P. Very true.

Mrs. G. Says I, we'll spare no expense to give Belle a superior edication. Miss Praxis, money's no object when advantages are concerned. I've always said so to Gushover. My child shall have advantages if money'll buy them.

Miss P. You are very right in your views concerning the future of your child!

Mrs G. Just what I've always told Gushover. Belle is a smart girl. She's the smartest of the family.

Miss P. Remarkable!

Mrs. G. She knowed every one of her letters before she was four, and could count like everything when she was six. I said then to Gushover, says I that child shall be edica'ed.

Miss P. Have you destined her for any particular work in life?

Mrs. G. Well, I can't say as I have. *Arithmetic* is her strong point. Don't you think so, Miss Praxis?

Miss P. She does very creditably in arithmetic and in fact in mathematics.

Mrs. G. I don't know much about them *mathematics* you speak of. I never studied them but one term when I went to school. Grammar and 'Rithmetic was my strong points.

Miss P. Ah! I dare say!

Mrs. G. It was, indeed. I believe in *strong points*, and it's a teacher's business to bring them out. Belle's a good girl. She'd never cause her teacher a spark of trouble if she knowed it. She never complains of her teachers and they never complain of her. Anybody can get along with her when they learn her ways.

Miss P. I soon learn the ways of my pupils. Belle is an excellent girl. She is inclined to be a little merry, but that is doubtless caused by her fine physical organization.

Mrs. G. I want to know! I declare I never noticed it. She is the quietest girl I ever seen. She is the bashfullest girl at home you ever heerd tell of. She wont even look at the young gentlemen who used to be playmates at the public school. Says I to Mr. Gushover, says I, Belle's so bashful we never will get her out into society at all; and says he, don't worry, Mary Ann, says he she'll come out some of these days.

Miss P. Her coming out will be easy enough, I apprehend, Mrs. Gushover.

Mrs. G. Gushover is a peculiar man I'm compelled to say, Miss Praxis.

Miss P. Oh, no! Don't say so, Mrs. Gushover. I think Mr. Gushover a model man!

Mrs. G. Yes, I vow he is, Miss Praxis. I took him because he *was a model* man. I could a' had a dozen men when I got Gush-over. They were just dyin' for me, but I took up with him. I knowed he'd suit me. Says I to myself, says I, I'll furnish the sentimental and style, and Gushover will furnish the practicalities of life. He don't care a straw about style. When I talked of sendin' Belle to school I said to him, says I, Gushover we must send Belle where there's *style*. And, says he, I agree with you decidedly Mary Ann, for we need some style in the family. D'ye see? He was jokin'. That man 'll be the death of me yet with his jokes, for you see he married me right out of a fashionable boarding school. (*Laughs.*) Now I spose really Belle must take after her Pa if she's inclined to fun.

Miss P. It 's quite probable. Such traits are often hereditary. You need not regret Belle's liveliness. She is a very good pupil, an exemplary one, in fact. Mrs. Gushover, would you like to visit some of the rooms where the young ladies are at study. You will find them busy as beavers. The occupants of this room have, I presume, obtained permission from Miss Sourtop, the matron, to visit some other room. Study hours end at eight, but the young ladies have permission to study until nine, and I'm glad to say that many of them avail themselves of the privilege. We are workers here, Mrs. Gushover.

Mrs. G. So you are! I see it on every hand. Now I venture Belle studies every evening till the last minnit. I could hardly git her away from her books at home. We'll drop into her room just before nine and surprise her.

Miss P. Perhaps she expects to spend the evening with you in the parlor? Possibly, it would not do justice to her to expect to find her studying on this occasion.

Mrs. G. Now don't you mind that, Miss Praxis. She's an obedient child and I told her she should go right along as if I wan't here. Don't you fear for her. I venture she'll be hard at work when we come, and we'll just visit round and see what the others are doing. Your discipline is so good, I know they'll all be hard at work.

Miss P. Ah! I'm glad you think so well of us. You appreciate a *good* school. Our discipline is indeed fine. Miss Sourtop is invaluable to me. She spends all her time seeing after the girls during hours when they are not in class. You can't *surprise* our girls much, for they are always at work. We *never* find them idle.

Mrs. G. Indeed your school is really perfection.

Enter SOURTOP.

Miss P. On the rounds as usual, Sourtop?

Sourtop. Yes, Miss Praxis, I'll strive to do my duty by these young ladies. Dear things, they need constant care and I love to bestow it. (*Exeunt Miss P. and Mrs. G.*)

Sourtop. One must keep up appearances when strangers are around. (*Looks around room.*) Now if the girls haven't left their closet door open. I can't teach them that such things are *very* improper.   Of course everything inside is disarranged. (*Steps inside.*)

Enter ANNIE and JULIA.

Annie. Goodness, if I haven't left my closet door open, (*Mimickingly*) Sourtop says that is very improper. (*Locks door and puts key in her pocket.*) Let's see what's in my box. (*They bring box from bed room and proceed to open it with a hatchet.*)

Julia. (*Pulling out an overcoat*) Good gracious, Annie! what's this?

Annie. Well, did you ever? I declare I've got somebody else's box. (*Pulls out various articles of gentlemen's dress.*) Ha! ha! ha! If mother hasn't sent me brother John's box, and of course mine has gone to him. How provoking!

Julia. It's real mean.

Annie. Wait a minute, Julia! I know Ma would send John something to eat too. Good! Here it is. (*Produces large cake, bag of nuts, etc.*)

Julia. It's too bad that Belle's mother is here. Suppose she'd find out all about our little supper.

Annie. No danger! She told Belle that she would spend the evening with Miss Praxis.

Julia. Splendid! Then Sourtop will be in the parlor too. She'll want to hear all that's said by Miss Praxis and Mrs. Gushover. Annie, I wouldn't prowl around these halls in the dark as she does, for the world.

Annie. Pooh, you little coward! you see a spook in every dark corner.

Julia. And I venture you would be just as much afraid as I, if you do think you are very brave.

Annie. Pshaw! All the girls know you're a regular little ninny! What do I care for your ghosts and haunted houses. I wish we could have a light.   It must be nearly time for the boys to come.

Julia. Hark! I hear footsteps.

Enter BELLE *and* NETTIE, *silently. Arrayed in white. They wave their arms silently.*

Annie. Good gracious! (*Darts into Passage L.*)

Julia. (*Screams.*) Annie! Annie! I shall die. (*Faints.*)

Nettie. (*Excitedly.*) Oh, dear, what shall we do? She's so easily frightened, and she may die.

Belle. Plague take it! She'll not die. But Sourtop will hear her screams. She'll be here in a minute, and then we're in a pretty fix. (*Footsteps heard outside.*) Gracious! She's coming! You'll not catch me in the scrape. (*Throws the sheet which is wrapped around her under the sofa, and runs into bed room.*)

Nettie. Well, they'll not catch me in a trap either. I'll just faint too. (*Throws sheet under the sofa and drops on floor.*)

Enter L, MISS PRAXIS, MRS. GUSHOVER, *and* BRIDGET

Miss P. It must have been here we heard the noise.

Mrs. G. Oh, where's my poor child? Belle would never leave her books unless it was something dreadful. (*They see girls on the floor.*) Mercy, save us, if it ain't murder! Call the police. We'll all be killed.

Bridget. Troth! an it's murder, it is!

Miss P. (*Calmly.*) Something serious has happened. But the young ladies have only fainted. Bridget run quick for water! Run into my office and bring my lancets, and a vessel to catch the blood. It may be necessary to let a little blood. Fetch my smelling salts too. (*Proceeds to lift the girls into sofa and easy chair.*) You see, I am something of a physician, and occasionally prescribe for the young ladies. I can bleed as well as any doctor.

Mrs. G. (*Rushes around frantically.*) Oh, Miss Praxis, don't mention blood! I can't bear to think of it. I can't bear to see a chicken's head cut off. Says I to Gushover before we were married, says I, one thing I never will do, I never will cut off a chicken's head! And I havn't. I'm as tender-hearted as a—a—

Miss P. (*Aside*) As a mouse! (*Trying to restore the girls.*) Calm yourself, Mrs. Gushover, really, I think it is nothing serious.

Enter BRIDGET *hurriedly L, with a large pail of water, containing large tin dipper; also, a long butcher knife, a wash-tub, a wooden tray of salt.*

Miss P. Mrs. Gushover, will you please assist me? Where can Sourtop be? Her assistance would be invaluable now.

Mrs. G. Oh, Miss Praxis, don't! You make me feel faint to hear you. Poor Belle! Miss Praxis, has anything happened to my child?

Miss P. Bridget, bring water. (*Bridget takes up dipper full.* MISS P. *raises* NETTIE'S *head and bathes her temple.*) Now, this way! (*They do same with Julia, latter shows signs of reviving. Turns to Nettie again.*) I'm afraid this is a more serious case. I think I will bleed her as the quickest means of relief. Bridget! where the basin to catch the blood?

Bridget. Shure, an' I brought the wash-tub.

Miss P. Dear me! Why did'nt you bring something else?

Bridget. Faith an' that will hould it, surely.

Miss P. The wash basin would have been quite sufficient.

Mrs. G. (*Excitedly.*) Oh! I shall faint! Help! To think of a wash-tub full of blood. It will kill the child.

Bridget. (*Takes handful of salt and puts under Mrs. G's nose*) Now, then, won't yez try a shmell of the salt?

Mrs. G. (*Severely.*) Take away them nasty drugs.

Miss P. Why, Bridget, what do you mean? What are you doing with the salt? Get the lancet for me, quick!

Bridget. Did'n't yez say that smellin' of salt would relave the pain of faintin'; an' isn't the lady a dyin' to faint? (*Takes butcher knife in one hand, and a dipper of water in the other. Hands knife to* MISS P.)

Miss P. Where's the lancet? Mercy, me! What's this for? Where's the lancet?

Bridget. Yez said yez wanted to spill some blood. I thought that would spill enough.

Miss P. You wretched blunderer. The girl might die before you could relieve her.

Bridget. Ay, an' I belave it.

Miss P. Water! Pour a little on her temples. (*Bridget pours dipper full of water on* NETTIE'S *face and neck. She jumps to her feet.*)

Nettie. You horrid thing! you've spoilt my new dress!

Miss P. Suddenly recovered! What is the cause of this?

Bridget. Faith, you've found spache at last, an' a very oncivil spache at that, when we've been trottin' the breath out of our bodies for yez.

Mrs. G. Do you feel weak, poor child?

Nettie. (*Snappishly.*) No! I don't. (*Annie slips in L unobserved.*)

Miss P. Miss Nettie, will you please inform us the cause of all this trouble?

Nettie. Oh, don't ask! Some one was coming in and frightened us terribly!

Miss P. What was it?

Annie. Something dreadful!

Julia. It was a ghost!

Miss P. Mrs. Gushover, I fear this is something serious. Bridget go and raise the alarm.

Mrs. G. Oh, don't leave us! That horrid thing may come back. Miss Praxis, what's that by the chair?

Miss P. (*Picks up coat.*) A man's coat, I declare. It must be a burglar and he's hid some where about. Bridget run for my revolver and call Sourtop. (*Bridget runs out L; Mrs. G. groans.*)

Annie. Aside to Julia.) What *shall* we do. The boys may be here any minute and she'll shoot them.

Julia. (*Aside to Annie.*) Oh, dear! Tell her it's your brother's coat. (*Sourtop with husky voice heard in the closet crying,* "*Let me out! I'm smothering!*")

Annie.
Julia. } Mercy!
Nettie.

Miss P. You're there, you villain, are you? (*Enter Bridget with revolver.*) Well, you shall not escape with impunity. We are armed. (*Bridget flourishes revolver.*) Come out, villain!

Mrs. G. Spare his life. I'll faint if you shed blood.

Sourtop. (*In closet.*) I can't get out. The door's locked! Oh, don't shoot!

Miss P. (*Sternly.*) Girls, if that door is locked from the outside there's a mystery some of you can unravel. Where's the key?

Annie. Indeed, Miss Praxis, I know nothing about it. I **saw** the door ajar a few minutes ago and locked it. That's all I **know.** (*Produces key. Miss P. puts key in the lock.*]

Mrs. G. Oh, don't let him out, Miss Praxis. He'll kill us all. Send for the police! I must find my poor child! *Will* you call the police?

Miss P. Stay where you are! I want no police prying around here.

Sourtop. Please let me out!

Miss P. Robber, are you unarmed?

Sourtop. Yes.

Miss P. Will you resist?

Sourtop. Mercy on us, no!

Miss P. Remember I have a revolver pointed at your head. (*Sourtop screams.*)

Bridget. An' I have a bloody big butcher knife pinted at your throat, ye murderin' villain. (*Sourtop screams again. Miss P. opens door cautiously; Sourtop rushes into her arms and screams "murder."*)

Miss P. (*Starts.*) Good gracious how you shock me! Miss Sourtop what does this mean? Why didn't you say it was you?

Sourtop. Oh, goodness! mercy! I was so frightened I didn't know you.

Miss P. (*Sternly.*) How came you in that closet?

Sourtop. Miss Praxis, I was inspecting the closet. As I found the door ajar I stepped inside and some one suddenly locked the door.

Annie. (*Aside to girls.*) Good enough for the meddling old thing.

Miss P. Then the burglar is concealed some where on this floor. I'll find him.

Mrs. G. Miss Praxis, I insist you shall find my child. I insist. Gushover pays his money. She's murdered in cold gore I know.

Miss P. It you're child is where she should be she is safe in bed, asleep. We'll try the bed room. (*Belle rushes out of bed room; Mrs. G. clasps her in her arms.*)

Mrs. G. My precious! Thank Heaven you're safe, darling.

Miss P. Miss Gushover, have you seen him?

Belle. Goodness, no! Seen whom? (*Aside.*) Have the boys been discovered?

Miss P. Seen whom! Why the burglar, of course. Miss Sourtop, did you observe this coat as you entered the room?

Sourtop. No! the villain must have followed me.

Annie. Miss Praxis, that coat belongs to my brother John. His box came to me by mistake, and mine went to him.

Mrs. G. Do tell! Well I never!

Miss P. (*Severely.*) Then why didn't you say so at once and save all this confusion, to say nothing of the danger to these young ladies. Your conduct deserves a severe reprimand.

Annie. If you please, Miss Praxis, what was the good in saying so when there was a villain in the closet.

Sourtop. Miss Annie, observe that such language toward your superiors is very impolite, not to say reprehensible. Your conduct, too, in locking that door was positively shameful. With your approval, Miss Praxis, I will make the penalty a week's detention at play hours.

Mrs. G. Bold thing! I'm glad my Belle haint taken up with *that* girl.

Julia. Please, Miss Sourtop, she wasn't to blame. I know some one else came into the room. They were ghosts! Gracious! I can't bear to think about it!

Sourtop. I am ashamed of you, Julia! To talk of spectres. Before *strangers*, too! One would think you read of nothing but ghosts. Shame!

Belle. (*Aside*) We must get them away before the boys come. (*Aloud.*) Indeed, Miss Praxis, Nettie and I are to blame. We were only in fun. We wrapped sheets around us to play a joke on the girls, and some one coming frightened us all.

Mrs. G. (*Laughs.*) Well, really, that child is gettin' quite jolly. (*Laughs.*)

Nettie. We thought you would not care! Please forgive us this time and we'll never do so again.

Belle. }
Annie. } No, never!
Julia. }

Bridget. (*Aside.*) Niver till there's another foine chance.

Miss P. Girls, you all see how your silly pranks might result seriously, but as the fright you have endured seems to be sufficient punishment, I will forgive you this time.

Sourtop. (*Aside.*) Well, I wouldn't! (*Aloud.*) Miss Praxis *I'm* convinced there's a *man* concealed about this house and I shall not rest till he's discovered.

Miss P. I think you are mistaken, perhaps?

Sourtop. The girls haven't made this matter clear to *my* mind. I'll see for myself. Miss Praxis, I'd be obliged to you for that revolver.

Mrs. G. Well, she must be a bold woman! I'd faint at the thought.

Miss P. If you must, I'll accompany you. Bridget, please bring a light.

Bridget. And the butcher knife?

Miss P. (*Laughing. Takes lamp.*) Yes. Mrs. Gushover will you accompany us?

Mrs. G. Oh, the idea of hunting in the dark for a horrid man. It's perfectly dreadful!

Bridget. Shure, an' if he knew who was after him he'd be lavin at onct.

Mrs. G. I'll retire to my room immediately. Go to your room precious. (*To Belle.*)

Belle. Yes, ma! (*Exeunt Miss P., Mrs. G. and Sourtop, Bridget following. The girls beckon to latter and she stops.*)

Annie. Oh, Bridget, will you tell on us?

Bridget. Faith, an' I think not, for I knows nothin' to tell yit. But I have me own opinions of the matter.

Annie. Cousin Fred was coming up with some of the boys. Run to the hall of the wing and watch for them. Sourtop will shoot them if they climb onto the roof.

Bridget. An' why do they be climbin' on the roof when there's a stairway up the stairs?

Annie. But Fred couldn't get permission to bring the others.

Nettie.
Belle. } Oh, do! They'll be shot.
Julia.

Bridget. An' you be wantin' me to desave Miss Praxis, the dear girl, an' ould Sourtop.

Annie. We promised her we'd never do it again, and we won't. I'll give you half my cake.

Bridget. Shure, an' it's no bribes I'll be taken' of yez, if you've a mind to make me a prisint of some cake, well an' good; I'll be after tellin' ould Sourtop the gintleman jumped off the roof and run away.

Nettie. Oh, No!

Annie. Don't say a word!

Belle. You mustn't tell for the world!

Bridget Troth an' be aisy darlints, I meant the burglars instid ot the gintlemen.

Belle. That will do! Hark! (*All listen.*) Hurry, Bridget, they're on the roof now. (*Bridget runs out L.*)

Julia. Mercy! I'm frightened to death.

Belle. Good land! That's nothing, if it hadn't spoiled all our fun.

Annie. I'll never risk it again!

Julia. Nor I!

Nettie. Nor I!

Belle. Well, I guess I'll not either, for it's too much risk.

Enter SOURTOP *L, with revolver.*

Sourtop. Young ladies! it is high time you were all in bed. Go to your rooms at once! Only think of the trouble you've caused. It's worrying the life out of me by inches! I'll never consent to stay here another term; I can't stand it.

Belle. (*Aside.*) That news is too good to be true.

Sourtop. Are you going to your rooms?

All. Yes, ma'am, we're going!

Enter BRIDGET *hastily, L.*

Bridget. If you plaze, ma'am, the gintlemen all jumped off the roof and cleared themselves (*Girls scream.*)

Sourtop. The gentlemen! What gentlemen?

Bridget. I mane the *burgulars!*

Sourtop. Then, why didn't you say burglars? The idea of calling a burglar a gentleman! Young ladies, to bed at once!

All. Yes, ma'am! (*Exit Sourtop, L.*)

Annie. Here, Bridget, is your cake! (*Cuts large piece of cake.*)

Bridget. Thank yez! Pat an' me will have a little tay party in the kitchen Pat's waitin' for me!

Annie. Well, I never!

Belle. Did you ever! Bridget, your time to be found out is coming.

Bridget. Troth, an' Pat comes in through the cellar windy. He'll niver be riskin' his bones climbin' a lightnin' rod. (*Exit L.*)

Julia. Thank goodness, we're out of this scrape!

Annie. It was a close shave, I tell you.

Nettie. You'll not catch me playing ghost soon again.

CURTAIN.

COUNTRY JUSTICE.

CHARACTERS.

JUSTICE OF THE PEACE.
SPLUDGE, Plaintiff.
FUDGE, Defendant.
ATTORNEY FOR PLAINTIFF.
ATTORNEY FOR DEFENDANT.
BULGE. ⎫
JENKS. ⎬ Witnesses.
SMITH. ⎭
JURY.

COSTUMES.

The "Jury" should have a rustic and somewhat dilapidated appearance. Spludge, plain suit; Fudge, very rustic, seedy and battered; Justice, plain and rustic; Lawyers, plain suits.

Note.—When there are not a sufficient number of characters to furnish a jury, by a very slight change in the wording of the piece, the jury may be omitted and the decision rendered by the Justice.

COUNTRY JUSTICE.*

SCENE.—*Room in a farm house; table with ink, writing paper, law books, etc.; chairs and spittoon; Justice of the Peace seated behind the table; Plaintiff and his Attorney right of Justice; Defendant and his Attorney left of Justice; Jury of six left of Defendant; three witnesses right of Plaintiff. Court discovered in session.*

Justice. The next case is Spludge versus Fudge. Counsel for plaintiff will please open the case.

Att'y for Plain. If it please your Honor, the facts of the case I will briefly recount as hereinafter enumerated, amplified and detailed (*Reads. Jury look wise and attentive.*) Spludge versus Fudge, *in re* sugar kettle. Be it known and understood that one Spludge (my worthy client, the plaintiff in this case,) was seized and possessed of an evaporating caldron, otherwise known as a sugar kettle. Be it also known that one Fudge, the defendant in this case (*Scowls at Fudge.*) was seized and possessed of a sugar camp. Be it further known that said Fudge was *not* seized of the requisite number of said metalic caldrons, otherwise known as sugar kettles, to evaporate to a granular consistency, otherwise known as maple sugar, the unelaborated fluids of said sugar trees, otherwise known as sugar sap or simply sugar water. Be it moreover and further known that said Fudge did apply to said Spludge for the loan of a sugar kettle, and that said Spludge, having every reason to suppose that said Fudge was acting in good faith, did loan said Fudge one sugar kettle, said kettle to be returned in good condition. (Mark me, in good condition.) Now, your Honor and honorable jury, said kettle has never been returned, and, to the best of the knowledge and belief of my worthy client, said kettle is now in a cracked and useless condition. Mr. Spludge brings action to recover the value true and proper of the aforesaid kettle. Your Honor, to sustain the facts hereinbefore enumerated, we offer the testimony of our worthy townsman Mr. Bulge, and others.

Justice. The counsel for defendant will state the defense.

Att'y for Def. Your Honor, and the very honorable jury: Our case is brief and as clear as day. We submit to this honorable court and jury the following points for your consideration:

First, The defendent is seized and possessed of a sufficient number of sugar kettles of his own to run his sugar camp.

* This dialogue is founded on the old story of the man who borrowed a sugar kettle, and was sued for its value on failing to return it in good condition. Although the author has never seen the story in print, it is probably familiar to most persons.

The inevitable conclusion then is, that he did not borrow one.

Second, The defendant has no recollection of having borrowed a kettle from plaintiff, and I ask this honorable court if my client *is a man likley to forget.* Look at him. I scorn the insinuation.

Third, The defendant is a man of very careful habits. Hence, we are forced to conclude that he did not break, crack, mar, deface, batter, pound, or otherwise maltreat the defendant's kettle.

Fourth, My client is a man of unimpeachable integrity and well known punctuality in his business, (Just look at him, your honor and gentlemen of the jury), hence the inference that he returned the kettle long ago crushes us with its ponderous weight of probability. The weight of this point is apparent when we remember that the kettle was alleged to have been borrowed in sugar-making, and that we are now in the midst of husking frolics and quilting bees.

Fifth, The damages claimed by the plaintiff, viz., one dollar and a half, are excessive. Just think of paying one dollar and a half for cracking a sugar kettle. Your Honor, it is absurd! (*Vehemently.*) Honorable jury, it is rank injustice. With due respect to the Court, I dont believe the plaintiff ever owned a kettle worth more than *six bits.* We are ready for the testimony.

Justice. Mr. Bulge, will you take the stand? (BULGE *takes witness's chair, right of justice, in front.*)

Att'y for Plain. Mr. Bulge, please state to the jury what you know about this case.

Bulge. I reckon Mr. Lawyer, that I don't know a great sight about it. I never seed the kittle in my life, as I knows on.

Att'y for Plain. What do you know about the *borrowing* of the kettle?

Bulge. I'm comin' to that. You see, I was down in the big woods one day in sugar makin', lookin' arter somethin' that hed been killin' my chickens. I hed forty big hens I was feedin' up on chopped meat and eggshells, so they would lay eggs for Easter. Nothin' like chopped meat—

Att'y for Plain. Please omit preliminaries.

Bulge. Which—what?

Att'y for Plain. Confine yourself to the essentials. (*Bulge looks puzzled, scratches his head.*) Come to the point at once.

Bulge. Dang it! that's jest what I'm doing if you'd let me. (*Takes out immense colored handkerchief and wipes his face, blows his nose, clears his throat.*) Kinder phthisicky weather, Squire.

Att'y for Plain. Please proceed.

Bulge. Well, as I was sayin', there's nothin' like chopped meat to make hens lay. But a coon or possum or some other varmint come an' tuk one every night for six nights hand runnin'. It riled me; it did, by jingo! I shouldered my gun determined to spoil that chap's fun if I could. I tuk straight down the crick, an' when I come to the lower end of the pint—

Att'y for Plain. (*Testily.*) Please tell what you know about this case. You will never get to the point at that rate.

Bulge. Wrong there, Mr. Lawyer, for I've jest got to the *pint*. I started straight up the pint through the woods, and found Bill Fudge's oldest boy haulin' wood for the sugar camp. He axed me if I could loan them a kittle, seein' as how they were one short, I told him—

Fudge. (*Jumps up excitedly.*) That aint so! We had plenty of kittles, but one had a sand hole in it an' we plugged that up.

Att'y for Plain. (*Jumps up excitedly.*) I wish to enquire, your honor, whether this Honorable Court and the witnesses are to be insulted, bullied, and intimidated by the defendant; instigated as he doubtless has been by other parties. (*Looks at opposing attorney.*) I will not say whom.

Att'y for Def. The fling of my opponent is unworthy of answer, and derogatory to the dignity of this court and the bar in general. My client may be excused any apparent hastiness of manner; realizing, as he does, the unscrupulous efforts made to crush him and blacken his character.

Fudge. I swear it's all a tarnation lie about my bein' short one kittle.

Justice. Silence, if you please! I reckon this court ain't obleeged to stand no sich interruptions nohow you can fix it. (*To Bulge.*) Go on with your testimony.

Bulge. Well, when Fudge's boy axed me about that ar kittle, I told him I 'lowed he could git one at Spludge's, an he said he would go up arter it.

Att'y for Plain. Then you understood that virtually the defendant's son borrowed Mr. Spludge's kettle at the time, by informing you he would accept the use of said kettle?

Bulge. Dunno about that! dunno, mister! All I know is, I told him I thought he *could* git it, an' he said he s'posed he *would* git it, an' I saw Spludge in the road goin' home an' told him I 'lowed they'd git the kittle.

Att'y for Plain. In the eyes of the law that constitutes a contract. (*Looks meaningly at jury.*) *That* point will impress itself upon all as conclusive.

Att'y for Def. Did you see the Defendant or his son get the kettle?

Bulge. No.

Att'y for Def. Do you know positively that either of them ever did get it?

Bulge. Well, not to a dead sartainty, but I believe they did. Couldn't swear to it.

Att'y for Def. The honorable jury will notice that the witness does not really know whether the defendant *ever got the kettle in dispute at all.* Call the next witness.

Justice. John Smith will take the stand.

Att'y for Plain. Mr. Smith, are you acquainted with the parties in this case?

Smith. Slightly!

Att'y for Plain. How long have you known them?

Smith. About twenty years, off and on.

Att'y for Plain. *Twenty years!* How old are you?

Smith. About twenty seven.

Att'y for Plain. *About* twenty seven! Mr. Smith you are un-der oath. Please state your age, exactly.

Smith. I was twenty seven last Friday, June 20th, at four o'clock in the morning.

Att'y for Plain. Ah, indeed! Remarkably precise, I see. State to the jury what you know about the case under consideration.

Smith. I don't know anything about it.

Att'y for Plain. Did plaintiff, Mr. Spludge, ever loan a kettle to the defendant Fudge?

Smith. Don't know.

Att'y for Plain. Why were you summoned in this case?

Smith. Don't know.

Spludge. I had him summoned to prove that I owned a kettle.

Att'y for Plain. Does the plaintiff, to your knowledge, own a kettle?

Smith. He does.

Att'y for Def. How do you know that plaintiff owns a kettle?

Smith. Spludge's wife told Nate Ripley's wife, last spring, that they bought a new kettle, and Mrs. Ripley told my wife she guess-ed we could get a kettle there when we wanted one.

Foreman of Jury. Square, if it aint agin the rules, I'd like to ax a question.

Justice. I reckon nobody will object.

Foreman. Mr. Smith, moughtn't this ere kettle of Spludge's be an *apple-sass* kittle. My old woman 's borrowed Spludge's apple-sass kittle nigh onto sixteen year, I reckon.

Smith. Couldn't say. Never saw it.

Att'y for Def. Your honor, the testimony of the witness is en-tirely irrelevant. I object to its introduction.

Justice. I heerd nothin *irreverent* about Smith's langwige. I've heerd him spell a whole line at a time when he was plowin' in stumpy ground, but it's a leetle too much to say he cussed when he didn't.

Att'y for Def. I meant, your Honor, it was useless. It should be ruled out.

Justice. If it's useless I reckon we'll let it go for what its worth.

Att'y for Plain. Mr. Jenks will take the stand. (*Jenks comes to chair.*) Mr. Jenks, state briefly what you know concerning the facts in the present case.

Jenks. Last spring, about the close of sugar making, I was down in the big woods hunting squirrels. I passed Fudge's su-gar shanty and stopped awhile. Fudge's boy was tending the ket-tles and I had a chat with him. He said they had a kettle bor-rowed from Spludge and that it was cracked. He asked me if I would tell Spludge, if I saw him, that the kettle was cracked, and say to him that they would make it all right.

Att'y for Plain. Did you inform Mr. Spludge, as requested?

Jenks. Fact is, I did not see him for a right smart while, and then I clean forgot it.

Att'y for Def. Do you know positively that said kettle was never returned?

Jenks. I do not.

Att'y for Def. Then considering the unimpeachable character of my client, the presumption is overwhelming that it was, and the damages made good. Is that all your testimony? (*To Att'y.*)

Att'y for Plain. Our case is so clear we shall introduce nothing more. I shall not even submit an argument to the honorable jury. A mere statement of the facts plainly proved, will be all sufficient. In the first place, we have clearly proved by two men good and true, that all the intents, purposes and determinations of defendant Fudge were to borrow said sugar kettle of plaintiff Spludge. Secondly, we have proved beyond the peradventure of a doubt, that said Fudge did, through his son, obtain and use to its detriment, said caldron or kettle. Said detriment consists of a crack beginning, according to the best information, at a point near the lower portion of said vessel, and ascending thence obliquely and sinuously to the perimeter of the caldron, otherwise known as the rim, and terminating at a point where the suspensory apparatus is attached, known as the bail. Thirdly, that the kettle referred to has ever been returned, or the damage made good, the defense do not even pretend to assert. (*Eloquently.*) Gentlemen of the jury, can the sun in the heavens at noon-day be more plain than the facts in this case? I have no doubts of the position of my client. I can have none. There can be but one verdict, and in that verdict I see with prophetic eye the vindication of the majesty of the law; justice triumphant; the evil doer punished; the down trodden lifted on high, and righteousness exalted. That verdict will tear asunder with the hand of a giant the slimy folds of the mighty serpent *fraud*, which would crush the very vitals of society, and strike a death blow at the institutions of our glorious country. Gentlemen of the jury, we trust to your patriotism, your love of justice, and above all to the more than ordinary intelligence I see in every feature of the honest countenances before me. (*Takes his seat.*)

Att'y for Def. Gentlemen of the jury, few words are necessary in closing this argument. My client's case is based on the bed rock of eternal justice, and no wily sophistry nor high-flown oratory can pluck it thence. (*Looks hard at Att'y for Plain.*) The prosecution has failed to prove that my client ever borrowed a kettle of Spludge. No one saw him borrow it. No one heard him say he borrowed it. He avers he did not. The fact that the kettle was broken rests on the unsupported evidence of a single witness. Not the most reliable, I am sorry to say, either.

Jenks. (*Jumps up excitedly and collars speaker.*) Take that back Mister, or I'll punch your head! I won't be called a liar.

Justice. Order! Order in the court. (*Several seize Jenks and seat him.*)

Jenks. (*Struggling.*) Let me at him! I'll break the rascal's head for him!

Justice, Order! Order!

Att'y for Def. Concerning the return of the kettle it is unnecessary to speak, as the prosecution have entirely omitted that point. Now, gentlemen of the jury, I will draw a picture. My client is a poor man. He toils for his daily bread. Unlike the plaintiff, he is not possessed of a broad estate. His little farm is scarce sufficient to furnish sustenance for his estimable family, consisting of a wife and sixteen children, ranging from the cherub in the mother's arms up to the sturdy, honest-hearted youth who tends the sugar camp. Does anyone suppose for an instant that my client, a man of unimpeachable character, would willingly commit waste on the property of another? Why, gentlemen, the pangs of conscience would carry him to a premature grave. Every time he sweetened his tea during his frugal repast, conscience would whisper in his ear, "You hav'nt paid for that kettle yet." Every time his little prattling child toddled to the cupboard, and in artless tones lisped its wishes for maple sugar, the thoughts of that damaged kettle would rise like a spectre of doom, and harrass him. Every time he visited the country store and saw the tempting bars of sugar arranged on the shelves, his conscience would prick him with a thousand darts. Such a life would be unendurable, and would leave its traces. Gentlemen of the jury, does my client look like a man whose conscience troubles him? (*Pauses.*) Not a bit of it. "*Fiat justitia ruat coelum.*" Which means, freely translated. "Give the poor man the benefit of a doubt." (*Seats himself.*)

Justice. The jury will now retire and bring in a verdic'. I have no particular instructions, only stick to the law and facts. And don't forget that you are tryin' to heal differences between neighbors. (*Jury retire and return in a few seconds.*)

Foreman. Mr. Square, an' feller citizens: we've decided unanimous onto the follerin' verdic'. Fudge must take that ere kettle and get it fixed. Bulge and Jenks orter pay the cost of the fixin', Spludge orter pay the cost of the lawin'. We thought we'd make it as easy as we could by sorter *everagin'* it.

Att'y for Plain. Your honor, I object to that verdict. It is not according to law.

Att'y for Def. It ought to relieve my client of *all* responsibility. Besides, Messrs. *Bulge* and *Jenks* are not parties to the suit.

Bulge. (*Excitedly.*) Jest what I was goin' to say, Jedge. I can't see as *I'm* mixed up into this ere suit, nohow you can fix it.

Jenks. Hanged if I'll pay any costs for other people's business.

Justice. I 'low that verdic' had better stand. If it aint *law* it's *justice.* Sposin' Bulge hadn't said anything about that kittle! It wouldn't been borried, and if Jenks had spoken to Spludge about the damages when Fudge's boy told him to, there most likely would have been no lawsuit. So I reckon they'd better come in for their share of the cost.

CURTAIN.

BORROWING TROUBLE.

CHARACTERS.

Mr. Borrow.
Mrs. Borrow.
Miss Sophy Borrow.
Mrs. Mehitable March.
Mrs. Wiggins.
Lina.
Detective Spotem.
Dr. Drench.

COSTUMES.

Any clothing suited to the social standing of the character.

SITUATIONS.

R means right as the actor faces the audience; *L*, left; *C*, center.

Steam Press of
Cushing, Thomas & Co., 170 Clark St.

BORROWING TROUBLE.

SCENE.—*Lodgings in tenement house. Room rather cheaply furnished, with attempt at display. Table and chairs. Sofa rear. Overcoat visible hanging on wall.*

Mrs. W. (*Pacing floor.*) Well, I never did see in all my days the like of these Borrows. I've been a widow twenty long years, and have kept lodgers for fifteen of that time, and the likes of them never before set foot in my house. (*Picks up a shawl.*) I declare, if there is n't Mrs. Wait's shawl. Mrs. Borrow got the loan of that two weeks ago, just to wear that day, as she said, and here she's kept it ever since. And if here is n't my Jack's shoe brush that Mr. Borrow got a month ago, and the boy thought it was lost ever since. (*Takes shoe brush.*) Well, really, I suppose they've borrowed every last thing they have, so I'd better look out for my rent and not wait any longer for that *little remittance.* Goodness knows! why dont they *board* instead of keeping house. They've borrowed enough of me to keep a small family. First, it is a cup of sugar, next a pint of milk, then a half dozen eggs. And, strange to say, they never think of returning them.

Enter L. DETECTIVE SPOTEM.

Spotem. Good day, Madam! Are these the lodgings of Mr. Borrow?

Mrs. W. They are, sir.

Spotem. Have I the honor of addressing Mrs. Borrow?

Mrs. W. Oh, no sir. I am Mrs. Wiggins, who owns this building and lets rooms to married or single persons. Do you wish rooms, sir?

Spotem. No, Madam. My business is with Mr. Borrow. Could you inform me where he can be seen?

Mrs. W. I think the family have gone out. I can ascertain definitely by asking their servant. (*Exit R.*)

Spotem. Now Mr. Borrow, I've got you. In spite of your cunning and your assumed names, you can't escape me this time. You may be out, but you'll return. (*Looks around the room; sees overcoat on wall.*) Ha! the very proof I wanted. That is the overcoat I've been shadowing all last spring. So I've run into your den at last, and before two hours you and your counterfeit money will both be mine. (*Chuckles quietly.*) Well you've manged this pretty cute, old Spotem. You have, for a fact, and the whole country will be ablaze with your fame. It was

lucky I didn't share this case with any one. It will make my
fortune, and the name of Detective Spotem will soon be on everybody's tongue. People will say, "He's a sly fox," "Sharp as a
steel trap," etc.

Enter Mrs. W., R.

Mrs. W. The family have gone, sir, for a walk, Will you
leave any word?
Spotem. No! I will call again shortly. Good day, Madam!
(*Exit L.*)
Mrs. W. Now what does he want, I wonder? These strangers
who take rooms, have *so* many callers that one *never can find out
anything about.*

Enter LINA, R.

Mrs. W. Lina, who was that gentleman that just passed down
stairs?
Lina. Don't know, Missa.
Mrs. W. Your master has a great many friends, has n't he,
Lina?
Lina. If he has, dah's a good many of dem not berry good
ones.
Mrs. W. Why, Lina?
Lina. Case *good* friends *gives* to each other, but Massa's
friends don't give him anything, so he's 'bliged to borry nearly
everything he buys for family use. It was an awful trouble last
place I was at to cook de wittles, but it's a mighty heap bigger
job here to get a meal ready, 'case I has to *borry* de eatables fust
an' *cook* 'em arterward. An' then Massa and Missa worrits so if
de wittles ain't good, an' folks don't lend 'em de *best.*
Mrs. W. Do they scold or ill treat you?
Lina. Law save you no! They're the resignedst folks you
ever seen, as Missa has said a thousan' times. Why one day
Massa worritted so he couldn't eat, 'case one of de eggs I borried
wasn't prezactly fresh. It got broke into de skillet fore I knowed
an' spiled de dish, for de family leastways. I pitied him, I did, I
could jest crammed de eggs down the throat of ole Mrs. Smith
who lent them. De idee of sendin' rotten eggs to a family of
quality! Missa an' Miss Sophy jest grieved their eyes nearly out
because of that disastah. De women folks are jest de most
tenderest angels I eber seed.
Mrs. W. (*Going L.*) Then you are happy here Lina, are you?
Lina. Happy as a tree frog in a wet day! But I'll be awful
glad when pay day comes. Been here a month an' hain't had a
cent, but Massa says he expects *permittances.*
Mrs. W. I wish he hurry and get them. What use are
promises to a widow with a family? (*Exit L.*)
Lina. It's a shame that as good a man has Massa hain't got
money. He says he's the wictim of circumstances, an' I believe
it for a fac' I do.

Enter MR. and MRS. BORROW and SOPHY, L.

Mrs. B. (*Throwing off bonnet and shawl.*) Lina, have you made arrangements for tea?

Lina. Beg pahdon! but dah's nuffin to arrange.

Mrs. B. Oh my! when will our remittances arrive, my dear?

Mr B. Not until next week I fear, love.

Mrs. B. Lina, you must manage it somehow. Try the neighbors again.

Lina. De fac' is I've *managed* nearly all de neighbors already.

Mrs. B. Try a new place. Have we any butter?

Lina. No, Ma'am.

Mrs. B. Any milk?

Lina. No, Missa.

Mrs. B. Any bread?

Lina. Law sakes, don't you 'member there wasn't enough for dinner?

Mrs. B. Lina, run down to Mrs. Lamb's and ask her for a loaf. Tell her we'll return it to-morrow.

Lina. Laws Missa we's borried two or three loaves from her, to say nuffin about eggs an' sugar an' coffee. 'Spose 'praps likely you's forgot it, but de *articles* haven't been returned home again.

Mrs. B. Never mind that, Lina. Mrs. Lamb is such a good soul she'll let you have the loaf and say nothing about it. Ask Mrs. Grey for a small piece of butter, and Mrs. Wiggins will let you have milk. Hurry up, Lina, it is tea time.

Mr. B. Hold a minute, Lina. Mrs. Borrow, I've told you often that the cares of housekeeping are too great for you; I *will* relieve you, in spite of yourself. I brought a can of oysters on trial, a new brand. The groceryman is *giving* samples away at first to build up custom; wants my trade. Bring plenty of milk for a stew, Lina. Have you salt?

Lina. No Sah!

Mr. B. Mrs. Wiggins will attend to that. Have you plenty of pepper?

Lina. Not a speck.

Mr. B. Mrs. Wiggins is very kind. She will manage that also. I must have oysters well seasoned. My stomach isn't what it once was. Vinegar, butter! I can't go into details. Just bring one of Mrs. Wiggins' castors, pepper, mustard, vinegar and all. (*Exit Lina, L.*)

Mrs. B. Poor man! Trouble is just wearing you out! Mr. Borrow, do sit down and rest yourself, so you may have an appetite for dinner. You know your stomach needs attention.

Mr. B. Yes, madam, I am aware that it does. I am sorry to say it often needs attention that a man who is the victim of circumstances is unable to bestow.

Mrs. B. It's a shame that such a noble, kind-hearted man, who has devoted a whole life to the service of the "Society for the Advancement of Benevolence, Philanthropy, and Exalted Fellowship among the Jarring Elements of Discordant Mankind," should be the victim of hard-hearted, relentless circumstances. I hate circumstances. They are the bar to all true progress! (*Enter Lina, with castor, loaf of bread and pitcher of milk. She proceeds to set table, R C.*)

Mr. B. A very true observation, my dear, which we toilers for the benefit of mankind have painful occasion to verify.

Mrs. B. Sophy, will you prepare your Pa's tonic? He must have an appetizer, you know. Here is the physician's prescription. (*Reads.*) "Whisky, gin and water, one-half oz each. Add sugar and flavoring to taste. Take before meals."

Sophy. (*In mincing, affected voice*) Oh my, don't trouble me with such affairs. They properly belong to the servant, and you know the fumes of those horrid drugs affect my eyes.

Mrs. B. So they do, my dear. I quite forgot that. I will prepare the medicine myself. Your Pa must have his tonic. His appetite is not what it once was.

Mr. B. Quite true! Quite true! Indeed I think sometimes it is better that it is not so good. One might be tempted too far in the way of luxuries, and people working for the good of mankind set an example whether they will or not. They should be careful and above all avoid luxuries. (*Mrs. B. enters kitchen R, and gets materials for Mr. B's "tonic."*)

Sophy. Why Papa, our example is quite good, isn't it?

Mr. B. Certainly my child!

Sophy. I did not dance at Mrs. Flighty's grand ball just on that account. I thought of our circumstances and the *cause* you have devoted us to, and that nerved me to the sacrifice. (*Languishes on sofa.*)

Mr. B. You did very right my child to abstain from dancing. Had you participated in the vanities of the dance it would have been a constant reproach to your poor Pa in his society work. (*Mrs. B, enters with tonic*) Ah! that is very inspiring. (*Smacks his lips.*) Just the thing for a weak stomach!

Enter MRS. MEHITABLE MARCH.

Mrs. M. Oh howdy! I'm so 'fraid I'm intruding. (*Rushes up to Mrs. B. and kisses her.*)

Mrs. B. Not at all; we're so glad to see you!

Mrs M. How are you, Miss Borrow? Are you well, Mr. Borrow? (*Shakes hands with him.*)

Mr. B. Very well thank you! This visit is indeed as pleasant as unexpected.

Mrs. M. (*Mrs. M. always speaks as fast as possible without indistinctness.*) Mr. Borrow, you don't know how I feel for you. Mrs. Borrow, it does me just as much good to know that he is well as to know that Ephraim is well, or to feel well myself. His loss would be a loss to humanity.

Sophy. (*Aside*) That old fright has just stopped for her supper.

Mrs. M. (*Taking off bonnet and shawl.*) I didn't think of stopping any time; but you are so cozy here really I must. You are *so* kind I have n't the heart to leave without chatting a while. you will please take my things, Miss Sophy. (*Sophy drops bonnet and shawl on the floor at the end of the sofa.*)

Lina. (*Aside to Mrs. B.*) Missa, dah ain't nigh likes enuff wittles for company.

Mrs. B. (*Aside.*) I wont ask her to tea. She shan't have it.

Mrs. M. I dont visit much, and I dont call on everybody. Dear me! I don't like to say much about such things, but ever since Mrs. Wilson eloped and left her husband, I don't know who to trust. Since we moved up town we've been gitting sorter *select.* Ephraim says we're too *select.* Only this morning, at breakfast table, he said, "Mehitable, why don't you call on the Borrows?" An' says I, I will. So I just run in this afternoon to chat a minute. It does me good to hear Mr. Burrow talk. I heard him lecture once.

Mr. B. Ah! Indeed?

Mrs. M. The sentiments he expressed was very beautiful. Mrs. Borrow, you've got a mighty smart man, I tell you.

Mrs. B. (*Coldly.*) I was aware of that long ago.

Mrs. M. (*Glances at table.*) I just said to Ephraim this morning that I would run in an' hear that man talk. It's as good as stump speaking any day, or a circus, for that matter. (*Mr. B. fidgets nervously. Mrs. M. glances at the table.*)

Mrs. B. (*With offended air.*) Of the merits of a circus *I* can not speak. *We* do not attend circuses.

Mrs. M. Land sake now! do tell!

Mr. B. *I* did attend a circus *once, a very long time ago.* While doubtless entertaining to many, I did not find the performance of the kind calculated to satisfy the longings of a man with aspirations to accomplish high, moral and philanthrophic purposes.

Mrs. M. Well I do say! Your ideas are *so* original, I never thought of that. Dear me! I heard to-day that Mrs. Jenkins and her husband quarrel dreadful, and they've not been married a month!

Mrs. B. I dare say! I thought as much.

Mrs. M. (*Looks at table.*) But did you hear about the cholera. They say it's come to town at last. They say they're going to take off everybody to the hospital who takes it. It's dreadful to think of dyin' in that nasty hospital! People can't be too careful what they eat. I told Ephraim so to-day. Speakin' of eatin', I see you have the table set. Don't let your tea spoil on my account. I'll just sit down with you, for company's sake.

Mrs. B. (*Aside.*) Well I never! Mr. Borrow, tea is ready. (*All sit to table.*) You see we are unprepared for company. We have nothing but the plain repast we usually spread for own family.

Mrs. M. Now don't worry on my account, Mrs. Borrow. You know you've just the nicest table. Have you heard about Callie

Brown? Don't say anything about it, but they do say she takes on dreadful, because her father forbid that beau of hers from comin' into the house again

Mrs. B. It's just like *him*, to be so cruel.

Mr. B. Wife, perhaps, we should add some other little delicacy, since we have company.

Mrs. B. Mr. Borrow, remember your health. Don't worry about such trifling matters.

Mrs. M. Goodness me! if he don't attend to domestic affairs the same as other men. Who'd 'a thought it!   •

Mr. B. I consider home duties equally as sacred as those more important ones with which I am burdened, and the duties of home should be attended to whenever opportunity offers a minute from weightier affairs. Lina, will you step into Mrs. Butler's and get one of those cans of strawberries? Explain! Company you know. And if she wouldn't mind it, a small matter of cake. (*Exit Lina, L.*) You see, Mrs. March, we are entirely unprepared for visitors. But it shall never be said that *my* family want for anything while *I* am able to provide for them.

Mrs. M. But ain't you afraid to set sich a bountiful table when there's so much sickness round? Cholera comes on awful sudden. They take desperate pains and turn sick in a minnit. An' the least thing will do it. A spoonful of fruit, or a mess of cucumbers. Pears like this tea tasted queer.

Sophy. Just what I was going to say Ma!

Mrs. B. (*Tastes tea.*) It has a queer taste. What can ail it?

Mr. B. Perhaps it's the milk. (*Pours out milk and tastes it.*) Mrs. Borrow, I fear there is something wrong. This milk has a horrible taste.

Sophy. Ma, I'm real sick! (*Jumps up from table.*)

Mrs. M. Land 'o goodness we'll all die. I know we will. It's the cholera! (*All jump up from the table.*)

Mrs. B. Mercy me! I feel it in my stomach!

Mr. B. Don't be alarmed, my dear. I will watch over you.

Mrs. B. (*Groans.*) Dear me, take care of yourself. Aren't you sick, too?

Mr. B. I feel the subtle poison, but even death shall not frighten me from my post of duty. Lina, run across the street for the Doctor. Call Mrs. Wiggins!

Lina. Lord 'a mercy! what's de matter? If it's de cholerum we'll all be dead afore de Doctor gets up de fust flight of de stairway! (*Runs out L for Doctor.*)

Mrs. M. (*Groans.*) What an awful suddint case! Oh, Mr. Borrow, won't you take me to Ephraim? I can't die among strangers, and they will take me to the hospital. (*Clasps her hands tightly across her stomach.*)

Sophy. Ma, I'm sinking fast! (*Groans.*)

Mrs. B. We will go together, daughter. (*Groans.*)

Mr. B. (*Paces around frantically; hands on his stomach.*) **Don't despair! I will never desert you!**

Enter L, DETECTIVE SPOTEM.

Mrs. M. (*Frantically.*) Oh take me to Ephraim!

Spotem. Couldn't do it, Madam. I haven't Ephraim's address.

Mr. B. Who are you, sir, who come into this tenement of stricken humanity to mock the sufferings of your fellow man? Wnat do you want?

Spotem. Well, sir, I will give you the information you seek to the best of my ability. I am Detective Spotem of the force and I want you.

Mr. B. You want us! Then all is over!

Sophy. Oh, Pa, don't let him take us! It would be horrid to die in that place. (*Groans.*)

Mrs. B. Protect us for a few brief hours more! It won't be long! (*Groans.*)

Mrs. M. Well goodness knows I just won't go into that nasty place for any policeman. Do take me to Ephraim till I can die in his arms. (*Groans and holds her hands on her stomach tightly.*) This pain is gettin' too awful for human perseverance!

Sophy. It is perfectly dreadful!

Mrs. B. It is excrutiating.

Mr. B. This pain is certainly very—very—(*Holds his stomach with both hands.*)

Spotem. Painful, eh?

Mrs. M. Oh Ephraim! Ephraim! It would rend your *vitals* if you knowed what pain your Mehitable suffers. Oh take me to Ephraim!

Spotem. Well this case is deuced singular. Have they been partaking too freely of green corn, or are they putting up a job on me? I guess it's the latter, for whole families seldom have trouble like this all of a sudden. (*Patients all groan.*)

Mrs. M. Won't you listen to a dying woman's request and take me to my Ephraim?

Spotem. (*Looks intently at Mrs. M.*) She'll live to see her Ephraim yet, I think. I guess they are playing it on me. Can't fool me, though. But it is singular. I'll make a note of it for my great book entitled "Secrets of the Great Detective Agency." (*Writes rapidly in a book.*)

Mrs. B. Oh, Mr. Borrow, that officer is writing out a commitment for us. (*Groans.*)

Sophy. Ma, I shall faint if you mention it.

Mr. B. Resign yourselves to fate my poor darling. We must go, I suppose.

Mrs. M. (*Indignantly.*) *I won't! I'm* going to Ephraim, if I walk every step of the way.

Spotem. Don't think of walking, Madam. I'll call a hack if I think it best for you to go at all.

Mrs. B. Oh, don't send us!

Sophy. It's real mean!

Mrs. M. It's perfectly horrid! (*All groan.*)

Spotem. Well, this beats all! Queer case! (*Reads.*) "Case of Borrow, the counterfeiter. When detective Spotem was about to make the arrest, the whole family of the prisoner were suddenly taken with violent cramps in the region of the stomach, so well feigned as to appear real. Ruse to gain time. One old lady, apparently a visitor, but really a shrewd accomplice, kept crying continually to be taken to her Ephraim." (*Patients groan.*)

Enter Doctor, Mrs. Wiggins *and* Lina, *L.*

Spotem. (*Stepping aside to R.*) Hello! What does this mean?
Lina. Here dey is, Doctor! Here's de patienters, if dey's not all clean gone dead.
Mrs. W. Oh dear! (*Wrings her hands.*) Just think of it! Cholera in my house! It'll kill us all, and ruin my business.
Doctor. (*Examines patients, feels pulses, bustles around.*) Violent cramping pains in stomach, eh?
All. Yes! yes! (*Groan.*)
Doctor. Then it is the incipient stages of genuine Asiatic cholera, and no mistake. It is a dangerous case, but with proper care I'll try to get you all through safe. I see the patients are not yet reduced in strength, which is very favorable. (*Busies himself with medicine case.*) (*Aside.*) It's lucky that I was called in. It is one of the first cases in town. It won't make a bad item for the morning papers. I see there is a reporter already present. A neat item. "*Cholera.*—An entire family stricken down. Doctor Drench called in. Under his skillful care they are doing well, etc., etc."
Mrs. M. Oh, Doctor, won't you take me to Ephraim?
Doctor. Madam, do not be alarmed, skillful hands are ready to wait on you. (*Gives each patient a draught from a colored mixture in a goblet.*)
Spotem. Well, this thing does really look serious. Doctor, can I be of any use?
Doctor. Ah, reporting! (*Sees Spotem's note book.*) No, I believe not, (*Pauses*) except in a professional way; you understand.
Spotem. But I don't understand.
Mrs. W. Doctor, can't I help you some way. If you want any herbs, I always keep 'em. I lived on a farm once. I always make catnip tea an' "penneroil" tea when my boy Jack gits sick.
Doctor. Madam, I'm sorry to say that only *professional* skill can baffle this most dangerous and deadly disease. (*Busies himself making powders.*)
Mrs. M. Doctor, is it ketchin'?
Doctor. Excuse me, madam, I didn't understand.
Mrs. M. Is it ketchin'?
Doctor. Madam, I am glad to say that when fumigation is properly attended to the disease is not contagious.
Mrs. M. Laws a me! How long is it before *fumigation sets in?* I wouldn't have Ephraim take it for twenty dollars.
Doctor. Take one of these every ten minutes. (*Displays on*

table a large number of powders done up in preposterously large papers.) I will return in an hour. If anything happens in the meantime, let me know.

Spotem. (*Aside.*) *I* should expect something to happen if those powders are all taken.

Sophy. Oh deah! if theh's anything I have an aversion to it's powders.

Mrs. M. I can't bear them! Oh, won't some one run to Ephraim and say his Mehitable is dyin'?

Mr. B. We will do our best, sir, to follow your instructions. What is your theory of the cause of the disease?

Doctor. Doubtless detective sewer-pipes!

Mrs. W. Goodness, no! The pipes froze up last winter and haven't been connected since.

Doctor. Then doubtless it is the hydrant water!

Mrs. W. It aint that either, for *I have a good well for my lodgers.*

Doctor. (*Annoyed.*) Of course the *immediate* cause is something the family have eaten. (*Looks at table, lifts can of strawberries triumphantly.*) This explains it all!

Lina. Doctor, I jes fotched dem berries in a few minutes ago, an' de family didn't have the smell of a single berry.

Mrs. B. Doctor, we seldom eat fruit. We first tasted something in the milk.

Doctor. (*Takes up milk pitcher.*) Why, there is something in this milk. It looks yellowish.

Lina. Well, I nebber hear of de like. 'Spect dat's my fault! Comin' up de stairs I dropped de mustard out of de castor into de milk, I was so hurried I teetotally forgot all about it. (*All laugh except Sophy, Mrs. M. and the Doctor.*)

Sophy. How perfectly disgusting!

Mrs. M. It's a shame to treat *visitors* so, a downright shame. If Ephraim—

Doctor. (*To Borrow.*) It's a trick, sir, a conspiracy to ruin my professional reputation. I'll make it a costly trick. My fee is fifty dollars, and the sooner it is paid the better for you, sir. (*To Spotem.*) And you, sir, are a party to this infamous piece of business. I wager your paper will make a rare display of head lines over it. I'll prosecute you for libel, sir.

Spotem. Sir, there is evidently some mistake here I was as ignorant as yourself of what has transpired here to-day.

Doctor. Aren't you a reporter?

Spotem. Reporter! no; I am Detective Spotem, and seeing that you are through with your professional business, I will begin mine. Mr. Borrow, my business is with you. For some time you have been suspected of being in league with counterfeiters; yesterday a counterfeit $10 bill was traced directly to you. You are my prisoner. (*Women scream.*)

Mrs. B. Oh, sir, my husband is innocent!

Spotem. That he will have opportunity to prove.

Mrs. M. (*Aside.*) Well, I always thought these Borrows weren't what they ought to be.

Mr. B. I borrowed the bill to which you refer.

Spotem. It is probable that a man in your circumstances would *borrow* a paltry $10 bill.

Mrs. W. He's a great borrower; he is indeed, sir; I can testify to that, besides I heard the queer gentlemen on the third floor say he loaned Mr. Borrow ten dollars.

Spotem. That may do, but Detective Spotem don't hang all his clothes on one peg. Do you know that coat, Mr. Borrow? (*Points to overcoat.*) A man wearing that overcoat has been seen under very suspicious circumstances at various places, for several weeks back. Isn't that your coat?

Borrow. I borrowed that from the gentleman on the third floor.

Mrs. W. From the queer gentleman!

Spotem. Did you borrow everything you have?

Mr. B. Pretty much all.

Spotem. And where is the queer gentleman?

Mrs. W. Left uncommon sudden a week ago! But he paid up like a gentleman.

Spotem. *Botheration! Vexation! Cremation!* He's given me the slip again and my great case is ruined. (*Tears leaf from his note book and stamps it.*)

Doctor. Give me your hand. You have my sympathies.

Spotem. (*Moodily.*) What is sympathy to a man whose reputation is ruined?

Doctor. My professional reputation has received a very disagreeable blow, but I'll see what a fee will do towards healing it. Mr. Borrow, my bill is just fifty dollars, terms cash.

Mr. B. It strikes me that is a large fee for a man who can't tell the effects of mustard from those of Asiatic cholera.

Doctor. (*Excitedly.*) What! do you mean to insult me? I won't stand it! I'll have satisfaction. But I see you are a trifler! To get rid of this disagreeable business I'll make it twenty five.

Borrow. Too much!

Doctor. Fifteen then!

Borrow. That's more reasonable. Mr. Spotem, will you oblige me with a small loan until to-morrow? I've remittances coming.

Spotem. Good heavens! Doctor, come. (*Seizes Dr. by the arm.*) This fellow would swamp our reputation with mortgages and then borrow money from us to lift them. (*Drags Dr. out L.*)

Mr. B. This is quite an episode, my dear.

Mrs. B. Oh, I'm so nervous! I was frightened nearly to death! Mr. Borrow, has it affected your stomach?

Mr. B. I believe not dear. I am spared for higher purposes.

Sophy. It's perfectly horrid. I shall not recover for a week. (*Languishes.*)

Mrs. M. Law sakes, Mr. Borrow! you are the luckiest man alive. The Lord favors the righteous. But I must go home. This 'll be just the best kind of news for Ephraim. (*Exit L.*)

CURTAIN.

T. S. DENISON'S CATALOGUE OF
NEW PLAYS,
FOR SCHOOLS and AMATEURS.
1879.
PRICE 15 CENTS EACH, POSTAGE PAID.

These plays have been prepared expressly to meet the wants of teachers and amateur clubs. They are simple in construction, and require no scenery, or only such as is usually at hand. They afford opportunity for "*acting*." They are *pure in tone and language*. The six first on the list were before the public last year, (published at DeKalb, Ill.) and met with a most favorable reception.

"If the succeeding numbers are as good as the first, we predict for them a large demand."—*National Teachers' Monthly, N. Y. and Chicago.*

"These plays appear to be full of fun and to teach many good lessons withal."—*Wis. Jour. of Education.*

"The farces are full of fun."—*Daily Inter-Ocean, Chicago.*

"These plays are supplying the dearth of good literature in this department."—*N. Y. School Bulletin.*

ODDS WITH THE ENEMY.

A drama in five acts; 7 male and 4 female characters. Time, 1 hour 50 min. Contains a good humorous negro character.

"It took splendidly. 'Tabbs' made it spicy."—*C. E. Rogers, Dunkirk, Ind.*

SETH GREENBACK.

A drama in four acts: 7 male and 3 female characters. Time, 1 hour 15 m.

"'Seth Greenback' has one very good Irish comic character, and some pathetic and telling situations. The plot is simple and dramatic, and culminates well."—*Iowa Normal Monthly.*

WANTED, A CORRESPONDENT.

A farce in two acts; 4 male and 4 female characters. Time, 45 m. Very interesting and amusing.

INITIATING A GRANGER.

A ludicrous farce; 8 male characters. Time, 25 m.

"'Initiating a Granger' brought down the house."—*J. L. Sharp, Burlington Iowa.*

THE SPARKLING CUP.

A temperance drama in five acts; 12 male and 4 female characters. Time, 1 hour 45 m. A thrilling play, worthy the best efforts of amateurs. Pathetic song and death scene.

"It is just the thing for dramatic clubs."—*The Anvil, Washington, D. C.*

A FAMILY STRIKE.

A spicy farce, illustrating "strikes"; 3 male and 3 female characters. Time, 20 minutes.

LOUVA, THE PAUPER.

A drama in five acts; 9 male and 4 female characters. Time, 1 hour 45 min. Contains a good Yankee character and a humorous darky character. This is an intensely interesting and pathetic play. It admits of striking scenic effects, and is a *strong* play for amateurs.

Act I. Louva's tyrants. Act II. Freedom promised and denied. Act III. The trial. Act IV. Flight. Act V. Pursuit; Death in the mountains; Retribution.

TWO GHOSTS IN WHITE.

A humorous farce based on boarding-school life; 7 female characters. Time 25 m. Abounds in ludicrous episodes.